The Grave Soul

ALSO BY ELLEN HART

The Grave Soul

ELLEN HART

MINOTAUR BOOKS ✹ NEW YORK

THE GRAVE SOUL. Copyright © 2015 by Ellen Hart. All rights reserved. Printed in the United States of America. For information, address St. Martin's Press, 175 Fifth Avenue, New York, N.Y. 10010.

www.minotaurbooks.com

The Library of Congress Cataloging-in-Publication Data is available upon request.

ISBN 978-1-250-04770-0 (hardcover)
ISBN 978-1-250-04781-6 (e-book)

Our books may be purchased in bulk for promotional, educational, or business use. Please contact your local bookseller or the Macmillan Corporate and Premium Sales Department at (800) 221-7945, extension 5442, or by e-mail at MacmillanSpecialMarkets@macmillan.com.

First Edition: October 2015

10   9   8   7   6   5   4   3   2   1

For Karen Maranville and Bruce Clausen, with much love

In loving memory of Charles Vinson

Cast of Characters

Jane Lawless: Owner of the Lyme House Restaurant in Minneapolis. Partner in a private investigation company—Nolan & Lawless Investigations.

Cordelia Thorn: Part-owner of the new Thorn Lester Playhouse in Minneapolis. Jane's best friend. Hattie's aunt. Octavia's sister.

Laurie Adler: Doug's wife. Onetime English teacher. Bartender.

Dr. Hannah Adler: Doug and Kevin's sister. Doctor of Gastroenterology, Eau Claire, Wisconsin.

Doug Adler: Forklift operator. Onetime owner of the *New Dresden Herald*. Laurie's husband. Hannah and Kevin's brother.

Kevin Adler:	Owner of the Sportsman Tavern in New Dresden, Wisconsin. Grace and Kira's father. Delia's husband.
Delia Adler:	Waitress. Kevin's wife. Grace and Kira's mother.
Guthrie Hewitt:	Owner of the Hewitt & Hewitt Teahouse in Uptown, Minneapolis. Kira's boyfriend.
Kira Adler:	Nursing student at the University of Minnesota. Daughter of Kevin and Delia. Grace's sister. Guthrie's girlfriend.
Grace Adler:	Kevin and Delia's daughter. Kira's sister.
Evangeline Adler:	Doug, Hannah, and Kevin's mother. Grace and Kira's grandmother. Wife of Henry Adler, onetime owner of the *New Dresden Herald*.
Father Michael Franchetti:	Catholic Priest. St. Andrew's Parish, New Dresden, Wisconsin.
Walt Olsen:	Onetime police chief in New Dresden, Wisconsin.

Katie Olsen: Walt Olsen's daughter.

Steven Carmody: Part-owner of the Carmody & Sons Funeral Home in Union, Wisconsin. Todd's brother. Brian Carmody's son.

PART ONE: NEW YEAR'S

The grave soul keeps its own secrets, and takes its own punishment in silence.

—DOROTHY DIX

NEW YEAR'S EVE

New Dresden, Wisconsin

Failures were like bread crumbs. A woman could, without much difficulty, follow them back through the dark fairy-tale forest of her life, noting the dead ends, the seemingly small mistakes, the hubris and lack of courage, the dearth of judgement, and eventually arrive at the primary failure which, without her knowing it, would inexorably become the fulcrum on which the rest of her life turned. In Laurie's case, at just eighteen years old, an epic failure of imagination had sealed her fate.

Light snow drifted across the highway as she sped toward town. The sky had been a bleak winter white all day. By tomorrow morning, according to the weather report, six more inches would be making life miserable for the New Year's Day revelers. Because the tires on her ancient Ford Windstar were almost bald, she hesitated to drive in this kind of weather, though because her husband hadn't answered his cell phone all day, she felt she had little choice.

This was one of Doug's many tests—the "If-You-Love-Me-You'll-Come-Looking-For-Me" test. She scanned the road ahead, squinting into the fading light. He could be anywhere—a restaurant, or more likely, a bar. He could have stayed late at work, although she wasn't sure what a forklift operator would do on New Year's Eve when everyone else at the lumberyard had left early. She silently prayed that the New Year's Eve dinner she was preparing wasn't turning into a burnt offering in the oven.

With only four miles left before she hit the outskirts of New Dresden, she slowed the van so she could scan the sides of the road for his gray Buick LeSabre. It was possible that he'd had car trouble. The cell phone service in New Dresden was hit or miss at best. The winter twilight made seeing difficult. Not even the headlights helped much, swallowed as they were in the expanse of white.

Laurie had bought a special German chocolate cake—Doug's favorite—at a local bakery on Saturday afternoon. They could ill afford the expense, and yet she needed this New Year's Eve to be festive. She also needed a gesture that would send the message that she still cared about him without her having to say it out loud. These days, words got stuck in her throat and, no matter how hard she tried, she couldn't force them out. Just another failure to toss on the pile, she supposed. One day, if she kept living her life the way she had these last fifty-five years, she'd be able to climb up on top of that pile and touch the moon.

Gripping the wheel, Laurie watched a dim figure emerge from a patch of woods. "Doug?" she whispered.

Half limping, half stooped, the figure moved to the shoulder and sank down on one knee.

Laurie pulled over to the shoulder and jumped out, relieved

to discover that it wasn't her husband. Long, dark hair obscured the woman's face. Bending toward her, Laurie reached out her hand. "Are you all right?"

The woman's left elbow was pressed hard against her side. "I need to get out of here."

"Are you hurt?" When the woman looked up, Laurie felt a moment of panic.

"Can you help me?"

Taking hold of the woman's free arm, Laurie pulled her to her feet, alarmed to see how much pain she was in.

"I need to get . . . to a hospital."

"What happened? Were you in a car accident?" She didn't see a car.

They moved haltingly to the van.

Once they were back on the road, Laurie switched on the overhead light, sneaking looks at the blood dripping from the woman's nose and mouth; her disheveled hair; the blood on her hands; the wet, dirty, ripped right leg of her jeans. The closest emergency room was in Henderson. With only a twenty-dollar bill in her pocket and little gas in the tank, there was no way Laurie could take her there. Even if she could, this was a situation that called for caution. "Where does it hurt?"

"Everywhere."

"How did you get like this?" She tried to sound concerned, but mostly she was scared.

The woman leaned back and closed her eyes. "I can't quite . . . it's . . . all confused."

"Uh huh. But, I mean—"

"They brought me."

"They?"

"I . . . I just need a minute. To pull things together."

Laurie decided not to press her, mainly because she felt she already knew the answer. She pulled the van into her sister-in-law's driveway a few minutes later. Hannah Adler was a doctor with a practice in Eau Claire, which was where she had her primary residence. Laurie tried not to be jealous, though it was often a losing battle. Hannah maintained an old bungalow in New Dresden to be close to the family.

Laurie guided the injured woman up the front steps and rang the doorbell. Hannah was in town because New Year's Day was a big family event, a command performance, dictated by Evangeline Adler, the family matriarch. When the door drew back, Hannah appeared in a sweatshirt, sweatpants, and slippers; a wineglass in her hand.

"Help me get her inside" said Laurie, maneuvering the woman through the doorway. If anything, the woman was more out of it now than she had been on the road.

The frightened look on Hannah's face matched Laurie's.

"Where can we put her?" asked Laurie.

"In the spare bedroom."

They helped her down the hallway and lowered her onto a double bed. While Laurie removed the woman's sodden boots, Hannah covered her with a quilt.

"What the hell's going on?" whispered Hannah.

"I found her like this about four miles out of town."

They exchanged worried glances.

"She's pretty confused," added Laurie.

"Good. I hope she stays that way." Bending over the bed, Hannah said, "I need to examine you. Does your head hurt? Are you dizzy?"

The woman searched the two faces gazing down at her, settling on Hannah.

Laurie held her breath.

"My ribs. On the left side."

"On a scale of one to ten, what's the pain like?"

"Eight."

Glancing back at Laurie, Hannah lowered her voice and said, "Probably bruised or broken ribs. She needs more help than I can give her."

"This is really bad."

Loud banging on the front door interrupted them.

"You expecting someone?" asked Laurie.

They raced back down the hall. Hannah parted the curtains in the living room. "It's Kevin and Doug. They look upset."

Grabbing Hannah's arm, Laurie said, "We can't let them in."

"They know we're in here. Your van is in the driveway."

"They did it. They took her out into the woods and beat her up."

"We don't know that."

"Who else would do it? Hannah, please. You know I'm right. If they find out we've got her in here, who knows what they'll do."

Hannah hesitated, then said, "I'll go out and talk to them. I'll tell them . . . hell, I'll figure something out. While I'm outside, you get rid of her. You hear what I'm saying?"

"What about her pain?"

"Get *rid* of her. She's poison."

Laurie gave a solemn nod. Rushing back to the bedroom, she found the woman sitting up, head in her hands. "You've got to get out of here."

"What?"

"Come on. Put your boots back on."

Ducking into the bathroom, Laurie opened the medicine cabinet and searched through the prescription bottles for a painkiller. If nothing else, she could give her a bottle of ibuprofen, though that hardly seemed strong enough. When she found nothing, she noticed her sister-in-law's medical bag on the floor next to small oak cabinet. Opening it, she found a white paper sack stapled at the top. She ripped it open and scanned the front of the prescription bottle: "Endocet 325 milligrams," she whispered. "One to two tablets ever six hours as needed for pain." Perfect. She grabbed the cup next to the sink, dumped out the toothbrush, and filled it with water. Returning to the bedroom, she found the woman struggling with her second boot. "Good. That's good. You're not safe here." She handed the woman the pills and the glass. "Take them fast."

"What are they?"

"Painkillers. Come on. Quick, quick." It was beyond frustrating to watch the slow, labored effort. Laurie helped her to her feet and steered her out into the hallway, this time heading toward the kitchen at the back of the house.

"Who's yelling?" asked the woman, twisting her head around.

"Listen to me," said Laurie, stuffing the prescription bottle into the woman's leather jacket and then plucking her last twenty from her own pocket and tucking that in that as well. "When you get outside, go straight through the yard. Keep walking out to the road. Hang a right and the road will take you back to the highway. There's a truck stop about a quarter mile to the west—which means you go right again. Got that? You'll be able to see the lights. You can hop a ride to . . . wherever someone's willing to take you."

"Okay," the woman said weakly.

"I know you're hurt, but you've got to run." Opening the back door, Laurie pushed her out, watching as she dragged herself through the back gate. Once the woman had disappeared into the darkness, Laurie shut the door and leaned against it. "Don't come back," she whispered. "Ever."

2

Before approaching one of trucks in the parking lot, the woman spent a few minutes in the restroom cleaning the blood off her face. She'd have a black eye in the morning for sure. She touched her nose gingerly, tried to assess the damage, then studied herself in the mirror, rearranging her tangled hair as she struggled to bring her chaotic thoughts into focus. The pills seemed to be helping. She eventually gave up trying to figure out what was going on and instead decided to concentrate on finding a ride.

Walking up to a guy who was about climb into the cab of his truck, she asked him where he was headed. When he responded Fargo, she asked if he might be going through the Twin Cities.

"Here to Eau Clair, then I-94 through the Twin Cities, and finally up the interstate to Fargo," he said.

She asked if she could hitch a ride. He thought about it for a few seconds, looked her over a little, then said she could.

Once in the cab, before they drove off, she took an envelope out of her pocket, the only piece of evidence she had that suggested a possible destination. She asked the driver if he knew the address.

Flipping on an overhead light, he took a look. "I think so. It's close to downtown Minneapolis."

"Any chance you could drop me off near there?"

"Don't see why not."

The driver, a burly, middle-aged man with a dark tattoo peeking out from under the right cuff of an old Pendleton, didn't say much for the first few miles. Eventually, he glanced her way and said, "Your husband do that to you?" He nodded to her face.

"No."

"Boyfriend then? A lot of shit happens around the holidays. Not that it's an excuse. I'd give anything to be home with my wife and kids tonight."

"Where are you from?"

"Cedar Rapids, Iowa."

He tried to get her to open up and talk about what the problems were, said he was a good listener, but she put him off by explaining that she needed to close her eyes, try to get some sleep. She ended up dozing most of the way. When she finally sat up and looked around, the driver said they were on the outskirts of Minneapolis.

Watching quietly as the lights whizzed past, the woman took out the envelope she'd discovered back at the truck stop. The return address was the only indication she had that she might know someone in the city. If it turned out to be a dead end, then she was at a complete loss for what to do next. Along with the envelope, she'd found a bottle of painkillers and a twenty-dollar bill. Her billfold, which would have answered so many questions, appeared to be gone.

After climbing out of the cab near a Holiday station, she thanked the driver and wished him a good trip up to Fargo. She stood on the sidewalk, blowing on her hands, watching her safe, warm cocoon gear off into the night, leaving her feeling adrift and utterly alone.

Limping into the gas station, she asked the man behind the counter if she could use his phone to call a cab. He offered to call one for her. Stoically assessing her banged-up face, he tapped in a number and spoke in a heavily accented voice, giving the address.

Snow had begun falling about an hour ago. Limping outside to wait, the woman felt suddenly nauseous and dizzy. The cab driver took his time, but finally appeared. She gave him the address and asked if twenty dollars would get her there. He answered that it would.

After easing into the backseat, she pressed a hand to her mouth, hoping like hell her stomach calmed down. The modest houses quickly gave way to more upscale homes. Stopping a few minutes later at the end of a cul-de-sac, the driver turned around and held out his hand for the twenty. The ride had cost almost eighteen dollars. She asked for two dollars back.

"Are you kidding me?"

"It's all the money I have."

He gave her a disgusted look as he handed back a couple of ones.

Stepping out into the snow, the woman checked the address on the envelope against the number above the front door. It wasn't really a house. It looked more like a mini English abbey.

Standing under the deep front portico, she rang the bell. Lights were on all over the house. Half a dozen cars were parked in the circular drive. It wasn't a stretch to conclude that a party might be going on inside, which meant that it wasn't exactly great timing for an uninvited guest.

She was about to ring the bell again when a giant woman in a red-sequined flapper outfit drew back the door.

"Janey, where the hell have you been? I've been texting you for hours. Get in here." Motioning with a jeweled lorgnette, the owner of the abbey held the door open, tapping her foot impatiently. "Couldn't you dress up *a little*? I mean, ripped jeans? Your fashion sense astounds."

3

My name is Janey?"

"Don't be silly," said the giant woman, turning away and heading into the house. "Now, listen. You're going to be angry with me. Let me state this up front, it's not my fault. Julia's here. She slithered in on the arm of an *invited* guest. Who knew I would need a bouncer? I mean, I suppose I could have strong-armed her out the door myself, but—" Holding the lorgnette up to her eyes, she stopped and peered closely at Jane's face. "What on earth happened to you? Are those bruises real?"

"Um . . . yeah. Listen, I wonder if I could sit down. And . . . could I get a glass of water?"

"Water? You look like you could use something stronger than that."

"I need to take some pain medication."

Narrowing her eyes, the woman moved in close. "What's going on? Did one of the Adlers do that to you? You told me you had everything under control. I need details, Janey. Facts. You keep Cordelia Thorn out of your affairs at your own peril."

"Cordelia?"

"Yes?"

"We're friends, right?"

"What is *wrong* with you?"

She had no memory of ever seeing this woman before. "The water?"

Cordelia sniffed, considered the request, then said, "Follow me."

So this sequined-covered Amazon's name was Cordelia? And hers was Janey? She felt as if she'd emerged from a fog only to find herself lost in wonderland. Something was definitely wrong with her mind.

"Sit," said the giant as they entered the kitchen. She found a glass in one of the cupboards, filled it from a filtered tap and handed it over, then stood behind the center island, raised her chin and appeared to be assessing the situation. "Jane?"

"Yes?"

"What's going on?"

With a grimace, Jane eased down on a stool. An inner voice urged her to focus on the physical pain instead of the feeling of dread growing in her stomach. She needed the pain pills badly. That and a bed in a quiet room. The giant, however, seemed to want to talk.

"Someone did this to you. Was it Kevin? Doug? OMG, was it Father Mike?"

Instead of answering, Jane downed the pills.

"You don't seem like you're tracking very well."

"If I could just lie down—"

"You need to tell me what happened. Why you're like this."

"I'm just a little confused, okay? It'll pass." She had no idea who

15

any of those people were. None of this made any sense. She was in a free fall, with no way to anchor herself in time and space.

"Are you actually saying you don't remember who hurt you?"

Jane glanced at the bottle of rum on the counter behind the giant. Even though she knew pain pills and alcohol didn't mix, she wanted a drink. "My memory is kind of . . . fuzzy."

"Define fuzzy."

"I have a bad headache. And I'm dizzy. Can we have this conversation another time?"

"We need to get you to a hospital."

"Can you just tell me where I could find a bed or a couch? If I could just lie down for a few minutes—"

Cordelia arched an eyebrow. "You know this house as well as I do."

"Humor me."

Tapping her long red talons on the granite countertop, the giant said, "How much *don't* you remember?"

Jane massaged her temples.

"You remember me, right?"

"How could anyone forget you?"

"Then tell me about myself. How wonderful I am."

"Well, yes. You're . . . Cordelia. That says it all."

"You haven't got a clue, do you? I am your oldest friend. Your partner in crime. Your confidant. The shoulder you cry on. I am the world famous Cordelia M. Thorn, theater director extraordinaire. For heaven's sake, Janey, we've been BFFs since we were sixteen!"

"Okay," said Jane. "Great. Then can I stay here tonight?" At the sound of a child's laugh, she turned to find a little girl, dressed in a black cat outfit, skipping into the room. "Hey, Hattie. Happy New Year."

"You know my niece," boomed Cordelia, backing up against the kitchen counter and waving air into her face. "But you don't know *moi?*"

Jane smiled at the little girl, then grimaced because it made her face hurt. She did recognize Hattie. Maybe she had landed somewhere familiar and her memory was slowly coming back. "See, I'm getting better. So no doctors, at least not right now."

"Can we open the sparkling grape juice?" asked Hattie, hip thrust coyly to one side.

"Not until midnight," said Cordelia. "That's a couple more hours."

Hattie made a pleading face. "But I'm thirsty *now.*"

"Then go drink some punch."

"I feel like drinking bubbles."

"When the clock strikes midnight, you'll get all the bubbles you want."

She pulled on her cat whiskers. "If I *have* to wait."

"Go play with Jason and Lisa. You're their host tonight. You have to show them a good time."

"We all want bubbles," mumbled Hattie, dragging herself out of the room.

"A place to lie down?" repeated Jane. "Somewhere quiet."

After climbing the stairs up to the second floor, Cordelia led her to a room near the end of a broad, oriental-carpeted hallway. She opened the door and nodded for Jane to precede her.

Seeing the double bed, Jane all but fell onto it.

"The least you could do is take off those wet boots."

"Could you help me?"

Grumbling, Cordelia said, "I've *always* wanted to be your valet."

"That's nice." Jane closed her eyes.

"Why are you holding your side like that?"

"Because it hurts."

"Let me look."

"I just need to sleep."

"You are the most stubborn——" She paused. "Aren't you going to take off your coat?"

"No."

"I guess I'm glad Julia's here after all. She can come up and examine you."

"I'll see a doctor tomorrow."

"You'll see a doctor tonight. Julia."

As Cordelia covered her with a blanket, Jane opened her eyes. "Do I own a restaurant?"

"One of the best fine-dining experiences in the Twin Cities."

"What's the name?"

"The Lyme House."

"Right," she whispered. "It's on a lake."

"Lake Harriet. And before you ask," said Cordelia, brushing the tangled hair away from Jane's forehead, "no, there's no Lake Ozzie."

"That's a good one." She closed her eyes again.

The words "Adler brothers" continued to swirl around inside her mind as she began to drift toward a fitful, drugged sleep.

NEW YEAR'S DAY

Jane felt a stabbing pain as she tried to roll over in bed. Opening one eye—the other was swollen shut—she struggled to orient herself. She didn't recognize the room—and then it hit her. The abbey. The Amazon she'd met at the front door. Cordelia. Her best friend. Turning her head to look for a clock, she was startled to find a woman sitting next to the bed.

"Don't be frightened. I'm only here to help."

With her one good eye, Jane studied the woman. She was blond, trim, maybe mid-forties. Dressed for a party in a long, shimmering gown. She looked like a princess in a fairy tale. "Who are you?"

"Julia Martinsen. That mean anything to you?"

"Not really."

"I'm a doctor. A friend. I was at Cordelia's party last night. She was worried about you so she asked me to come up and look in on you. I asked you a few questions, did a few simple tests."

"You did?"

"You were pretty out of it."

"How long have you been sitting here?"

"All night.

"What time is it?"

"Seven-thirty."

"A.M. or P.M.?"

"Boy, you are out of it."

Jane lifted the quilt off and tried to sit up.

"Want to take off your coat?"

"Why do I have my coat on?"

"Here," said the woman, handing her a water glass and two pills. "These will help."

Jane downed them gratefully.

"How's your memory this morning?"

"Not great."

"Tell me what you remember about last night."

Swinging her legs out of bed, Jane sat up, pressing a hand to her ribs. She'd hoped that after a few hours of sleep, her mind would be clearer. "Riding in the cab of a semi. Knocking on Cordelia's front door. Lying down in here. That's about it."

"And who are you?"

"Jane. I own a restaurant."

"Last name."

She shrugged.

"Lawless. Jane Lawless. I'd like to examine you again. I'm concerned that you may have a concussion."

"Now?"

"Well, yes, briefly. And then, after you're dressed, I'd like you to come over to Abbott Northwestern, where I can run a more sophisticated battery of tests." She rose and stepped over to the windows to open the blinds. Early morning light flooded into the room. Moving back to Jane, she leaned in close to examine her facial bruises. "Boy, somebody sure did a number on you. You said last night that your vision was blurry. Any light sensitivity? Double vision?"

"No."

"Are you dizzy? Do you have a headache?"

"Bad, throbbing headache. And yes, I think I was pretty dizzy last night."

Julia held up several fingers. "How many fingers to you see?"

"Three."

"Good." Sitting down on the bed, she held a penlight up to Jane's eyes. "Look to your left. To your right."

Jane did as she was told. "What do you see?"

"The world in miniature."

"Huh?"

"What year is it? Who's the president? What city are we in? Where do you live?"

"Slow down."

She touched Jane's nose. "I don't think it's broken. How's the pain in your side this morning?"

"I'm pretty bruised all over, but that hurts the worst."

"You may have a bruised or fractured rib. Who did this to you?"

"Don't know."

"No memory at all?"

"None," said Jane.

"And . . . you have no memory of who I am?"

"You said you were a friend."

Julia arched an eyebrow. She was about to say something, but stopped herself.

"What?"

"We were . . . more than friends."

"We were?"

"Lovers. For several years."

Another puzzle piece fell into place. "It ended?"

"Badly."

"Why?"

"Because I lied to you one too many times. Because you couldn't trust me."

What a strange situation this was. As far as Jane knew, she was meeting Julia for the first time.

"I'm not always a good person," added Julia. "I want to be, but I also want . . . what I want."

"Sounds fairly human. Why not lie to me now? You could tell me whatever you want and I wouldn't know the difference."

"Good point. Let's try this one on for size. You still love me, Jane. The passion we felt for each other never died. You do your best to deny it, but you can't bring yourself to let go entirely."

"Is that true?"

"Yes."

"But you could be lying."

"I could be."

"You like to play games, don't you?"

Julia smiled.

Even in the shape she was in, Jane could hardly deny that she found Julia attractive. "I don't think I have the energy for this conversation."

Cordelia poked her head inside the door. "Is she harassing you, Janey? Just say the word and I'll give her the boot."

"Good morning to you, too, Cordelia." Julia rose from the bed. "Jane's agreed to let me run some tests. I thought I'd drive over

22

to Abbott Northwestern and get everything set up." Looking back down at Jane, she said, "If you want to shower, that's fine. You might want to eat something. Painkillers can be hard on the stomach." She picked up the orange plastic bottle from the dresser. Reading the front, she said, "Who's Kevin Adler?"

"One of the Adler brothers," said Cordelia.

"That may be axiomatic," replied Julia, "but it tells me nothing."

"He owns a bar in New Dresden, Wisconsin. We'll talk about it later."

"Fine." She checked her watch. "If you could bring Jane to the hospital at nine, I'll have everything all arranged." As she passed Cordelia, she repeated, "Nine sharp."

"Yeah, right," said Cordelia. "Like doctors are always so big on punctuality."

Jane felt ridiculous wearing the pink angora scarf, gloves, and hat Cordelia demanded she don before going outside. "I'm not sick," said Jane.

"I'll be the judge of that," responded Cordelia.

Even with her memory problems, Jane knew she wasn't a pink sort of person.

"Now," said Cordelia, straightening Jane's hat, "I'll go out to the garage, get the car, and bring it around to the front."

"Where's Hattie?"

"Still in bed. So's Bolger. You remember Bolger, yes?"

"Hattie's nanny?"

"Bingo. You're making progress. Even the cats are still asleep. It was a late night for everyone." She swept toward the door. "Oh, hey, bring my purse when you come out. It's hanging on that ladder-back chair under the stairs." She pointed, twirled, and left.

23

Even with the painkillers, Jane hurt pretty much everywhere a person could hurt. It took her a full minute to walk over and get the purse, and another full minute to return to the door. She felt fragile, unstable, like she could shatter if she moved too fast. Hearing a loud "Moo" come from inside Cordelia's bag, Jane opened it and found that her friend's cell phone was making the noise. It mooed several more times before she decided to click it on. "Hello?" she said, holding it to her ear.

"Cordelia?" It was a man's voice.

"No, she's not here right now. Can I take a message?"

"Jane? Is that you?"

"Who's this?"

"My God, it *is* you. I called you a dozen times last night. I figured I'd try Cordelia this morning, thinking she might know where you were, why you weren't answering your phone. It's Guthrie. You left me a message yesterday. Said you'd call later in the day, that you had something to tell me. Is Kira okay? Did you talk to her?"

Jane had no idea what he was talking about. "Guthrie? Guthrie . . . Hewitt?"

"Yeah. Absolutely."

"I was in an accident last night. My memory's a little foggy."

"What kind of accident?"

"Just give me a few more details."

"You've been in New Dresden. New Dresden, *Wisconsin*. I hired you."

"Hired me? To do what?"

"Are you kidding me?" He was beginning to sound angry. "You're a licensed P.I. I came to you because I knew you—I used to be a waiter at your restaurant. I hired you to look into the death—the murder—of my girlfriend's mother."

"Is that Kira?"

"Kira Adler, right."

There was that name again. "The Adler brothers," she whispered.

"Finally. Jeez, you had me worried there for a minute. So what did you find out? I've been going crazy. There's something sick about that town. It swallows people whole."

Jane eased down on a bench by the door. Rubbing her temple, she closed her eyes. "Look, Guthrie—" Crazy, tilted images began to burst inside her head. She felt suddenly dizzy. Dizzy and nauseous. Outside, a car horn honked.

"Jane? Are you there? Are you okay?"

"Not really," she said. Unable to sit upright, she found herself slipping onto the floor in a weird sort of slow motion. The cell phone dropped from her pink glove onto the oriental carpet. She was spinning—spinning and falling through stutter flashes of light, like an old black-and-white movie reel flickering into the final frames. She watched the front door open and heard Cordelia scream. And then everything just . . . stopped.

PART TWO: SIX WEEKS EARLIER—LATE NOVEMBER

"The truth." Dumbledore sighed. "It is a beautiful and terrible thing, and should therefore be treated with great caution."

—J. K. ROWLING, *HARRY POTTER AND THE SORCERER'S STONE*

5

Guthrie Hewitt woke to the sound of his girlfriend thrashing around in bed next to him. The sun leaked in around the edges of the plantation shutters, though since the alarm hadn't gone off, he knew it was still early. He wrestled his way out of a tangle of blankets just as an arm connected with his face.

"Whoa," he said, loud enough to startle Kira awake. "Come on, babe. This early morning mayhem is getting out of hand."

She blinked her eyes open. "What? What happened? Did I say something? My god, did I hurt you?"

His usual move was to lean over and kiss her, but this morning he'd finally had it with her nightmares. "Yeah, you did. You beaned me in the face with your arm."

"Oh, honey, I'm sorry. It's stress. My classes. Maybe I should sleep on the couch."

"You think that's a good solution?"

"Well—"

He turned over, propped his elbow against a pillow and played with her golden hair, tucking several delicate blond wisps behind her ear. "It's the same nightmare, right? The one about your mother?"

"I don't want to talk about it."

"Hey, you're shivering." He pulled her close and whispered, "It was just a dream. You're awake now. Safe with me." Kissing her cheek, he added, "I wish you'd tell me more about it? Maybe I can help."

"It's just too crazy."

All that Kira would ever say about the nightmare was that she'd had it ever since she was a child. Kira had grown up in New Dresden, Wisconsin, which was where most of her family still lived. It was a town of approximately three thousand, 180 or so miles northeast of the Twin Cities. The fall after she'd graduated from high school, she'd moved to Minneapolis to attend the University of Minnesota's School of Nursing. She went home fairly often the first year, but as time went on, especially after she met Guthrie during the summer between her freshman and sophomore years, her visits became less frequent.

On the day before she was supposed to pack up her car for a Fourth of July trip, the nightmare had hit with such force that it had taken three shots of vodka and a lengthy back rub before she calmed down enough to spend the rest of the night watching TV in the living room. The next morning, Guthrie had found her sitting on the couch, sobbing. That was when she finally explained that the nightmare was about her mother.

All Guthrie knew about Delia Adler was what Kira had told him on their second date. When Kira was five years old, Delia had fallen off the back deck of their house, which was perched over a steep ravine. At the time, there'd been some talk about the possibility of suicide, but because she hadn't left a note and no one really believed she was depressed, the family assumed it was simply a tragic accident. The temperature that December day was apparently well below zero. She wasn't found for many hours, and by the time she was located, her body was frozen solid. Kira had gone off to school that morning excited to continue her work on the Christmas gifts she was making for her parents and sister. When she returned to the house on the bus that afternoon, she found it filled with family—and a police officer. Gracie, her older sister, was perched on the couch, watching TV and ignoring the commotion.

Kira had cancelled last summer's Fourth of July trip back home. This Thanksgiving, however, her family, especially her grandmother, wasn't going to be put off. When Kira asked to bring Guthrie along, her grandmother had hesitated at first, but finally agreed that it was about time they met.

"Babe," said Guthrie, kissing Kira's hair, wishing he could do something to help her. "Seems to me that when you're about to go home, the nightmare gets worse. I think that's the stressor."

She bit her lip, looked away. "Maybe."

"We don't have to go tomorrow. We could make up an excuse."

"I promised them, Guthrie. They all want to meet you. And I miss them. I really do."

"Then . . . when we get back home, maybe you should see someone. A sleep doctor. A therapist."

She slipped her arm around his waist. Resting her head against his chest, she grew silent. Finally, she said, "If I tell you what the dream is about, will you promise not to think I'm totally crazy?"

"Of course, I promise," he said, assuming that she was simply being her overly dramatic self.

Hesitating, she drew back so she could look him in the eyes. "Okay. Please understand—this is hard for me." She took a ragged breath, then said, "The setting for the dream is always different. It takes place in a mall, or outside in a field. Once it happened in a tree house. Another time on a beach. But one thing never changes. In the dream—the nightmare—my mother is strangled."

"Kira—"

"I know. Let me finish. There's always a bright light behind her and it gets in my eyes, makes it hard for me to see. All I know is that someone has their hands around her throat and is choking her. The worst part is, I can't do a thing to help her. I can't move. Can't cry out. I'm frozen, and all I can do is watch."

"But you said your mother's death was an accident."

"No doubt in anyone's mind. Nobody was even home that morning, which includes me, so there's no way I could have seen what's in the nightmare."

"But if there's any truth in it, your mother was murdered."

Climbing out from under the covers, Kira turned her back to him and sat on the edge of the bed. In a voice barely above a whisper, she continued, "In the final moment of the nightmare, the murderer turns and comes for me. That's when, mercifully, I usually wake up."

Now he was shivering. "So, what does the nightmare say? Who did it?"

"That's the thing: I finally get a good look at the killer, but it's always someone different. The first time I had the nightmare it was my grandmother."

"Evangeline?"

She nodded. "The next time it was my Uncle Doug. And then my father. My Aunt Hannah—"

32

"Always someone in your immediate family?"

"Always."

"So, does that make you a little frightened of them? Do you think there's any possibility——"

"No, Guthrie. It's just a dream."

"But, then . . . why? There has to be a reason it reoccurs."

"It's the exact question I keep asking myself. Because that's it. I've been thinking about it a lot lately. I'm supposed to learn something from it. Until I do, no matter how much I want it to go away, no matter how badly it frightens me, it will never leave me alone."

6

THANKSGIVING DAY

New Dresden, Wisconsin

On the ride from Minneapolis, Guthrie noted that Kira seemed alternately subdued and excited. She'd spent all day yesterday baking ginger cookies, brownies, and lemon bars, saying that it was a mortal sin in the Adler family to arrive for Thanksgiving dinner without a homemade culinary contribution. He was told that the meal itself was always at the farm—her grandmother's place. Everyone in the family would be there. All would spend the night.

"If everyone lives in town, why not just go home?" he asked.

"It's tradition," said Kira. "You don't screw with tradition in my family. The house has six bedrooms, so when you add in the two of us, we'll all just fit."

He counted in his head. "No, there would still be one extra bedroom."

"One for my dad," said Kira, holding up a finger. "One for my grandmother. One for my Uncle Doug and Aunt Laurie. One for my Aunt Hannah."

"And one for us. That's five."

"You think my grandmother's going to let us to sleep in the same room?"

He looked over at her. "Isn't she? I mean, we live together."

"Not when we're under her roof. You better make your peace with the fact that we'll be staying in separate bedrooms."

"Until everyone goes to sleep."

She glanced at him and grinned. "We can't get caught. Gram is very religious."

"What flavor?"

"Catholic."

"I never knew that. When I asked you, you said you weren't religious."

"I'm not. My dad wasn't big on church stuff. I never went much as a kid—only when Gram made me. I mean, I'm sure Dad considers himself Catholic. My Aunt Hannah goes sometimes with my grandma, when she's in town for the weekend. My Uncle Doug thinks religion is a crock. Aunt Laurie is a wonderful woman, but she's a mouse."

"Is that a religious affiliation?"

She chucked him on the arm. "No, I just mean she's quiet. She blends in, makes an effort to go with the flow."

"You mean she stays under the radar?"

"I suppose that could be her motivation. For all I know, she's a practicing Buddhist. She was like a second mother to me growing up. I don't blame her for being quiet around my uncle. You know how they say every family has a few jerks? Uncle Doug's ours. He knows everything there is to know about politics and isn't afraid to tell you."

"Sounds like Thanksgiving at the Adlers may have a little drama."

"We're all pretty well behaved. Except, as I said, for Uncle Doug."

"Did your dad ever remarry?"

"Never."

"Your mom was probably a hard act to follow."

Kira chewed her lip and didn't respond.

"No interest in women?"

"How do I put this politely? Dad has a number of . . . friends in town. Friends with benefits. He rarely wants for female attention, but there's nobody special in his life."

They reached the farm just after eleven. Guthrie stood behind his ancient Subaru Impreza and lifted the luggage out of the trunk. As usual, he and Kira had both overpacked. Guthrie cut himself some slack because he wanted to make a good impression and wasn't entirely certain from what Kira had told him whether the family tended toward the casual or formal. He had to cover all his bases.

Grandma Evangeline's house, a rambling old farmhouse with white clapboard siding and Victorian pretensions, sat perched on a small rise surrounded by hoar-frosted fields dotted with trees. There was an old garage, the kind with doors that folded to the side, and a barn that looked new.

"It was a working farm once upon a time, right?" asked Guthrie, refolding his scarf over his wool cardigan.

Kira stretched her arms over her head as she gazed up at the cloudless late-autumn sky. "Dairy cows. When my Grandpa Henry inherited the place, he sold off a bunch of the land and all of the cattle. Did I ever tell you that Great-Grandpa Adler started the *New Dresden Herald* back in the early 1920s? He was minor royalty in town. He ran the newspaper until he retired and turned the reins over to Grandpa Henry."

"Did the royalty status transfer with it?"

She smiled. "Yes, for a time. There was more to it than just the newspaper. Henry married Jamie Carmody's daughter, Evangeline. Old Jamie C. was a wealthy businessman, owned property all over the county, bootlegged during Prohibition. He supplied—if not outright owned—every bar in a hundred-mile radius of New Dresden. Bars are big in rural Wisconsin, in case you didn't know."

"So I'm dating a princess of the realm."

"And I expect to be treated accordingly." She smirked. "Bring the bags in. I'll tip you later, when we're alone."

"You better," he muttered.

A slight, white-haired woman stepped out onto the long, open, front porch, fingers wrapped around a mug. She smiled and waved. Guthrie found himself smiling back at her. Kira rushed up the steps into her grandmother's arms.

As he hefted the luggage up onto the porch, Evangeline said, "You must be Guthrie. Welcome." Reaching out her hand, she added, "I've got rooms all fixed up for both of you."

"Thanks," he said, trying for, but not quite reaching, enthusiasm. The woman before him truly had been a beauty once, and in many ways, still was. With delicate features, high cheekbones, and fine white hair pinned into a loose bun at the back of her neck, she appeared rosy with health and vigor. She was dressed in a rough flannel-lined barn coat, slim-legged jeans and hiking boots, but still managed to look elegant. Except for the age difference, grandmother and granddaughter could have been sisters.

Coming into the house, Guthrie was immediately enveloped by the smell of roasting turkey. An Airedale in a red bandana and a black Lab in a yellow bandana burst out of the kitchen. The Lab began to sniff Guthrie's legs, while the Airedale headed straight for Kira.

"Where's Foxy?" asked Kira, bending over to rub the dog's ears.

"Out in the barn, resting," said Evangeline. "Our little girl is pregnant. A new litter is on the way."

"My grandmother breeds Airedales," Kira said to Guthrie. When the Lab nosed her hand, she turned her attention to him. "Wow, Sammy's getting so old. He's my dad's hunting dog," she explained, looking up. "Seems like he's been around forever."

"He can't hear very well anymore," said Evangeline. "But he still plugs along. He's almost thirteen, ancient for a dog his size."

The interior air felt deliciously warm. Scented candles burned on the mantel in the living room. Directly to Guthrie's right, the dining room table was decked in a fine linen tablecloth and the best family china and crystal. The furniture, he was happy to note, sacrificed beauty for comfort. The house looked lived in and loved.

He was about to head up the stairs when a muscular, broad-shouldered older guy came out of the kitchen carrying a load of birch logs. He had on threadbare jeans, beat-up hiking boots, a brown corduroy shirt, and navy blue quilted vest. Reading glasses hung from a lanyard around his neck. Apparently, the formal table setting didn't mandate formal attire. Score another one for the Adler family.

"You must be the boyfriend," he said, proceeding into the living room, where he dumped the logs next to the fireplace.

"Yup," agreed Guthrie. "That would be me."

"I'm Kira's dad. Call me Kevin." He nodded to the suitcases. "Need some help with those?"

"No, think I've got it covered."

"Turn right when you get upstairs. Your room is the last door on the left. Kira's is across from you."

Guthrie nodded his thanks, then headed up. When he came back down a few minutes later, he found a woman dripping with gold jewelry coming through the front door, carrying a pie in each hand.

"Take this," she said, handing a pecan pie to Guthrie and motioning for him to follow her into the kitchen. "I'm Guthrie," he said, setting the pie down on the counter next to a relish tray.

"Figured." She eyed him briefly. "You're kinda cute."

"Thanks. I think."

"I like tall and lanky. But . . . do you always wear your hair like that?" She twirled her finger. "Thought the ponytail look went out with the sixties." Not waiting for an answer, she asked, "Where's my mom?"

"No idea."

Kira sailed into the kitchen and gave the woman an extra-long hug. "This is my Aunt Hannah," she said, beaming at Guthrie as she tried to pry a pecan off the top of the pie.

"Stop that," said Hannah, lightly slapping her niece's hand. Removing her sunglasses, Hannah said, "You can call me Dr. Adler."

Kira burst out laughing. "Right."

Assessing Guthrie from head to toe, Hannah added, "Just kidding. You can drop the last name and just call me doctor."

"Ignore her," said Kira.

Hannah shrugged.

"Dad sent me in here to get some matches. He's building us a fire."

"My brother, the arsonist," muttered Hannah.

As they dug through the kitchen drawers, Guthrie edged toward the back door. Once outside, he sucked in a deep breath, thankful to have found a moment alone. The family seemed friendly enough. Still, it was going to be hard being the outsider all weekend.

Stepping down off the back step onto a graveled path, Guthrie walked around the back of the house, where he came upon a broad brick patio nestled up against a rock retaining wall. The outdoor furniture and large gas grill were covered by heavy tarps. Scanning the rear of the property, he was surprised to find Evangeline inside a small fenced-off area about twenty yards to the right of the barn. Rectangular stones stuck out of the ground at odd angles. It appeared to be an old cemetery.

Evangeline stood with her head bowed, arms crossed in front of her, holding a single pink rose. It seemed like such a private moment that he didn't want to intrude, but before he could creep silently away, she looked up and noticed him, motioning for him to come join her.

"You might as well meet the rest of the family," she said, watching him with her intense blue-eyed gaze.

He opened the weathered wood gate and stepped up to her. Crouching down, he read the names on the two oldest gravestones. "Adolf Adler, 1892-1951" and "Emma Adler, 1896-1968." Under Adolf's name was an inscription:

REMEMBER ME AS YOU PASS BY,
AS YOU ARE NOW, SO ONCE WAS I,

As I am now, so you will be,
Prepare for death and follow me.

How utterly grim, thought Guthrie, though he didn't say it out loud.

"They were my husband's parents," said Evangeline. "They bought the land and built the house. Adolf began the local newspaper, a job my husband, Henry, eventually inherited."

Guthrie examined several more stones, then came to Henry's, the tallest, made of gray-and-black granite. Henry's inscription was a quote:

"Where there is sorrow there
is holy ground." Oscar Wilde

Better, thought Guthrie. Some hope in that one.

"Henry and I were married for forty-seven years," said Evangeline, a sad smile tugging at the corners her mouth. "He wanted to be buried here, with his parents, but the county wouldn't allow it anymore. The recent stones mark the sites of cremation urns."

"You have three children?"

"Douglas is the oldest. Then Hannah. Kevin was my last. That's Kira's father."

"And they all still live around here?"

"Hannah lives in Eau Claire, but she maintains a small home here. And then, of course, Kira moved to the Twin Cities."

"Do you have other grandchildren?"

"I'm afraid not. It was a great sadness for all of us when Douglas and Laurie weren't able to conceive. I know it was Laurie's dream to have a large family." Transferring her gaze to a crow sitting at the edge of the barn roof, she said, "Hard to live a life without a dream. You have one, Guthrie?"

Pushing out of his crouch, he rose up next to her. "I do. Actually, it's tea."

"Tea?"

"I'm in business with my brother. We're importers and own a teahouse in Minneapolis. Eventually, I want to create and sell our own blends."

"When we have some time just for the two of us, I want to hear more about it." Evangeline placed the pink rose in front of a small white marble headstone, one that read,

GRACE ADLER.

1989–1996.

ONLY IN DARKNESS CAN YOU SEE THE STARS.

"That's Kira's sister, right?" asked Guthrie, pushing his hands into his back pockets. "I didn't realize she was only seven when she died."

"It was a car accident." Evangeline caressed the gravestone before straightening up. "Not three weeks after Delia passed. An awful time for the family."

"Delia was Kira and Grace's mother."

Evangeline nodded.

"I don't see her gravestone."

"No. Kevin——" She glanced up at Guthrie. "He wanted to scatter her ashes on the north shore of Lake Superior. It was a favorite place of theirs."

Seemed like the least they could do was put up a memorial

marker, thought Guthrie. As he considered the significance of the omission, a rusted gray Buick rumbled over the gravel into the drive and parked next to a white van. An middle-aged woman with dark hair and red lipstick got out of the passenger-side door. From the driver's side, a balding, heavyset man in a tweed sport coat with professorial-looking patches on the elbows emerged. Neither looked particularly happy, though when they caught sight of Evangeline, their expressions brightened. The man took a moment to tap out his pipe. Stuffing it into his coat pocket, he dug through the backseat and, once the door was shut, held up two white sacks.

"That's my oldest son, Douglas, and his wife, Laurie," said Evangeline, waving and smiling. Slipping her arm through Guthrie's, she asked, "You any good at peeling potatoes?"

"One of my best events."

"Good man. Let's get to work."

7

By one A.M., Guthrie still hadn't slept. He'd eaten too much, that
was a given, but it was more than that. Kira might be sleeping
peacefully across the hall, but, ironically, it was her nightmare
that was keeping him awake. Maybe he was being too sensitive,
looking for clues to prove something that had never happened.
Was it really possible that someone in Kira's family had murdered
her mother?

Kira's father, Kevin, was a friendly, straightforward kind of
guy. He'd spent time in the military—had served in the first Gulf
War. There was a picture of him in his army uniform on the
piano. As a young man, he'd been movie-star handsome—wavy
brown hair, strong square chin, broad shoulders, and a confi-
dent, cocky grin. He looked much the same today, though his
hair was shaggier and shot through with gray. He swore like a
man who'd served in the army, and yet there was a sweetness
about him, an empathetic appreciation of the others at the dinner
table.

Guthrie's mother had once pointed out to him that people

rarely asked questions of other people. Mostly, they waited around for a chance to talk about themselves. She told him that when he found someone who asked questions and actually listened to the answers, that he'd found a rare soul indeed. Kevin Adler was like that.

Hannah was an arch personality, liked to tease, to sit back and make acerbic comments. Doug had clearly staked out the position of family intellectual and curmudgeon. He was animated, opinionated, and surreptitiously downed hefty sips from a thin silver flask he kept secreted in the inside pocket of his sport coat. He also partook liberally of the Irish whiskey and Chardonnay Kevin had brought with him—his contribution to the meal. While Doug never seemed drunk, he clearly kept himself on the edge of inebriation throughout the day. Occasionally, he would slip in a comment that was so breathtakingly bitter, it brought all conversation to a halt.

As for Laurie, Doug's wife, Kira's assessment of her seemed accurate. She spoke very little during dinner. When she wasn't looking down, picking at her food, her attention was focused on Kevin or Doug. There was a lot more to her than met the eye— Guthrie was sure of it. She wasn't quiet because she had nothing to say.

Of all the people who'd been at the table, Guthrie liked Evangeline the best. She was warm and loving, and made every attempt to include Guthrie in the conversation. She might not allow two young unmarried people to sleep together under her roof, but she made no conspicuous show of her religious beliefs either. And she loved tea.

Like Guthrie's own family, Kira's had a hierarchy and its own kind of heartbeat. Because Guthrie had grown up with a drug-addicted mother and a father who steadfastly refused to believe he had a right to his own feelings and opinions, he'd learned early on to listen for subtext. Words weren't only used to communicate, they could also obscure. Beyond words, the truth of any interaction often lay in what wasn't said, in the emotions that underpinned whatever subject was on the table. Deciphering his parents had always given Guthrie a splitting headache. He'd been hoping that Kira's family would be a more easygoing group—what you saw was what you got. It was probably asking too much.

Slipping out of bed, Guthrie grabbed his bathrobe and headed out to the hallway in search of a bottle of Maalox, or failing that, something fizzy to drink. He rummaged through the medicine cabinet in the second-floor bathroom, but finding nothing, he tiptoed toward the stairs. He didn't want to wake the sleeping family.

Before he got halfway down, he heard voices in the kitchen. The stair treads creaked under his weight, so he stopped, wondering if whoever was in there had heard him. When they continued, he sat down to listen.

Kevin and Doug appeared to be the only two people in the room.

"You didn't vote?" said Doug's voice. "What the hell's wrong with you?"

"Didn't like any of the candidates," replied Kevin. "So what would have been the point?"

"The point? What's the *point*?"

"I'm not up for an argument, Dougie."

"Don't call me Dougie. You don't deserve citizenship in this country if you don't vote."

"Back the hell off or I'll take my bottle of Jameson and drink it somewhere else."

Doug muttered. "I'm just saying—"

"*Doug.*"

"All right, all right. Jesus."

They stayed quiet for a few minutes.

Guthrie was ready to head back up to his bed when Doug said, "You must really like working with Laurie."

"Why do you say that?"

"Because sometimes she doesn't get home until four in the morning."

"We do cleanup after we close the bar."

"For two hours?"

"Sometimes we sit down and have a beer together. You got a problem with that?"

"Maybe."

"Meaning what?"

"Hell, Kevin. You sleep with half the women in this town. Can't you leave my wife alone?"

"Oh Lord. I should have known you'd think that. It's not happening."

"No?"

"*No.* If you got problems in your marriage, it's not because of me."

Doug grunted.

More clinking glasses.

"Since we're on the subject of my wife," said Doug, his gravelly voice starting to slur, "I have to say, she kind of surprised me. She's usually so quiet. When I see her behind the bar, it's like she's had a personality transplant."

"She's quiet around you, asshole, because you suck up all the air in the room."

"You are so full of it." Chair legs scraped against linoleum.

"You wanna fight, Doug, or you wanna drink?"

Guthrie waited for the brawl to begin. Instead, he heard the sound of wood creaking as Doug resumed his chair. After that, neither man spoke for a while.

Finally, Doug muttered, "All the beds in this house should be taken out and burned. They're so old they probably have fleas."

"The price we pay," said Kevin.

"We all know about paying prices."

Kevin said nothing.

"I think . . . I . . . am officially drunk," said Doug.

"I think you've been officially drunk all day."

"Shut up. On my days off, I like to relax."

"Uh-huh."

"That kid," continued Doug. "You ask me, he had a lot of nerve asking all those questions about Delia. I felt like we were being interrogated."

"He's head over heels for Kira," said Kevin. "But yeah, he's definitely the nosey type."

Guthrie stiffened. He'd joined Doug and Kevin in the living room to watch the Green Bay game after dinner. Had he gone too far with his questions? After all, he and Kira were serious about each other. It stood to reason that he'd want to know about her mother.

"It just pisses me off," said Doug. In a voice apparently meant to mimic Guthrie's, he said, "Where'd you meet Delia? Was she depressed before she died? God, Kevin, I hope you weren't the one who found her."

"He doesn't know jack shit," said Kevin.

"Exactly," said Doug. "We covered our tracks. End of story."

"Except, it's not the end. I'm not sure it will ever end."

A wave of apprehension rolled through Guthrie's chest. *Covered our tracks?* What did they mean by that?

A new voice was added to the mix. Hannah's bedroom was on the first floor. Guthrie hadn't heard her moving around downstairs, but suddenly she said, "What are you boys talking about at this hour?"

"The usual," said Kevin.

"You gonna share that whiskey?"

When Guthrie heard chair legs scraping the linoleum again, he assumed that Hannah had joined them at the table. He was so freaked at how easily he might be caught eavesdropping from the stairs that he got up and headed back to his room. How could he ever tell Kira what he'd just heard, especially since nothing had been explicitly stated? Would she really want to know if her family was responsible for her mother's death—or, at the very least, was keeping some aspect of the death a secret?

If Guthrie took a cold, pragmatic approach, he supposed Delia's passing, however it happened, could be considered water under the bridge, unlikely to have any impact on Kira's life today. And yet, he knew himself well enough to realize that if he and Kira got married—and he was planning to pop the question on Christmas Eve—it was a scab he wouldn't be able to stop himself from picking. Even more worrisome was the fact that Kevin Adler knew that he was more interested in Delia's death than he had any right to be. That had been Guthrie's mistake, though there was nothing to be done about it now.

This trip hadn't turned out to be the kind of up close and

personal he'd been looking forward to with the Adler family. He'd be a fool if he didn't wonder, now that he'd linked his life with Kira's, what kind of a hornet's nest he'd just stepped into.

PART THREE: LATE DECEMBER

For every complex problem there is a solution—simple, neat, and wrong.

—H. L. MENCKEN

8

SIX DAYS BEFORE CHRISTMAS

Minneapolis

Jane leaned back in her chair and tossed her reading glasses on the desktop. She'd been concentrating for hours on the late-winter menu, sourcing possible options for specials, working on expanding some of the "Small Bites" options for the Lyme House's main-course menu. She needed a break. The dinner rush wouldn't begin for another couple of hours, which meant that this was the perfect chance for her to grab something to eat. She hadn't had a decent meal today and her stomach was growling so loudly it actually made her laugh. She called up to the kitchen and asked for a plate of bangers and mash—and some coarse grain mustard—to be sent down to her office.

After saving the page she'd been working on, she glanced through her calendar, seeing that she had an interview with a reporter for *City Pages* on Friday morning. It would be great PR for the restaurant, and also for the brilliant new sous chef she'd hired to develop a separate Scandinavian menu.

Rising from her chair, Jane headed down the hall to the

ground-floor pub. She still had a bunch of shopping to do before Christmas. This would be the first Christmas she'd spent in Minnesota without her brother, Peter, and his family. They were in Brazil, where he was shooting a documentary on the Latin American Spring. Their father had recently turned seventy and had also broken up with his on-and-off girlfriend, both big changes in his life. Jane wanted to make sure his Christmas was filled with warm fires, good food and wine, and family—the last part meant not only Jane, but her best friend, Cordelia, and Cordelia's niece, Hattie. Jane had recently ended a romantic relationship of her own, though it hadn't taken her long to rebound. In truth, she felt she was in a great place.

Stepping into the pub, Jane found a few regulars seated at the bar, as well as a foursome playing cribbage in one of the raised booths. The hearth in the back room was burning hardwood logs, low and slow, ready for those brave souls willing to negotiate the frigid temperatures in order to grab a beer and a burger after work.

Jane made small talk with the bartender while she poured herself a mug of coffee. She bent down to get a napkin and when she straightened up, she saw a familiar figure sitting alone at one of the tables.

"Guthrie?" she said, walking over to him. She hadn't seen him in years. In that time, he'd let his brown hair grow long. It was pulled into a ponytail and trailed midway down his back.

"Jane, hi," he said, standing, smiling at her. The strain in his voice betrayed a degree of nervousness.

Guthrie Hewitt had begun working for Jane as a busboy during his senior year of high school. The following summer, he'd graduated to waiter. At the time, he and his older brother were living at home, saving their money so they could rent an apartment together. Since they both worked two jobs, they saved a significant amount in a fairly short period of time. The following summer, they'd blown it all on a backpacking trip to Japan, China, Thailand, and India.

Jane remembered talking to Guthrie after he'd come back. Both he and his brother had developed such a passion for tea that they were thinking of getting into the import business. She didn't know the particulars, but after they renovated a space next to a busy smoke shop on Hennepin Avenue, the Hewitt & Hewitt Teahouse was born. It quickly became one of the trendiest spots in the uber-trendy Uptown area. Jane had never stopped in, though she'd always meant to.

"Great to see you," said Jane. "How's the tea business?"

"Good," he said, his smile fading as he sat back down. He folded his hands over a manila envelope.

Since he didn't have anything to eat or drink on the table, she asked if she could get him something.

"No thanks," he said. "I was sitting here wondering if coming to see you was the right thing to do."

"Can I help in some way?"

"Could we go back to your office? There's something I need to show you."

"Sure," she said. He seemed so hesitant that she glanced over her shoulder a couple of times as she led him down the hall, thinking that he might simply run off and never tell her why he'd come. Once she took her seat behind the desk and he'd chosen one of the chairs opposite her, she said, "What's up?"

He ran a hand over the stubble on his face. "I'm planning to ask my girlfriend to marry me on Christmas Eve."

"That's wonderful news." So why the long face, she wondered. "Who is she? How long have you known her?"

"Her name is Kira Adler. She's a nursing student at the U, will graduate next year. She's from a small town in Wisconsin. There's no doubt in my mind that she's the one for me. I am totally, one hundred percent, head over heels in love."

Jane nodded, grinned. "She feel the same way?"

"Totally. I met her family about a month ago at Thanksgiving. We drove to New Dresden and stayed at her grandmother's house for a couple of nights. I'd known that Kira's mother had died when she was quite young. She fell from the deck of their house. The thing is—" He paused, tugging nervously at his shirt—"Kira's had this dream—a nightmare really—for most of her life. Recently it's been getting worse. Two days before we left for New Dresden, she finally told me what the dream was about." He paused again, pulled at a small rip in his jeans. "See, in the nightmare, Kira sees her mother being strangled."

"Wow," said Jane, sitting up straight. "That's intense. Is there any way it could be true?"

"She says absolutely not."

"So who committed the murder in the dream?"

"It's always someone in her family, but the identity of the person changes."

"Huh. Strange. Nobody ever wondered if it was suicide?"

"Sure, they wondered, but since they had no proof one way or the other, they decided to come down on the side of accidental. Kevin, that's Kira's dad, got home earlier than usual that day. He was working construction at the time. When he couldn't find his wife, he went to see if her car was gone. It wasn't. And her purse was on the kitchen table. I don't have all the details, but the body was eventually found. The deck Delia fell from overhangs a ravine. That's where they found her. It was December. Below-zero temps. She had some injuries, but most likely died of exposure."

"How old was Kira when this happened?"

"Five. She was in kindergarden. Her older sister, Gracie, was seven."

"New Dresden has its own police department?"

"I called, talked to the patrol officer on duty. He said that besides the chief, they've always had four full-time officers and two part-time."

"Did you ask for a copy of the police report on Delia's death?"

"The guy looked but couldn't find anything. Since it was ruled accidental, he said the attending officer might not have filed one. And because it wasn't a crime scene, he doubted any photos had been taken. The only information I could get my hands on was Delia's death certificate, which was useless. I read it over and learned nothing. I mean, I already knew the cause of death."

"But you think there's some truth in Kira's nightmare?"

"I didn't. But——" Guthrie explained about the late-night conversation he'd overheard between Kevin and Doug. "They were talking about Delia's death. These were Doug's exact words: 'We covered our tracks. End of story.' Kevin disagreed. He said the story would never end. He also said that Kira was clueless about what happened. And then Hannah walked in——that's Kira's aunt. She asked what they were talking about and Kevin said, 'The usual.' Am I wrong, Jane? Seems to me those three know a lot more about Delia's death than they've ever said. I asked a few simple questions about Delia's passing and Doug got all hot and bothered——thought I was interrogating him and Kevin. I mean, come on."

"Did you tell Kira what you overheard?"

He looked down, shook his head. "How am I supposed to tell the woman I love that there's a chance her family did have something to do with the death of her mother? Especially, when I have no proof. That is, until a few hours ago."

"What happened a few hours ago?" asked Jane.

"This." He handed her the envelope. "Came in the mail."

Jane drew out a stack of five-by-seven photos. Stuck to the top photo was a yellow Post-it note. In black ink someone had printed:

> Proof Delia Adler was murdered. Stay out of it or the same thing will happen to you.

There was no return address. The postmark read Henderson, Wisconsin. Flipping quickly through the stack, Jane found that each photo showed a woman in dark slacks and what appeared to be a red ski sweater. Her body lay halfway down the edge of a steep ravine, caught between several large boulders and a clump of leafless birch. She was on her back, legs bent at unnatural angles. The shots were all taken from above.

"I wonder if the police did take photos."

"No idea," said Guthrie. "All I know is, someone wanted me to see them and hoped it would stop me from any digging any further."

"The problem is," said Jane, flipping through the stack a second time, "I see nothing here that proves Delia was murdered. And even if she was, these photos can't tell us who did it."

"But . . . see . . . that's where you come in," said Guthrie,

58

shifting forward in his chair. "I heard that you're a licensed PI now. You work part time with another guy—an ex-homicide cop."

"He's retired."

"Right. So, what if I hired you? The Adlers know who I am, but they don't know you. Maybe you could spend some time in New Dresden, investigate them. Figure out what went on all those years ago."

"You really want to pay me to prove that someone Kira loves is a murderer?" By the look on his face, he obviously hadn't thought that one through.

"I guess . . . maybe—" He scratched the side of his cheek. "Maybe I should tell her what I overheard. Show her the photos—"

"You think she'd want to see her mother like that?"

"Okay, I won't show them to her unless she wants to see them. But I can tell her about them and show her the note. If she wants to pursue it, then . . . we will. If not, I guess I wasted your time."

"I have to tell you," said Jane, putting the photos back into the envelope, "even if Kira agrees to the investigation, I'm not taking any new clients right now. I'm buried in work here at the restaurant." Guthrie looked so crestfallen that she added, "If you want, I could show the photos to my partner, A. J. Nolan. If, after you speak to Kira, you want to go ahead with it, he'd already be up to speed."

"Is he any good?"

"He's the best," said Jane.

Guthrie considered the idea for a few seconds. "Yeah, that

sounds perfect. Go ahead and show him the pictures. I'll talk to Kira tonight, when I get home."

He wasn't going to let it go. Jane stood up and offered her hand. "Good luck," she said, thinking it unlikely that Kira would give such an investigation a green light.

9

Jane drove by Nolan's house on her way home that night. Several lights burned on the first floor, so she parked her Mini on the street and headed up the walk, the photos tucked safely in the inner pocket of her leather jacket.

She rang the bell and was surprised when he answered it almost immediately. "Jane, what a surprise," he said, maneuvering his way back into the living room using two canes.

"Are you being sarcastic?"

"I love your nocturnal visits, especially when they interrupt a football game." He sat down heavily on his La-Z-Boy and switched off the sound on the TV, nodding for her to sit on the couch across from him.

Nolan was a big, strongly built, African-American man in his mid sixties. He'd taken a bullet while saving her life several years back, which was why he now walked with the help of two canes. It was a major step up from the wheelchair he'd been in for the first year out of rehab. Even before he'd taken that bullet, Jane had grown to love him like a father. Sure, he could be prickly and demanding at times. Roses come with thorns, he liked to say when he knew he'd crossed a line. And then he'd smile sweetly and raise his gray eyebrows at her.

Glancing at a suitcase by the front door, Jane asked, "Going somewhere?"

"Glenda and I are hitting the road in the morning. We'll spend a couple days in Chicago with her daughter, then head to St. Louis for Christmas with my family."

Glenda was Nolan's neighbor. Early in the friendship, he could barely stand to be in the same room with her. In his opinion, she never shut up, and what she talked about bored him silly. She'd won him over, little by little, with her homemade pies. These days they played Scrabble together several nights a week. Jane had wondered for months if a romance might be in the cards. Nolan, being Nolan, refused to comment.

"Then I guess my reason for stopping by is moot," said Jane.

"Let me guess: A new client."

"One I was hoping you would handle."

"Okay. Tell me about it." He picked up his beer bottle and sat back, ready to listen.

Jane detailed what Guthrie had told her, ending with the note and the pictures.

"Let me see them."

She handed the photos over.

He flipped through them quickly, then reached over to an end table and removed a loupe from a small drawer. Switching on the lamp next to him, he examined the photos more closely, taking his time, making lots of "mmm" sounds.

With nothing else to do, Jane watched the silent football game on the flat screen.

Finally, Nolan gave a satisfied grunt.

"What?"

"Come over here and look at this."

Jane got up. "You think they're police photos?"

"No."

"Why?"

"They're all taken from one angle: directly above. The police shots would have been taken from many angles."

She should have thought of that. Nolan always told her she had good instincts, but she still had a lot to learn. Thankfully, she had a great teacher.

"The officer your friend talked to was probably right. If it wasn't a crime scene, no photos would have been taken."

"So who took these?" asked Jane. "And why?"

He handed her the loupe and one of the enlargements. "Look closely at her neck. Squint if you have to."

"Oh my God," said Jane. What she'd dismissed as a shadow now looked like a series of dark bruises.

"The woman was strangled," said Nolan. "No other way to get that kind of discoloration. It was a homicide all right. In a case like that, the husband would likely be the primary suspect, at least initially. But since it was ruled accidental, nobody was ever investigated. Which makes no sense at all. Unless—"

"Unless what?"

"The officer who was called to the scene couldn't have missed all the bruising around the woman's neck."

"You're saying the police were part of a cover-up?"

"Had to be. I'm not suggesting the entire police force was in on it, but the officer who showed up sure was."

"Then why document the murder scene with photos?"

"Good question. I'm just guessing here, but I'd say those shots were taken from the deck, the place she fell from." He held one of the pictures closer to the light. "See here? There's a slice of white at the edge of this frame. I'll bet it's part of the deck rail. Somebody photographed the scene, then tucked the evidence away."

"Why?"

"An ace in the hole? Leverage? Or to use in some future blackmail scheme? However you look at it, this investigation isn't going to be a simple case, Jane. If you take it—"

"I don't see how I can."

"Well," said Nolan, leaning back in his chair, "maybe that's for the best. If you ask me, that family's been keeping some mighty big secrets for an awfully long time. That kind of stress can distort people, make them do things they never thought possible. I'd bet money that one of them took those photos."

"And now passed them on to Guthrie."

He shook his head. "Tell him to call Thomas Foxworthy Investigations. He loves a good dysfunctional family saga. Me, I'd rather track a nice, straightforward, gangland hit."

10

When Guthrie inserted a key into his apartment door that night, his palms were sweating and his stomach was churning. He'd stayed at the teahouse later than usual, thinking through the conversation he needed to have with Kira. He knew what he felt needed to be done, but wasn't at all sure they'd be on the same page.

Three evenings a week, Kira worked as a health unit coordinator at Cedar-Riverside hospital near the university. She mainly answered phones, helped the staff as needed, and directed visitors to various waiting rooms. She rarely got home before ten. Since it was going on eleven, Guthrie assumed he'd find her in front of the TV, drinking a glass of wine and snacking on her usual cheese and crackers. Tonight, however, the apartment was dark and quiet.

After turning on a couple of lamps in the living room, he went into the bedroom. The bed had been made and all the dirty clothes had been picked up and dumped in the hamper. He hadn't seen or talked to Kira since morning. He'd showered as usual and then wolfed a bowl of Cinnamon Toast Crunch. Before leaving, he'd gone back into the bedroom to give her a kiss good-bye. She wasn't asleep, just dozing, putting off the inevitable for as long as possible. Sometimes he wished he was the kind of guy who allowed himself to chuck his duties, put his desires ahead of his responsibilities. He wanted so badly to crawl back under the covers with her. As usual, his one and only superpower—Dependability Man!—took over and guided him out the front door. Long days were the norm for both of them.

Walking into the kitchen, Guthrie switched on the overhead light. Scanning the kitchen counter, he spied a handwritten note propped up against a open can of Coke. He dropped his keys next to the sink, picked it up and read:.

> Guthrie—Tried calling you, but was
> put through to your voice mail. Blah.
> Gram phoned. She asked me to drive
> to New Dresden today. Family meeting
> called for this afternoon. I've never been
> included in one of those before, not that
> they happen often. She said she had some
> good news and some bad news. Sounded
> important. She didn't want to get into
> it on the phone. Anyway, so I'm leaving.
> It's just after ten. I'm planning to spend
> the night with her. Will be home tomorrow.
> I didn't eat the leftover pizza, so you can
> have that for dinner if you're hungry.
> Love you, sweetheart. Miss me.
>
> K.

Guthrie sank down on one of the kitchen chairs. For many reasons, this new turn of events made him uneasy. He supposed he was overreacting. He did that sometimes, especially when it came to Kira. She'd be back tomorrow, and that meant tomorrow night he'd tell her about what he'd received in the mail. He had no idea what her reaction would be, but he did believe one thing firmly: she needed to know what he'd been sent, wherever it might lead.

Late the next morning, Guthrie sat at his desk in the back room of the teahouse, working on ordering, when he felt his cell phone rumble inside the front pocket of his flannel shirt. Switching it on, he saw that it was a text from Kira:

> HEY BABE. CHANGE OF PLANS. NO GO FOR MEETING
> YESTERDAY. TRY AGAIN TODAY. HERE 1 MORE
> NIGHT. WILL CALL LATER.
>
> LOVELOVELOVELOVELOVE

"Damn it," he said under his breath. A winter storm watch was in effect for the entire region beginning this evening. He'd been hoping she'd get on the road and be back before anything hit. Predictions were for three to eight inches. He punched her preset, then waited through six rings until her voice mail picked up. What the hell, he thought, as her message played in his ear. If she'd just texted him, why wasn't she answering? After the beep, he said, "Kira, it's me. There's a winter storm watch. You need to check your weather app. Do you really have to be at the meeting? If you leave now, you'd beat the storm. Call me back. I need to talk to you." He didn't doubt that she could hear the frustration in his voice, and he didn't care. He set the phone next to him on the desk and then tried like hell to concentrate on tea prices.

By ten that evening, as snow began to pile up outside his apartment, Guthrie was still waiting for a call from Kira. He'd left her half a dozen texts, all unanswered. She'd never been this out of touch before. He couldn't understand it. He'd left her two more voice-mail messages, both of which she'd ignored. Something was wrong, he could feel it in his bones.

Scooping his phone up off the coffee table, he called her again.

"Kira, I'm really getting worried. Why haven't you texted or called? What the hell's going on? If I don't hear from you tonight, I don't care if we get three feet of snow. First thing in the morning, I'm driving to New Dresden. Call me," he said, all but growling.

The red numbers on Guthrie's digital clock read 3:18 A.M. when the call finally came.

"Hey, sweetheart, it's me," said Kira.

She sounded weird, her voice tight.

"Where have you been?" Guthrie struggled out of the blankets and rubbed a hand across his eyes.

"Don't be angry."

"Why didn't you call me back?"

"That's what I'm doing."

"It's the middle of the night."

"I needed to hear your voice."

"Are you okay?"

"Yeah."

Her tone seemed unusually strained. "Did you have the god-damn meeting?"

"We did."

"And?"

"It's too long to get into over the phone."

"When are you coming home? The storm mainly hit south of here. You should be okay in the morning to drive."

"Honey, I think I'm going to stay through the weekend."

"What? Why?"

"Just . . . a lot going on."

"Why are you whispering?"

"I don't want to wake Gram."

"This feels so incredibly weird."

"I love you. I miss you."

"You'll be home for Christmas Eve on Monday night, right? Promise?"

"I'll be there."

"I don't believe you."

"Everything's fine, Guthrie. It's just some family stuff. Nothing I can't handle."

He considered telling her about the note. He wanted to shock her, to get her to open up to him. "I've got nothing better to do than talk to you. Tell me what you learned—your grandmother's good news and bad news."

"I will. When I get home."

"On Monday."

"Right. I've gotta go now, sweetheart."

"No . . . don't hang up."

"I love you so much. Don't ever doubt that. Give me this time, Guthrie. Don't call or text. Just let me have these few days. Okay?"

"I don't know. Kira, I'm scared."

"Why? That's crazy. I'll see you very soon."

11

Jane found Guthrie sitting alone at a back table in the Hewitt & Hewitt Tearoom, staring intently at his laptop. This was her first visit, although after seeing the place, it wouldn't be her last. She counted fourteen tables scattered around the room, all but three filled with customers enjoying tea and baskets of fresh bread as they talked to their companions or lingered over the morning paper.

The bold, eclectic decor was what impressed her most. Indian and Asian elements had been mixed together, though the Indian detail, especially the wall art and the hand-loomed, block-printed tablecloths, predominated. For a moment she had the sense that she'd stepped into an Indian curio shop during the British Raj. A large statue of Siddhartha Gautama had been given pride of place near the front. The sitar music floating through the air was soft and soothing, making her wish she had the time to sit, relax, and enjoy a cup of tea herself. Alas, this initial visit would have to be short. She had information to deliver, and then she needed to get over to the restaurant for that interview with *City Pages*.

As she approached Guthrie's table, he looked up.

"Oh, Jane. Hi." He started to rise.

She motioned for him to stay seated. Folding herself into a chair across from him, she removed the photos he'd given her from her pocket. Since she wouldn't be taking the case, she needed to give them back. She also felt he deserved to hear Nolan's conclusions. "Did you get a chance to talk to Kira about your concerns?"

He shook his head. "Her grandmother called Wednesday morning and asked her to drive to New Dresden for a family meeting. I didn't find out about it until I got home that night. She won't be back until Monday."

"How far away did you say New Dresden was?"

"Two and a half hours, give or take."

She handed him the photos. "I showed these to my partner. He used a loupe to look at them and then he asked me to do the same."

"And?"

"What you see with the help of magnification is the extensive bruising around Delia Adler's neck. Nolan thought it was clear evidence of strangulation."

Guthrie's startled eyes took a moment to focus. "Then . . . it's true. Kira's dream. Her mother was murdered."

"You mentioned that there was a police officer present the day her body was found."

"That's what Kira remembers."

"If that's true and he saw the marks on Delia's neck, then the next question is, why wasn't the death ruled a homicide? Since it was an unattended death, a medical examiner would also have been called to the scene. There's no way he could have missed those marks. Whoever helped remove her body from the side of the ravine, whether it was family or the authorities, they had to know it was a murder. The funeral director, the one who prepared her body for viewing, would also have known."

"Her body was cremated," said Guthrie.

"Why doesn't that surprise me? I'm stating the obvious here. You've stumbled into one major cover up. Probably includes not only the family, but public officials."

Guthrie stared at his laptop screen. "Jane, you've got to help me. I can't handle this alone. I don't have a lot of money, but I could pay you in installments. I don't care anymore if Kira's on board or not. Every minute she spends in that town, I feel like her life's in danger. I mean, I know her family loves her. But what if she stumbles across something . . . inadvertently. Something that proves someone in her family murdered her mother. Remember, I just asked a couple of simple questions at Thanksgiving and her dad and uncle acted like I was performing a military-style interrogation. Am I overreacting? Do you think I'm blowing this all out of proportion?"

"I wish I did," said Jane, feeling sorry for him, but also feeling torn. She wanted to help, she really did. But taking this case went against a solemn promise she'd made to herself in early November to spend the remainder of the year concentrating solely on the Lyme House. She'd seen the kind of toll her way of life—the constant pressure she put on herself to work two jobs, always overextending, agreeing to do too much, saying yes when she should've said no—had taken on both her restaurant, the main source of her income, and her health. Neither were small matters.

"Look," said Jane. "I asked Nolan if he could work on this for

73

you. Unfortunately, he's going out of town for the holidays. And I'm buried at the restaurant. I just can't take on anything new." She pulled a paper napkin in front of her and pointed at the pen resting next to Guthrie's computer. When he handed it to her, she wrote down *Thomas Foxworthy Investigations*. "Give him a try. You can look up his number online."

Guthrie seemed deflated by her response. "Okay. If you can't you can't. I get it. You've already helped me a lot, and for that I'm grateful."

"Call Tom," said Jane. She wished she could offer more, but under the circumstances, this was the best she could do.

After locking up the back office, Guthrie left a message for his brother. He pleaded with him to take his afternoon shift at the teahouse. The counter guy could handle it until he arrived. "And if you can't make it," said Guthrie, struggling into his coat, "I guess all we can do is close the place. I'm sorry, but something really important's come up. I'll explain later."

Guthrie rushed out to his car. Kira's safety was the only thing that mattered to him. He vowed to set a new speed record on his way to New Dresden.

Flying down Main Street, stuffing the last bite of a burger into his mouth, Guthrie drove straight to Evangeline's farmhouse. He wished he'd asked Kira last night what she had planned for today. His heart sank when he rolled up to the house over the unplowed drive and saw no other cars. There weren't even any tracks in the snow.

He jumped out and made straight for the front door, where he rang the bell and then looked around, blowing on his hands, wishing he'd thought to bring gloves and a scarf. Then again, when he'd left his apartment this morning, he never thought he'd end up here. Banging on the door, he called, "Kira? Are you in there?" He peered through the glass, hands cupped around his eyes. Inside, the house looked quiet. No lights were on. No fire in the fireplace. The TV was off. No grandmother bustling about. No dogs. No nothing.

It was the lack of car tracks in the fresh snow that gave him the biggest pause. He had to think it through. If nobody was home, and it seemed clear that nobody was—unless they were hiding, which seemed extreme, even in Guthrie's current state of mind—that meant they had to have left before the snow came through last night. Evangeline parked her Jeep in the two-stall garage next to the barn. If snow was coming, Kira had probably parked her old Chevy Cobalt inside, too. Since there were no windows in the garage, and there was a heavy padlock on the door, Guthrie had no way to know if either car was gone.

Kira had called Guthrie from her grandmother's house in the middle of the night. She'd whispered because she said she didn't want to wake Evangeline. That meant they were both inside at three in the morning. The snow would have stopped falling well before that. If Kira and her grandmother had gone out today, where were the car tracks? The footprints? "What the hell?" he said, surveying the property.

Think it through, he told himself. Logically, Kira and her grandmother were either still in the house and were ignoring him, which he didn't believe, or they'd left before the snow arrived last night—and that meant when Kira called him, it wasn't from the farmhouse.

Rushing back to his car, he gunned the motor and fishtailed

out of the drive back onto the county highway. If anyone knew where Kira was, it would be her dad.

When Guthrie had come for Thanksgiving, Kira had taken him into town, to her dad's bar. She'd walked him through the apartment on the second floor that had been her home from the time she was six until she left for college. Her father still lived there. Feeling a surge of hope, Guthrie felt certain he knew where she was.

The Sportsman's Tavern was one of six bars in town. Kira had casually mentioned once that her home state had more bars than any other state in the union, with the exception of Montana and North Dakota. She described her dad's place as blue collar, with the occasional fistfight, but also with a loyal group of regulars. A large flat-screen TV hung above the back bar, always tuned to a game—any kind of game. A back room accommodated monthly meetings, everything from the Lions Club to the local horticulture society.

Pushing through the front door, Guthrie found a heavyset older woman in a Green Bay Packers sweatshirt and pearls standing behind the bar. "Is Kevin around?" he asked.

"Sorry."

"How about his daughter, Kira?"

"Nope."

"You're sure."

"One hundred percent." She wiped a cloth across the counter.

"You one of the regular bartenders?"

"Hell, no. I sub from time to time, when Kevin makes it worth my while. This ain't exactly my idea of a great time, if you know what I mean." She winked.

"When will Kevin be back?"

"He said he'd be here to close up on Sunday night."

"Do you know where he went?"

She leaned against the counter. "I don't keep his social calendar, son. Can I get you something? A beer? A bump?"

He eased down on one of the stools. "Just information."

"Might cost you more than the booze."

He wasn't sure if she was kidding or if she meant it. "Look, I'm trying to find Kira. She's my girlfriend. She's not at her grandmother's place. I know she has an uncle in town. Doug Adler. I don't suppose you know where he lives."

"As a matter of fact, I do. We're neighbors. It's called the Jack Pine Trailer Park. If you drove into town on Highway 30, head back out that way. You'll see a sign about six miles out, on your left. Can't miss it."

"How do I find his trailer?"

"It's white with rust-colored trim. Only one there with those colors." She leaned an arm on the counter. "Course, if you're looking to find him, he's not there. I talked to Laurie—that's his wife—yesterday morning. She said they were planning a little weekend getaway."

"With the rest of the family?"

"No idea."

Guthrie held on to the edge of the bar to steady himself. "Kira has an Aunt Hannah—"

"The doctor. Yeah."

"Do you know where she lives?"

"Nope. Me and her don't run in the same social circles."

Guthrie opened his wallet and pulled out a five-dollar bill.

"I was kiddin' about that," said the woman.

"No, I appreciate your time and the information." He left it on the counter. As he rose to go, he stopped. Turning back, he said, "Do you have a phone directory for New Dresden?"

"As a matter of fact, I do." She reached under the bar. "Here you go." She shoved it across to him.

He quickly found Hannah Adler's name. "1459 Ogden Avenue," he said, repeating the address out loud. "You know where that is?"

She gave him directions, said it wasn't far.

A few minutes later, Guthrie pulled his car to the curb outside a one-story stucco bungalow. It was a nice enough middle-class neighborhood with large, ancient elm trees, though the houses were all small, as were the yards. Cutting the engine, he trotted up the front walk and rang the bell, noting that, at the doctor's house, the driveway and walks had all been shoveled. When no one answered, which, by now was what he expected, he banged for almost a minute, taking out his frustration on the door.

"Damn it," he shouted, whirling around. He scanned the street, then turned back and examined the front picture window, which was covered by a heavy curtain. Opening his cell phone, he was about to punch in Kira's number when the garage door opened and a black Lexus backed out. As it eased into the drive, the passenger-side window lowered.

"What are you doing here, Guthrie?" Hannah's expression was impatient on the way to being pissed.

"How come you're still in town?" he asked, trotting down the steps. "Why aren't you with the rest of your family?"

"Right, like I want to spend the next few days getting yelled at. Answer my question. Why are you here?"

"I need to see Kira."

The car continued to back toward the street. "Have you heard of an amazing little device called the cell phone? Works wonders for general communication."

"She won't answer."

Hannah stopped the car. "Then give her some time and she will."

"Where are they? What's going on?"

"None of your business. Now, if you'll excuse me, I've got patients to see in Eau Claire." With that, she closed the window, backed out onto the street, and drove away.

12

Jane carried an old dusty box of Christmas ornaments up the stairs from the basement, amazed to think that she hadn't opened it in more than fifteen years, not since her longtime partner, Christine, had died. Ever since that time, she'd spent Christmas at her father's house or at Cordelia's. This year, she'd made the decision to host Christmas at her home. It was all part of the decision she'd made to live life at a more respectful pace, to stop and smell the roses, and all that.

Coming into the living room, she found Cordelia bending over the tree base, filling it with water. Bolger Aspenwall III, Hattie's part-time nanny—also in his final year of an MFA program at the university—stood on a ladder attempting to affix a glittering gold star to the top of the tree. Hattie was on her knees in front of the fireplace, perched between Jane's two dogs—Mouse, a brown lab, and Gimlet, a miniature black poodle. All three were staring raptly at Bolger.

"Make sure it's straight," said Cordelia, helping Jane set the cumbersome box down on the couch.

Hattie scrambled to her feet as Jane removed the cover. "Ooh," she said, touching the red tissue paper surrounding all the delicate ornaments. "Can I help put them on the tree?"

"That's the plan," said Cordelia. "You work on the bottom half and I'll do the top."

"And I'll string the lights," said Jane, standing back to assess the tree. "I can't believe you talked me into buying such a big one." A seven-foot Scotch pine was now enthroned in her living room, in front of the picture window.

"I forgot to bring my extra lights," said Cordelia, grumbling as she dug through a paper sack.

"No worries," said Jane. She lifted out three flats of ornaments to reveal what was at the bottom.

Cordelia peeked inside and turned up her nose. "I don't like those larger bulbs. They're old fashioned. I like the tiny new ones."

"Not me," said Jane. "I've even got a string of bubblers that Christine bought for our first Christmas together." She removed the lights and began to untangle them.

"Can I assume," said Bolger, climbing down the ladder, "that you're preparing some spectacular edibles for the party?"

"I'm still working on the menu," said Jane, though in truth, she hadn't had time to give it much thought.

"Who all's coming?" asked Bolger, lifting the ladder away from the tree.

"Cordelia, Hattie, and me," said Jane. "And then my father. I doubt he'll bring a date."

"And me and my boyfriend," said Bolger. "That's six."

"And Daddy Radley," said Hattie with a delighted cry.

Radley Cunningham had been number seven in Octavia

81

Thorn-Lester's extensive husband collection. Octavia was Cordelia's sister—Hattie's bio mom—though Cordelia had been the constant in Hattie's life. Radley was an Englishman, a movie producer who had formed a strong bond with the little girl during the time he and Octavia had been together. He liked to take Hattie on location shoots when it didn't interfere with her schooling. A charming, decent, gentle man, Radley was the closest thing to a real father in the little girl's life.

"I think Radley's bringing his sister this trip," said Jane.

"What about Octavia?" asked Bolger, retrieving the bottle of pinot from the mantel and pouring everyone more wine.

"She's making the rounds of casting couches in Hollywood at the moment," said Cordelia. "And I mean that in the literal sense."

"What's a casting couch?" asked Hattie.

"Oh, sweet pea," said Bolger, scooping her into his arms. He straightened her black satin cat outfit, which she insisted on trying out before her auntie's New Year's Eve bash. "Auntie Cordelia was just being silly."

"Couches aren't silly," said Hattie, poking the cleft in his chin.

The doorbell rang, causing the dogs to bolt into the foyer.

"You expecting someone?" asked Cordelia, sitting down on the edge of the couch to unwrap the ornaments.

"Not that I know of," said Jane. When she drew back the door, she found Guthrie outside.

"Uh, hi," he said tentatively, removing his watch cap. "I'm sorry to bother you like this, out of the blue. Do you have a second? I really need to talk to you."

"Sure," said Jane. He was breathing hard, almost hyperventilating, and he looked so frazzled, so wired, that she couldn't turn him away. "Come in. Can I get you something? Water? A glass of wine?"

"I'm fine," he said, though he clearly wasn't.

Jane was glad now that she'd filled Cordelia in on Guthrie's situation over lunch. Cordelia had known Guthrie almost better than Jane had because she'd employed him so often to staff her legendary theatrical soirees back in the late nineties. Cordelia might see herself mainly as a theatrical diva, and yet another persona she claimed was Earth Mother. In that capacity, she felt it was her duty to listen to anyone with a problem, especially romantic problems, which Guthrie seemed to have in abundance as a younger man. Cordelia freely dispensed what she considered to be golden advice.

"Guthrie," cried Cordelia, sweeping out of the living room and nearly lifting him off his feet with in a hug. "Oh, my poor boy, how are you? Jane has told me all."

"She has?"

"You look terrible. Come sit by the fire and let Auntie Cordelia help."

Guthrie started for the living room, but stopped when he saw the tree. "You're decorating your Christmas tree. This is a family evening. I shouldn't be here."

"Oh, blither," said Cordelia, dragging him over to the rocking chair by the fireplace. "Sit," she ordered.

He sat stiffly as the dogs sniffed his hands before moving on to his pants and shoes.

"They're very friendly," said Jane.

He gave a weak smile.

"Not an animal lover, are we?" asked Cordelia.

"No, they're fine."

Jane introduced Bolger and Hattie to Guthrie. "Hey, Bolge," said Jane as she joined Cordelia on the couch. "Could you take the dogs and Hattie downstairs to the rec room? You'll find lots to eat in the refrigerator, and ice cream treats in the freezer. There's an entire wall of games and movie DVDs. Help yourself."

"Treats?" repeated Bolger. Both dogs whipped their heads around, pricking up their ears at a favorite word. Since he was still holding Hattie, he clapped a hand to his thigh and ordered the dogs to follow.

"I feel awful about interrupting your evening," said Guthrie, stuffing his watch cap in his pocket, then holding his hands closer to the fire.

"Stop with all the apologizing," said Cordelia, "and tell us why you're here."

"Well, see, after you left the teahouse this morning, Jane, I decided to drive to New Dresden. I had to talk to Kira in person, see her face when I told her what I'd learned. But she wasn't at her grandmother's farmhouse. I eventually figured out that the entire family had gone off for a few days. Nobody knew where. I called Kira and begged her to call me back. That was around three. I still haven't heard from her." Leaning forward, pressing his hands together, he said, "I don't understand it. She's never been like this before. It's like she's been sucked into a black hole."

Jane and Cordelia exchanged worried glances.

"So, why are you here?" asked Jane.

His shoulders sank. "I called that guy, Tom Foxworthy, the PI you suggested. He wouldn't take the case unless I paid him five hundred dollars up front. I don't have that kind of money. I know you said you don't have any time to work on the case. I'm not even sure what you charge, or if you'd let me pay it off slowly."

"Fear not," said Cordelia, puffing out her ample bosom. "You have my word. Jane and I will do what we can."

"Cordelia?" said Jane.

"We'll leave for New Dresden in the morning. Spend the weekend digging."

"Are you a PI, too, these days?" asked Guthrie.

"I'm"—she put a finger to her lips—"covert. I keep a low profile."

"Oh. Okay."

"We'll come up with something," Cordelia assured him. "I've always been the brains behind Jane's cases. She probably didn't tell you that." She paused. "Well?" she said impatiently. "Did she?"

"Um, no?"

"Doesn't surprise me." Slapping her knees and standing, she said, "We better finish trimming the tree. I've got to get home and pack my trunk."

"You probably won't need a trunk for only a couple of days," said Guthrie.

Jane figured she might as well give in. Two days, in the scheme of things, wasn't all that much to ask. Besides, she hated to admit it, but she'd become fascinated by the mystery. It was the way it always started, the reason she often said yes when she should have said no. "We'll take my CR-V. That way, even if you decide on two trunks, we'll have enough room."

"Good thinking," said Cordelia. Towering over Guthrie, she added, "I like an adventure every now and then. Gets the juices flowing."

At least, thought Jane, she hadn't said anything about going into "sleuthing mode." Jane needed to be grateful for small mercies.

13

The crack of dawn, for Cordelia, was somewhere between ten and noon. Thus, at ten after ten on Saturday morning, Jane sat in her SUV outside Cordelia's fortress, waiting for one of the help to drag out the various trunks. Cordelia and her sister had hired a "house man," James Merriman, when they first moved in. He was a retired actor, and though he radiated a certain gravitas, thanks mostly to his resemblance to Ian Richardson and his penchant for spouting verse, he was so beset by arthritic back problems that it was more a charity hire than actual employment. Just to be "subversive," as he termed it, he'd taken to wearing an Edwardian butler's uniform, a la *Downton Abbey*. Actual Merriman sightings were rare, as he stayed mostly in his third floor lair. On his good days, however, Jane would sometimes see him moving gravely through the house wearing white gloves and touching tables and vases to make sure they were sufficiently dust free.

Startled by a knock on the driver's window, Jane turned to see Cordelia, dressed in a red cape and black Cossack boots, holding up a leather satchel.

Rolling down the window, Jane asked, "Where are the trunks?"

"Bolger convinced me to travel light."

"Score one for Bolger." She unlocked the rear hatch and Cordelia tossed the satchel inside.

As soon as Cordelia had clipped on her seat belt, Jane handed her a file folder.

"What's this?"

"I called Dad's paralegal last night." Norm Toscallia was a wizard at ferreting out information quickly. "Those are background checks on Kevin, Doug, Hannah, and Delia Adler."

"Criminal background?"

"Everything." Jane pulled out onto Irving and headed back to Hennepin, where they would catch I-94.

"Have you read them?" asked Cordelia, paging through the documents.

"That's what you're here for." The entire stack had been faxed to Jane at the restaurant, arriving just before she'd left. "Read through them and give me the high points."

After slipping on her reading glasses, Cordelia silently studied the pages for the next few minutes. "So, who do you want to hear about first?"

"Your choice."

"Okay, Delia. Born Delia Teresa Howell, in Louisville, Kentucky, in 1965. Father an army chaplain, mother a homemaker. Delia grew up at various army bases around the country. One brother, Thomas, two years older, also in the military. Mom and dad divorced when Delia was four. Kids stayed with the father. Delia graduated from Russell County High School, in Seale, Alabama. No college. Married Kevin Leighton Adler in 1983 at Fort Hood, Texas. She was arrested near Fort Benning, Georgia, for drunk driving in 1984 and 1986, and again in New Dresden, Wisconsin, in 1994. No other arrests. Worked half a dozen minimum wage jobs in New Dresden. My analysis?" said Cordelia, lifting a finger. "Delia had a peripatetic childhood, a drinking problem, and wasn't much good at keeping a job."

"Read Kevin's next."

"Kevin Leighton Adler. Son of Henry Erhard Adler and Evangeline Ruth Adler, nee Carmody. Raised in New Dresden. Graduated from Richmond High School in 1980. Five months later he entered the army. He served in the first Gulf War, attained the rank of staff sergeant before he was mustered out in 1992, whereupon he moved his wife and two daughters, Grace and Kira, back to New Dresden. Started his own construction company. Inherited the Sportsman's Tavern from his uncle, Hugh Carmody, in 1996."

"The year after Delia died."

"No criminal record."

"What about Doug?"

"I thought I got to pick."

As they reached the outskirts of downtown St. Paul, traffic on the freeway began to thin. "My apologies."

"Damn straight." Pulling a pack of bubble gum out of the pocket of her cape, Cordelia unwrapped a lump and popped it in her mouth. "Care for something to rot your teeth?"

"Thanks. I'll pass."

"Douglas Adolf Adler." She glanced at Jane. "Gives you the urge to salute, doesn't it?"

"Keep going."

Cordelia hummed and chewed as she scanned the information. "Three years older than Kevin, two years older than Hannah.

Degree from U-Madison in journalism in 1981. Worked at the *New Dresden Herald* until he inherited it in 1994. Married Laurie Ann Sherman in 1980. No children. Closed the doors in 2003. No criminal record, but he has . . . let me count." She paused. "Nineteen speeding violations over a period of twelve years. Jeez, he's really got a lead foot. One DUI a year ago. Nothing since. He currently works as a forklift operator at Vaughn's Lumber in New Dresden."

"A big comedown from being the editor of the local paper," said Jane. She never expected a lot from background checks, though she never knew what piece of information might turn out to be important. "And finally, Hannah Adler?"

Cordelia blew a bubble and flipped to the last report. "Hannah Justine Adler. Medical degree in gastroenterology and family medicine from U-Madison medical school. Never married. No children. Primary employer is Northside Medical Care in Eau Claire, Wisconsin. No criminal record. Boring, boring, boring." She took off her reading glasses and replaced them with sunglasses "That was an exercise in futility. Where's all the good stuff? The dirt. The gossip. The *real* grist for our sleuthing mill."

Jane had spent last night assembling a list of information she was hoping to ferret out in the next two days. Anything that moved her closer to understanding who Delia Alder had been, what problems and issues she'd been dealing with in the months, weeks, and days before she died, would push Jane nearer to the reason for her murder, and hopefully, ultimately, shine a light on the identity of her killer.

Beyond family members, Jane needed to locate several significant players: the police officer who'd come to the scene of Delia's death; the coroner who, in the face of all the evidence to the contrary, had ruled that death accidental; and finally, the name of the undertaker who'd handled Delia's remains, sending them off to be cremated.

To break this case open, all Jane needed was to convince one of those last three people to tell the truth. Straightforward enough, though hardly a simple task. Twenty years after the fact, with a potential prison sentence hanging over their heads for colluding to cover up a murder, getting even one of them to talk would be next to impossible.

Still, Jane had made a promise to give Guthrie two days. And two days it would be.

14

The Timber Lodge Motel on Birch Lake had been recently renovated. It was pure north woods kitsch, here and there even a little garish, though taste aside, most of the carpeting and furnishings were new. Jane stood at the reception desk and signed for two rooms on the second floor. When the woman behind the counter gestured to the stairs, saying that the motel didn't have an elevator, Jane sent up a silent prayer of thanks that all trunks had been left at home.

As Cordelia freshened up in her room, Jane sat down in her connecting room with the background information on the Adlers. She was specifically interested in the address of the house where Kevin and Delia had been living when Delia had died. She found it fairly quickly and tapped it into her phone's GPS. Checking the distance, she saw that it wasn't more than two miles away.

Once back in the car, Jane commented on Cordelia's change of attire. Instead of the cape and Cossack boots, she was wearing a buffalo-plaid hunting jacket, black jeans, and a Batman T-shirt. "Where'd you get the T-shirt?" asked Jane.

"You think I'm going to tell you that? So you can run right out and buy one for yourself? No way, dearheart. This is *my* fashion statement."

Jane was a bit nonplussed to think Cordelia thought of her as the Batman-T-shirt-type.

"Did you try out your bed?" asked Cordelia.

"Never thought about it."

"Well, mine's lumpy."

"You have terrible luck with motel beds."

"Only in fleabags."

"This isn't a fleabag."

"Just because they've put down some new carpet and added a few, may I say hideous, pieces of new furniture, doesn't mean this place doesn't qualify for fleabag status. In fact, I may start giving fleabag star ratings. One flea. Two fleas. You get the picture. We seem to stay in so many when we're off in search of evildoers."

"You sound like George Bush."

"Ah, the halcyon days, when I was driving that Hummer and thought if I pressed the wrong button, I might end up launching a missile."

Jane had never understood Cordelia's Hummer period. It was best left buried in the mists of time.

"Where are we going?" asked Cordelia, fiddling with the heat.

"Forty-nine Amberwood Trail. Delia and Kevin's old house."

"The scene of the crime."

"One of them," said Jane.

Driving up a fairly steep hill to the house, Jane parked her

CR-V in the unplowed driveway. The home was two stories, covered in weathered wood shakes, and had obviously seen better days. The green paint around the doors and windows was peeling, and the screens were old, rusty, and full of holes. There were a few other houses around, but all were at least a block away and none as close to the ravine.

"Do you think anyone's living here?" asked Cordelia, peeking in the window of the one-stall garage.

"Looks pretty derelict to me."

They tramped through snow to the rear of the house, where they found a chain-link fence preventing anyone from gaining access to the ravine.

"I wonder if the fence was here when Delia fell," said Jane.

"I can't imagine building a house this close to something so dangerous without a fence," said Cordelia. "Seems like it would be a kid magnet." She shuddered.

Jane was surprised by how rugged and steep the ravine was. Turning back to the house, she studied the deck. Like the rest of the place, it was in rough shape. Several of the upright posts had broken off. "Makes you wonder why the murderer needed to strangle her. Just pushing her off would have done the trick. If she didn't die immediately, the subzero temperatures would have finished her."

"You saying the strangulation was overkill?" asked Cordelia.

"I think it shows rage. Makes me wonder about premeditation." Jane took a few photos with her cell phone.

"Must have been hard to haul her body up, especially in the ice and snow," said Cordelia, shivering.

Studying the angles, Jane concluded that if Delia had dropped from the deck like a rock, she would have landed ten to fifteen feet down the incline. If there'd been any force at all, if she'd been ejected, she could easily have landed twenty or thirty feet down. With all the trees and rocks, there was no possible soft landing.

"Okay, we've seen it," said Cordelia, tugging on Jane's arm. "Let's get out of here. Where to next?"

"The town library."

"What do you expect to find there? Besides books and librarians?"

"Have patience and all will be revealed."

They spent the next half hour scoping out the downtown area. It was a charming small town. Most of the buildings were old and some of them were quite beautiful. New Dresden gave the impression of being well cared for and prosperous. Pine boughs and decorations hung above most of the shop windows. On Main Street, minilights wound around street lights, providing color and more Christmas cheer.

"Very middle America," said Cordelia. "I'm getting high breathing in all the family values. Not to put too fine a point on it," she added, lowering her sunglasses for effect, "I've counted six bars, in case you become overwhelmed by irony and need a libation. Hey, there's the Sportsman's Tavern." She pointed.

Jane slowed the car. "Looks like a dive." A dive with a HELP WANTED sign in the window.

"They all look like dives to me," said Cordelia. "Not that I've got anything against a good dive bar every now and then."

"It's the long cold winters," said Jane. "Takes a lot of grit to live in the upper Midwest."

"Grit and cheese and brats," agreed Cordelia.

"Let's check in at the library, and then we can have an early dinner."

The New Dresden library was located in the government center. It was a small room off the central hallway, across from the Dresden PD, and was packed to the rafters with books, DVDs, music CDs, and even a few computers.

Jane stepped up to the counter and waited until a fiftyish looking woman came out of a back room. She was plump, with short salt-and-pepper hair and the smile of a woman who loved her job.

"Can I help you?" she asked pleasantly.

"Do you have copies of the *New Dresden Herald*?"

"Oh, goodness, that died years ago. Always thought it was sad, you know? A town should have a newspaper. I used to read it from cover to cover."

"Have any copies been saved?"

"I believe we have them all. Our archive is in another room. Any particular year, day, month, you're looking for?"

"December, 1995."

"Okay, sure. Just give me a sec." She bustled out the door.

Jane found Cordelia kneeling next to one of the bookshelves.

"Think Hattie would like this." She held up a hardcover. "*Classical Physics for Kids*."

"Wonderful," said Jane, raising her eyebrows and turning away. She moved around the room, picking up a mystery here, a cookbook there. It only took a few minutes before the woman was back, a stack of yellowed newsprint in her hand.

"Here you go," she said. "Is there some particular issue you're interested in?"

"I'd just like to browse." Jane didn't want to call attention to her search.

"Sure thing. There's a table in the back. You can spread out."

Jane thanked her, took the newspapers, and nodded for Cordelia to follow her back.

"Do we have the date of her death?" whispered Cordelia, trying to wedge herself into one of the small chairs. "I think we're in the children's section."

"All I know is that it was before Christmas. We need to check all the obituaries. I wouldn't doubt, since Delia was Doug's sister-in-law, that we might also find an article."

They divided up the eight papers. Ten minutes later, while perusing the last newspaper, Cordelia erupted.

Jane put a finger to her lips. "What?"

"Here it is." She pushed the paper between them and they both read in silence:

NEW DRESDEN HERALD, THURSDAY,
DECEMBER 18TH, 1995
DEATH OF NEW DRESDEN WOMAN
Delia Adler, wife of Kevin Adler, owner of
Adler & Thompson Construction, tumbled
to her death from the back deck of her
home on 49 Amberwood Trail on Wednesday.
The deck overhangs Gauthier Ravine.
She was discovered by her husband when he
came home for a late lunch.

A spokesperson for the New Dresden police
said it appeared that Mrs. Adler had

97

accidentally fallen to her death sometime during the morning hours. In a short phone interview, Evangeline Adler, Delia's mother-in-law, said, "My family is devastated, stunned by this tragic, senseless loss. Delia was a loving mother, wife, and member of our family. She will be deeply missed."

Delia Adler is survived by her husband, Kevin, and her daughters Gracie (7) and Kira (5). Her life will be celebrated during a private ceremony to be held at the home of her sister-in-law, Dr. Hannah Adler. No wake, public viewing or funeral is planned at this time.

Brian Carmody of the Carmody & Sons Funeral Home in Union, Wis., will handle the cremation. Mr. Carmody will also be accepting flowers and donations on behalf of the family.

"If I'm remembering correctly," said Jane, "Evangeline Adler's maiden name was Carmody. It was in the background checks you read me."

"Small towns, small worlds," said Cordelia.

"How does that article strike you?" Jane asked, reading through it again.

"As perfunctory. Not cold, exactly, but there's nothing personal in it, nothing but the usual token response."

That was how it struck Jane, too. She stood up and used her cell to take a few photos of the article. "Come on. Let's give these back and get out of here."

"Kind of a bust, huh?" said Cordelia.

"Bust? Are you kidding me? We just learned the name of the funeral director who handled Delia's remains. He *saw* her body. He knew her death wasn't accidental. That means he was part of the cover-up. In my book, that's a huge win."

"Then let's go celebrate with a greasy cheeseburger and fries."

And tomorrow morning, thought Jane, they would drive over to Union to pay a visit to one Brian Carmody.

15

Union was a town of some five thousand people located twenty-two miles southeast of New Dresden. Light snow had begun falling by the time Jane and Cordelia drew up in front of the Carmody & Sons Funeral Home the following morning.

"Let's find a cafe before we hit the funeral home," said Cordelia.

"Work first, then rewards," said Jane. She was itching to talk to Carmody.

"Am I supposed to survive on bubble gum?"

"Just think how much more you'll enjoy your pancakes after we get some answers."

The funeral home was an impressive brick two-story that had once been, during an earlier incarnation, a family home. The richly paneled foyer was octagonal, the floor covered in a rose-patterned carpet. A round oak table sat directly in the center, adorned by a stunning blue-and-white flower arrangement in a crystal vase.

"This place makes me think there's serious money in death and dying," said Cordelia, picking up one of the brochures.

For today's visit, Jane decided to disguise her normal look just a bit—to be on the safe side. She wore a pair of fake horn-rimmed glasses and had tucked her long hair up under a baseball cap. There wasn't much anyone could do to disguise Cordelia, except, perhaps, toss a tarp over her and order her to keep her mouth shut.

As they stood in the foyer looking around, a ginger-haired man emerged from what had once probably been the living room and now appeared to be a chapel. He greeted them with subdued warmth.

"Good morning," he said, his smile muted, his tone soft. "I'm Steven Carmody. How may I help you?"

"Anybody ever told you you're the spitting image of John F. Kennedy?" asked Cordelia, openly studying the handsome, forty-something man.

His smile turned to a grin. "Actually, yes. I do a pretty fair imitation of a Boston accent, too."

Jane handed him her business card: *Nolan & Lawless Investigations.*

Giving it a cursory glance, Steven said, "You two are private investigators?"

"She is," said Cordelia, nodding at Jane. "Me, I'm a theater director."

"Really," said Steven. "What theater?"

"For the last sixteen years, I've been the creative director at the Allen Grimby Repertory Theater in St. Paul. I'm opening my own theater in Minneapolis next spring."

"I *love* the Allen Grimby. What's your name?"

"Cordelia Thorn."

"Oh my god," he said, his eyes popping. "I can't believe you're standing here . . . that I'm talking to you. I'm such a huge fan."

"How lovely of you to say that," said Cordelia, attempting but failing to look demure.

"I lived in New York for a few years, acted in a couple off-Broadway productions. That was before I followed my boyfriend to San Francisco. You know how it is. It was silly, but I was young and in love."

Cordelia turned to Jane and lifted an eyebrow.

"How did you end up here?" asked Jane.

"Oh," he said, adjusting the silk handkerchief in the breast pocket of his suit coat. "That's a long story." He spread his hands under the flower arrangement and fluffed the bottom flowers.

"Do you do the flower arrangements yourself?" asked Cordelia.

"Twice a week," he said, plucking off a brown petal. "My brother thinks I'm spending money needlessly, but I believe fresh flowers, especially in winter, create a certain mood. I mean, nobody wants to come to a funeral parlor. At least in ours, you're met with something fragrant and *alive*."

"Did you ever watch the TV show *Six Feet Under*?" asked Cordelia.

"I had *such* a crush on Michael C. Hall. Then he turned into Dexter." He grimaced as he flipped the business card back and forth in his hand. Switching his gaze back to Jane, he said, "So you must be the PI. Is there some problem?"

"We just need information," said Cordelia.

Jane was delighted that Steven was in awe of Cordelia. It might make this much easier. "In December of 1995," she began, "a woman named Delia Adler died."

"Sure, Kevin's wife. I remember. Kevin's my cousin. Evangeline, his mother, is my father's sister."

"Delia was cremated?"

"I'm not sure. I was living in New York then. My brother, Todd, was in Milwaukee that year, getting his degree in mortuary science. I assume Kevin used our funeral services. Most family members do. My father would have handled everything."

"Is his name Brian?"

He nodded.

"Is he here?" asked Jane. "Could we talk to him?"

"We lost him to a heart attack four years ago."

"Oh, I'm sorry," she said.

"I'm not. He was a nasty bastard. Made my life miserable growing up. He was the kind of guy who thought he got his marching orders straight from the Almighty. After he was gone, Todd asked me to move back and work the business with him. Since things had fizzled with my boyfriend by then and I was financially at loose ends, I took him up on it. You know, as I think about it, I do remember that Delia was cremated. That's very unusual in our family."

"How does cremation work?" asked Jane. "The body arrives at your facility. And then what?"

"Dad would have contacted the crematorium over in Pine River and sent her remains there. The ashes would have come back here and we would then return them to the family."

"Do you have a record of Delia's cremation?"

"I'm sure we do. Technically, I'm supposed to get the family's permission before I release any information to a nonfamily member."

"Can't we bypass that little detail?" asked Cordelia.

He grinned. "I shouldn't. But for you, anything." He opened the paneled doors directly across from the living room and led them past an ornate carved buffet to a hallway, then into a business office. Along the rear wall were six tall filing cabinets. "Have a seat," he said, motioning them to leather chairs in front of a massive oak desk. "That was 1996, right?"

"Ninety-five," said Jane. "December."

He flipped through the files until he came to what he wanted. Removing a folder, he sat down behind the desk and began to leaf through the documents. "Here we go," he said, lifting out a page. He read it over and then said, "Huh."

"What?" said Cordelia. "Something wrong?"

"No, not really. It's just . . . we have a form that we generally use. These are my dad's personal notes. Guess that, since it was a cremation, he dispensed with the usual protocol. Of course, he was the one who would have written the coroner's report. I don't have that here."

"Why would he write the coroner's report?" asked Jane.

"My dad was the county coroner from 1990 through 1998. It's an elected office in Wisconsin."

"Wait a minute," said Cordelia, raising a finger. "They give the job of county coroner to a funeral director? Isn't that like putting a fox in charge of security at a henhouse?"

"Like I said, it's an elected position. The guy who's the current coroner is a schoolteacher. When I was a kid, the coroner was a plumber. I remember he was bald. Looked like Mr. Clean."

"You don't need some sort of training?"

"I believe some requirements are being considered by the state legislature," said Steven, "but I doubt it will be much."

"Crazy," said Cordelia, lifting her sack purse into her lap. "This calls for stiff piece of bubble gum." She removed a pack and popped a lump into her mouth.

Steven smiled at her. "You're going to have to tell me all about your new theater."

"I'll do better than that. If you give me your address, I'll send you comps to the first production."

His smile grew even brighter. "This is so cool." Returning to the page, he continued reading.

Cordelia winked at Jane.

"Okay, here's what happened. Walt Olsen—he was the chief of police in New Dresden for many years—called Dad and asked him to come over to Kevin's place."

"Is Walt still alive?"

"Last I heard, he was in a nursing home. Not sure where. His daughter would know. Her married name's Bauer, but I think she went back to her maiden name when she got divorced a few years ago. Katie Olsen. She lives in New Dresden."

"Is Walt another member of your family?" asked Jane.

"No. No relation. Anyway, Dad ruled the death accidental. Looks like Delia fell from the deck of her house. Cause of death was exposure. Boy, that's a sad business. The body was removed from Gauthier Ravine and brought here. No viewing. Cremation was ordered. The cremains were returned on December 22, 1995. No notation about selling a burial urn. That's usually part of the service we provide, but I would assume they probably had a family heirloom they wanted to use." He looked up. "So, that's what I can tell you."

"This is much appreciated," said Jane.

"It's probably none of my business, but I have to ask: Why are you so interested in Delia Adler's death?"

Before Jane could answer, another ginger-haired man, this one older, heavier, and less Kennedy-esque, popped his head into the room.

"Oh, Todd," said Steven, closing the file folder and folding his hands on top of it. "I didn't think you were coming in today."

"I'm sorry to interrupt," said Todd, using the same fakey soft tone Steven had when they'd first walked in. "I need to talk to you when you get a second."

"We were just leaving," said Jane.

"You were?" said Steven. "I thought we could talk a while longer."

"Don't worry," said Cordelia, tossing her gum wrapper in the garbage can next to the desk. "I'll send those comps here. Maybe we can have lunch when you come to Minneapolis next spring."

"Really? I would absolutely adore that."

Jane shook his hand. "Again, many thanks." She waited for Cordelia to move in front of her, then nodded to Todd on her way out.

On their way back to the Honda, Cordelia asked, "Do you think Steven thought he'd get in trouble with his brother for giving us that information?"

"He sure covered up that file fast," said Jane. She opened the doors with the remote. "Which works in our favor. The fewer people who know we're looking into this, the better."

They followed traffic to the main drag—Elm Street. "There's a restaurant," said Jane. "The Corner Cafe."

"An oasis," said Cordelia, clutching her sweater like the ingenue in a silent film.

"Probably won't give us ptomaine poisoning."

"You have such faith in the restaurant profession."

"I'm a realist."

"You're also in a good mood."

"When I'm getting somewhere on a case—and when I know I get to sleep in my own bed tonight—I sure am."

"Such simple needs you have. Simple Jane. Simple, basic, reliable Jane."

"Aren't you afraid you'll turn my head with such magnificent praise?"

Lowering her sunglass, Cordelia shot her a half-lidded look. "Buy me breakfast and a vat of life-sustaining coffee, and I'll come up with some better adjectives."

16

Hasn't anyone ever heard of cell phones in this town?" demanded Cordelia, tapping frantically on her iPhone's keypad. "I had service when we were in Union. A bunch of texts downloaded, but now that we're back, nothing. And I've got a stage manager at the theater who's freaking out. If I don't talk him down off the ledge in the next few minutes, I'm afraid he's going to jump."

"I'll take you back to the motel," said Jane. "You can use the landline. You can also pack up for both of us. Just to be on the safe side, why don't you ask at the motel office for a late checkout."

"Why on earth would I do that? There were only three cars in the parking lot last night. They're not exactly overflowing with guests."

"Just play nice, okay? I'll try to make my visit with Katie Olsen fast. I'd like to get on the road before the snow starts piling up."

"What*ever*," Cordelia spluttered, still tapping on her phone.

• • •

A smiling, sandy-haired woman, about the same age as Jane—midforties, or perhaps a little older—answered the front door. "Can I help you?"

"Katie?"

"Yes?" She brushed her hair away from her eyes.

Jane explained who she was, handing the woman a business card. "I wonder if I could talk to you."

"What's this about?"

"I'm looking for some information on Delia Adler."

"Delia," she repeated, her lips parting.

"If I could just ask you a couple of questions—"

"I guess," she said, eyeing Jane's baseball cap before leading her into a small den off the living room.

Jane understood now why Katie was wearing overalls splattered with paint. "You're painting your living room." All the furniture had been pulled into the center of the room and covered with a tarp.

"The house needs a lot of work before I can sell it."

"Are you moving?"

"I'm thinking about it. I've been offered a job in Madison."

Noting the half-eaten sandwich on a desk, Jane assumed she'd interrupted the woman's lunch. "I'm sorry," she said. "This is a bad time."

"You're doing me a favor. I'm sick to death of all of this do-it-yourself crap. I painted the kitchen last weekend. Two bedrooms the weekend before. With very little coaxing, I'd probably be willing to tell you my entire life story."

Jane noticed that bookcases covered one entire wall of the den. A few of the shelves had been cleared. Most were still filled.

"You like to read," said Jane.

"I've donated hundreds of books to the local library in the last couple of years, and yet I can't seem to part with these. They're my friends. I don't expect that most people would understand."

"I do," said Jane. "I feel the exact same way. Alas, I also collect cookbooks."

"Cooking's never been my thing. Now eating, that's another story."

They both laughed.

Jane was glad for the connection. It made asking questions easier. She sat down on a rocking chair as Katie resumed her seat behind the desk. "I understand your father was the chief of police in New Dresden."

"For twenty-four years, until he retired. He was the best chief of police this town ever had. He won a bunch of awards. Honest as the day is long. He was born and raised here, so he wanted to make sure the police department served the citizenry well."

"Where you born here, too?"

"Yup. That's why this Madison job, if I take it, will be such a big change. Of course, I'll be back on weekends to see my father. That's a given." She glanced down at Jane's business card. "I have to tell you, private investigators are fairly rare around these parts."

"I'm just looking for a few answers."

"About Delia. Are you investigating a crime?"

Technically, she wasn't. According to the police and the coroner, no crime had been committed. "No," she said, knowing it was a half-truth. "I just need some information."

With a shrug, Katie said, "Okay. I'm not sure I know anything that would help you. I'll throw you out if the questions get too personal."

Jane grinned. "Deal. How well do you know the Adler family?"

Katie crossed her legs and settled in. "Henry Adler, Delia's father-in-law, was my dad's best friend."

"Is that right." The chief of police might not have been family, but he was the closest thing to it. It might explain a lot. "How about you? Did you know the Adlers?"

"Sure. Our families did a lot of things together when my brother and I were kids. Skating and sledding in the winter. Swimming and barbecues in the summers. Kevin Adler and I graduated high school the same year. I had a supercrush on him. Most of the girls did. He was athletic, on the track team and the football team. He was never a top student, but he was good-looking and superfriendly, he loved to laugh and have fun, and he was sweet. He wasn't stuck on himself the way so many of the other jocks were."

"Did he date?"

"Yeah, but I don't think he was ever serious about anybody."

"What about Hannah and Doug?"

"Hannah was a pistol. She was always in trouble, never wanted to toe the line. If anyone in the family gave Evangeline and Henry gray hair, it was Hannah. But she turned out well. She's a doctor now. Since she's a couple years older than me, we didn't run with the same crowd, but I liked her. Doug was the exact opposite of Kevin—kind of a nerd. Where Kevin was easygoing, fun to be around, Doug was serious, intense, always with his nose in a book. He was a straight-A student, I think. Very smart. He was going places and he wanted everyone to know it. Some kids at school thought he was a jerk. I mean, he was physically awkward, walked with this sort of gangly stride, so he was easy to make fun of. It made me mad, you know? He was my friend. He could be hard to take, sometimes, but he had a good heart. The Adler kids were incredibly tight. Kevin stood up for Doug a lot. The thing is, Doug often acted like he was better than the rest of us because his dad owned the local paper, and he was going to inherit it one day. Big deal. A lot of good it did him."

"What do you mean?"

"The paper died after he took it over. Not right away, but everyone knew it was mostly his fault. See, the Adler family was always politically conservative and the *New Dresden Herald* reflected that. When Doug took over after Henry's death, the paper began to lean even more to the right. New Dresden's a conservative small town, so there was never a problem with Henry's point of view, but Doug's growing libertarianism was sometimes too much. Advertisers began to pull out. When Doug wrote opinion pieces against the wars in Afghanistan and Iraq—after 9/11—that was the last straw. People stopped buying it."

"Did he find another journalism job?"

"Last I heard, he was working at a lumberyard."

"Do you know his wife?"

"Laurie? Sure, she was in my high school class. She and Doug hooked up at the beginning of her senior year. Doug was away in college, but he'd drive back on weekends. I'd see them walking around town, holding hands."

"Did you ever meet Delia?"

"Sure. We weren't friends. I was married by the time Kevin brought his family back here."

"What did you think of her?"

Katie shrugged. "I knew that she liked to party. She could be funny, sometimes more sarcastic than funny, if you know what I mean. She'd order Kevin around—do this, do that—and he'd do it. Totally amazed me. My husband said he was whipped. Never thought he'd end up with a woman like her. Delia was hard. Thought she was the center of the universe. She loved giving people the finger. Maybe it worked for her in big cities, but it sure didn't in New Dresden."

"What was she like as a mother?"

"No idea."

"And Kevin? Did he seem happy?"

She looked down. "He never seemed happy to me after high school. He turned sort of silent during the last few weeks before graduation. Never understood why. And then he joined the military maybe six months later, which totally surprised everyone. I didn't see him for years. When we finally did reconnect, he was older, a man, not a boy. He was married, had a couple kids. But the spark that he had in high school, when I knew him best, was gone. I always wondered about that."

"Was he a good father?"

Her voice softened. "He was wonderful with his girls. Totally in love. When I saw them together, I could sometimes glimpse the old Kevin. Made me sad." She looked away for a few seconds, then back at Jane. "You know his wife's death was an accident, don't you?"

"I do."

"Well, okay . . . inquiring minds. I've been living in this backwater for so long that anything out of the ordinary—like a PI showing up at my door—makes me a little suspicious."

"Did the Adlers accept Delia into the family? I mean, did her personality cause any particular problems?"

"I would imagine she caused lots of problems. I saw her flirting with Doug once at the county fair over in Union. She really turned on the charm. I thought it was appalling. Maybe I'm wrong about this, but I think she might have been flirting with a priest that day, too. I'm not Catholic, so I didn't know him. She was like that. Always trying to get a rise out of some guy."

"Was Kevin there that day? Did he see it?"

"No, she'd come with her two girls—and with Evangeline."

"Do you think Evangeline noticed? Or Doug's wife, if she was there?"

"Not sure about Evangeline, but I'm positive Laurie did. Laurie was usually pretty quiet, but she wasn't stupid, and she had a wicked temper—something she didn't show very often. She seemed like the kind of person who smolders, keeps things in until they explode."

"Can you give me an example?"

Katie picked up her can of soda and gave it some thought. "We were on the girls' basketball team together our junior year, practiced after school. She was Laurie Sherman back then. There was this one girl who had it in for her. Not sure why. Laurie took the girl's crap—for weeks—but one day I guess she'd had enough. She jumped on her during practice, started pounding her, biting her. She wrestled her to the floor and got her hands around her neck. I think she might have killed her if the coach hadn't pulled her off."

Laurie hadn't really been on Jane's radar. Maybe she should be. "Do you think your father would be up for a visit? I'd really like to talk to him."

"About the Adlers."

Jane nodded.

Katie tapped her fingers on the arm of her desk chair. "I guess that would be okay. You really don't need my permission."

"But I do need to know where he lives."

She hesitated. "Right. It's the Bridgewater Nursing Home on Templemoore Avenue. Remember, he's a frail old man. I don't want him upset."

"Is his mind—"

"He's as sharp as he always was."

Jane nodded to a framed photo on the desktop. "Is that him?"

"In his prime. It's my favorite photo of my father in uniform. Handsome, wasn't he?"

"Very. How old is your dad now?"

"He just turned eighty-four. Say, you know . . . maybe I should come with you."

"I really need to speak with him privately."

"You're afraid he won't talk about . . . something . . . if I'm there. I sure wish you'd tell me what you're after."

"As I said—"

"Yeah, yeah. Can't be anything too serious. Nothing very serious ever happens in this town. Just the same old, same old."

"Some people might like that," said Jane, rising from the rocking chair.

"That's why I read novels," said Katie.

"Better to get your thrills and chills from a book than from a stranger with a knife pounding on your front door in the middle of the night."

"You make a good point. Something to think about. Maybe I shouldn't move to Madison." She thought about it for a few seconds, then smiled and said, looking up at Jane, "Nah. I'm still going to give that job offer some serious thought."

17

The Bridgewater Nursing Home was a depressing two-story, cinder-block building, with low ceilings lit by fluorescent lights. Jane signed in as a visitor at the front desk, then took the elevator up to the second floor. She found Walt Olsen's room easily enough, though he wasn't in it. Stopping one of the nurse's aides in the hall, she asked the young woman if she knew where Walt might be.

"He likes to sit by the large picture window on the other side of the lunchroom," the aide said. "Just keep going straight down this hall. When you come to the end, make a right, go past the lunchroom, and you'll probably see him."

Jane thanked her. She found Olsen right where the nurse's aide said he would be. She would never have recognized him from the photo his daughter had shown her. He was no longer that robust man with piercing blue eyes and a full head of dark hair. This man was frail, rail thin, with white wisps circling a bald crown. The only part of him that still looked vigorous were his fierce white eyebrows.

"Chief Olsen?" she asked.

He looked up at her with milky eyes.

"My name's Jane Lawless."

"Yes? Do I know you?" His voice wasn't much above a whisper.

"No. We've never met. I'm a private investigator. I'm here to ask you about Delia Adler." There was no way to sugarcoat the questions. She didn't even pull up a chair, figuring the conversation wouldn't last long.

His lips drew together. "Delia? What about her? She's gone. Died years ago."

"You were called to the scene."

He blinked, looked away, stared silently into the middle distance.

"Who called you, Mr. Olsen?"

No response.

"Was it Evangeline Adler? Did she ask you to do her a favor?"

"No, no favors. Just doing my job."

"And when you got to the scene, you found that Delia had been murdered."

He drew in a long, composing breath.

"Isn't that correct?"

"You have your facts wrong, Miss. I don't know who you've been talking to, but Delia's death was an accident. She fell off the deck of her house."

"Then why did she have all those marks on her neck?"

His lips parted, but no words came out.

"You called Brian Carmody, the coroner. Had him come over and pronounce her death accidental. But it wasn't. She'd been strangled."

The old man searched Jane's face. Reaching some sort of decision, he closed his mouth, then his eyes.

Jane felt terrible for him, for the questions, which must have hit him like blows. She hated herself for needing to inflict this kind of pain. "You, Henry Adler's best friend, and Brian Carmody, Evangeline Adler's brother, and others in the Adler family colluded to cover up a murder."

When he spoke again, his voice came out deeper, stronger, steadier. At the same time, he'd begun to tremble. "I want you to leave."

"Why did you do it? Lying like that. All these years."

"I'm an old man. Let me die in peace."

"Did Kevin do it? His brother, Doug? Or was it someone else in the family?"

Mustering what defiance he could, he said, "If you don't leave right now, I'll call a nurse and have you thrown out."

It appeared Walt Olsen would take the truth of the matter to his grave. He hadn't given an inch. Even so, Jane felt she'd found part of the answer she'd come looking for. Words could lie. Body language rarely did.

Gazing down at him with an overwhelming sense of sadness, seeing clearly what his actions had cost him, she said simply, "I'm sorry. Thanks for your time."

Why was your mother so upset with your sister?" asked Laurie, staring out the passenger's window of her husband's LeSabre as they sped along the snowy highway late Sunday afternoon, on their return trip to New Dresden.

"Because she didn't come to the family retreat," said Doug.

"But . . . I mean, she's had conflicts before. We all have."

"This time it was really important for all of us be there."

"Because of Kira," said Laurie. "I get it."

"Hannah's never played by the rules. Besides, I would imagine our usual cottage rental on Beaver Lake isn't exactly a draw anymore. The good doctor is way out of our tax bracket." Turning the radio down, he added, "What you probably don't know is that Hannah's been pushing Mom and Kevin to make some changes."

"At the farmhouse?"

"She won't get anywhere with her ideas."

"What does she want to change?"

"Doesn't matter. Mom's thinking on the matter is set in concrete."

"We all did make a commitment."

"Yeah, right. You're the poster child for that."

Every conversation these days eventually devolved into the same thing. Laurie didn't love him enough. She never had. "What do you want from me?"

"If I have to explain, what's the point?" He didn't say anything for almost a minute, then, "Are you cheating on me?"

"My God. Who on earth would I be cheating *with*? And where would I find the time?"

He grunted. "You sure did stay late at Kevin's bar when you were working there. Way later than you needed to."

His constant whining about her late hours was one of the reasons she'd quit. "I'm not cheating on you with your brother."

"Right."

"You actually believe I'd do that?"

"What if I said yes?"

"How do I know you're not cheating on me?"

"Maybe I am. If I was, it would serve you right."

Doug had put on so much weight in the last couple of years,

probably because of his drinking, that she doubted he'd be willing to risk the humiliation of getting naked with a woman who might find him physically wanting. Still, there had been a time, back in the early nineties, when she'd been fairly certain he'd been cheating on her with none other than Delia. It was before his dad died, before he'd inherited the paper. Two or three nights a week he would work late into the evenings. He covered by saying he needed to take the initiative—learn everything he could about the business, impress his dad with his dedication. He'd stumble into the house in the wee hours of the morning, weave noisily into the bedroom, strip, and climb into bed, snoring almost before his head hit the pillow. Since she was teaching at the middle school back then and had morning classes, she usually turned in around eleven. Doug undoubtedly figured she was asleep, though how she was supposed to sleep through the racket he made was beyond her.

Unwrapping a candy cane, Doug stuck the straight end in his mouth and sucked on it. "Tell me again why you decided to stop bartending at Kevin's tavern?"

"Are we going to argue all the way home?"

"Nothing new in that."

She removed her gloves. "The only reason you care is because I can't sneak free bottles of booze to you anymore."

The muscles along his jawline tightened.

She should never have responded with the truth. He'd been building all morning—that's how she thought of it. A building up. Twisting everything people said, using words to feed some unquenchable internal fire. At times like this, she couldn't help but wonder what had happened to the eager, ambitious young man she'd married. The answer was, of course, obvious: When his lifelong dream of running the *New Dresden Herald* had died, the best part of him had died right along with it.

"If you don't tell me," said Doug, "I'll pry it out of Kevin, one way or another."

She felt a wave of heat roll up her neck. "He thought I pocketed some money. The till was short forty dollars the other night and he blamed me."

Turning to look at her, he laughed. "You know, even after all these years, you still have the capacity to surprise me."

"I didn't do it."

"Is that right. Then where did the money go?"

"How should I know?"

"You saying Kevin made it up? He used it as an excuse to fire you?"

"He didn't fire me. I quit."

His amusement at her apparent disgrace suggested he'd chew on that one for a while. Her perceived pain would, in a weird way, assuage his.

"So that's why you were so cold to Kevin all weekend," said Doug.

"I wasn't cold."

"I believe I saw icicles dangling from your ears."

"Funny."

"I'm a stitch."

Especially when he'd been drinking. She'd caught him downing half a bottle of wine right after breakfast. She knew she should be worried about him, should urge him to talk to someone about it, but the truth was, she didn't want to fight with him. She had something else in mind. "I assume we're still planning to stay at your mom's house for Christmas Eve." All she

wanted was to go back home and stop thinking—and talking—
for a few days.

"If you don't want to come, don't," said Doug.

"You don't want me there?"

"Jesus, woman. You're the one who's bitching. Do what you
like. You do anyway, no matter what I want."

She let a few silent minutes go by. Finally, she said, "You know
how much I love Kira. She's like my own child."

"Oh, fabulous. Dumb me, right? I thought we'd put 'poor
childless Laurie' to bed years ago. So we weren't able to have kids.
Nothing we can do to change it. If you still blame me—"

"*Please*, Doug. All I meant was that I feel sorry for her."

He gripped the wheel and stared straight ahead.

"Don't you? She didn't know a thing about any of this until a
few days ago. There were times, in the last two days, when I felt
like she was being brainwashed. Like we're a cult and we were
trying to draw her in, indoctrinate her. You could see it in her
eyes. She's overwhelmed."

"We all felt like that in the beginning. If she can just help my
mom through the chemo, then she can go back to Minneapolis."

Laurie didn't believe him. A necessary decision, one that had
once seemed so right, so utterly essential, had grown to domi-
nate their lives in ways that none of them could have foreseen.

Kira would never leave New Dresden. And everyone in the
family—except Kira—knew it.

18

I can't thank you enough for everything you did," said Guthrie, walking Jane and Cordelia to the door of his apartment. They'd stopped at his place on their way home to fill him in on what they'd learned in New Dresden. Guthrie could now approach Kira with much more than a few photos of unknown provenance and an unsigned note.

"I wish we could've figured out who actually murdered Delia," said Jane.

It didn't matter. He could have hugged and kissed both of them. Kira would be home tomorrow night. He had the ring and the champagne, the strawberries, the whipped cream and the chocolate. Lots of chocolate. The conversation about her family would come later. He didn't want anything to spoil this one special evening.

"Before you go, we should probably talk about what I owe you," said Guthrie, his hand jingling change in his pocket.

"You can't afford us," said Cordelia, her gaze traveling to the framed drawings that covered a good section of one of the living room walls. "I love all the artwork. They look like something a child would do. Either that or a brilliant modern master."

He laughed. "Actually, they were all done by Kira's sister— when she was a child. Kira loves them. They've kind of grown on me." He scratched the back of his neck, watching Jane walk over to look at one more closely. "So, after I get your bill, will I be in hock for the rest of my natural life?"

"You don't owe us anything," said Jane. "We were glad to help."

"Let us know how it goes with Kira," said Cordelia, sympathetically chucking him on the shoulder.

"Thanks. I will."

"I assume we'll be invited to the wedding," she added.

"Absolutely." He knew his grin was ridiculously wide and he didn't care. "You two have a great Christmas."

After they'd gone, Guthrie switched on the Christmas tree lights and sat down to enjoy his handiwork. He hadn't been sitting for more than a few minutes when his cell phone rang. Checking the caller ID he saw that it was Kira.

"Hey, sweetheart, I'm so glad you called. What time will you be back tomorrow?"

"I've missed you so much."

"No more than I've missed you. So when should I expect you?"

"Guthrie?"

The way she said his name pulled him up short. "What?"

"I'm not coming home. Not quite yet."

"*What?* Why?"

"I've decided to spend Christmas in New Dresden with my family."

"I'm your family."

"Of course you are, baby. I didn't mean——"

"Kira, you promised."

"I know, but something's come up."

"It's not safe for you there."

"Safe? What?"

"I have so much to tell you, but I can't do it over the phone. It's important, Kira. Things you need to hear."

"About what?"

"Just come home, okay? Christmas Eve was supposed to be our time."

"I know, sweetheart. And I'm really sorry. Please don't make this harder than it already is."

"If it's so hard, I don't understand why you're staying. Something's wrong, Kira. I know it is. I can feel it. I'm back here, all alone, and I'm worried. I mean, what if you never come back to me?"

"Oh, Guthrie. Don't be ridiculous. That's never going to happen. Listen, I better—"

"No," he all but yelled. "Don't hang up. Just a few more minutes."

"I'm so sorry, honey. I love you."

"Call me later."

"I'll try."

"Don't just try, do it."

"Bye, sweetheart. Have a wonderful Christmas. I'll make it up to you, I promise."

Before he could say that was impossible, she'd hung up.

By six the following night, Christmas Eve, Guthrie alternated between bouts of fury at Kira and her family and a relentless anxiety that twisted his stomach and made him feel like the ground he was walking on was about to dissolve. His brother, on hearing that Kira wouldn't be back, had invited Guthrie to spend Christmas Eve with him and his wife and little boy. Guthrie knew he wouldn't be good company, so he thanked him, but declined the offer.

As he made himself a cheese sandwich in the kitchen, an idea occurred to him. He might be the only one who could save Kira from the clutches of her family. He normally didn't think in such melodramatic terms, and yet, in this situation, he felt it was justified. Stewing about it a few more minutes, he finally made a decision. And then, as he had just a few days before, he grabbed his coat, hopped in his car, and headed for the freeway: Next stop, New Dresden.

Evangeline's house, decked in Christmas lights, glowed warm and inviting in the winter dark. As Guthrie sat in the drive, going over his game plan—he'd formed several different approaches, depending on who answered the door—he worked hard to force his anger away, replacing it with a more calculated calm. He wouldn't get anywhere if he started a fight, though that's exactly what he felt like doing. He wanted to stomp into the living room and let it rip, tell those people that he knew one of them was a murderer and the rest were the murderer's accomplices. And then Kira would fall into his arms and he'd whisk her away from this wretched place forever.

Yeah. Right. And the earth was flat.

Stepping up on the porch, Guthrie rang the bell. He could hear the muted sound of a piano playing Christmas carols, singing, laughter. He imagined the dining room table loaded with food. Ham. Roasted turkey. More homemade pies. He hated himself, but he longed to be part of it. The door finally opened, though not by a family member, but an unfamiliar man wearing a black shirt and white clerical collar.

"Can I help you?" asked the stranger, peering over his reading glasses.

The man reminded Guthrie of the aging Dustin Hoffman—thin-lipped, perpetually amused expression, the kind of guy who smiled without ever showing his teeth.

"Oh my goodness, you're Guthrie," said the priest. "Kira showed me pictures of you on her smartphone." He pushed through the screen, then reached back and closed the heavy front door behind him. "I'm Michael Franchetti. Most people call me Father Mike."

"Ah, hi," said Guthrie. He wasn't prepared for this. Stumbling around in his mind for something to say, he finally offered, "I'm not Catholic. I'm Lutheran."

"Yes," said Father Mike. "A lot of that going on around here." He stepped farther away from the door and motioned for Guthrie to do the same. "Beautiful night," he said, looking up at the starry sky. "May I ask what you're doing here?"

"I came to talk to Kira. I'm not leaving until I do."

"I see. Forgive me, son." He placed a hand on Guthrie's shoulder. "I know you don't know me, but allow me to give you some advice: I don't think this is the best time."

"I don't care. I'll break the door down if I have to."

"Right. Well. You're admirably clear about your intentions."

"Damn right I am."

"Is there any way I can talk you out of this?"

"Look, how well do you know the Adlers?"

He seemed puzzled by the question. "They've been members

of Saint Andrew's parish since I first arrived in New Dresden, some thirty years ago. Where does the time go?"

"No, I mean, do you know them personally?"

"I like to think I do."

"Well, you don't."

"I can tell that you're angry. Maybe you'd like to talk about it. I'm a good listener."

"If you want to help me," said Guthrie, lowering his voice, "you'll go back inside and tell Kira I'm out here. Don't let anyone else know. I just need a few minutes alone with her."

"You're sure that's all?" asked Father Mike, tucking his hands under his arms to keep them warm. "You're not going to do anything rash?"

"Like what? I love her, man."

"And from what she said to me, I believe she loves you, too."

"Then do us both a favor and go get her."

The priest gazed up at the stars once more, appearing to think it over. Nodding silently, he went back inside. A few minutes later, Kira slipped outside.

They flew at each other, kissing with a hunger that made words unnecessary. Finally, Guthrie whispered, "Come home with me." He tried to release her so that he could look into her eyes, but she held on, unwilling to let him go.

"Oh, Kira," he whispered, his hand caressing her hair. "What's going on? You can tell me anything, you must know that."

"I do," she whispered back. "I'm freezing. Let's go sit in your car."

Guthrie started the engine and turned up the heater. Climbing into the backseat, they entwined their arms, holding each other so tightly it almost hurt.

"I wish we could stay like this forever," said Kira.

"I can think of more comfortable places," said Guthrie, kissing her hair. "Tell me why you can't come home with me."

She hesitated a second, then said, "It's my grandmother's bad news. I didn't want to get into it on the phone. I mean, it's all so painful, so scary. She was diagnosed with cancer a few weeks ago. After New Year's, she's scheduled to start chemo. Once a week for twelve weeks. Someone will have to drive her to Eau Claire each week, stay with her overnight because she has to be seen the next day. And then bring her back here until the next round the following week. It will be a grueling time for her. She's going to need a lot of help. She didn't ask me, Guthrie. She wouldn't do that. I offered. I want to be here for her. I plan to stay at the house for at least a few months—possibly longer, depending on the outcome. I've already called my advisor, told him I won't be attending next semester."

Guthrie could hardly argue with her decision. And yet, selfish man that he was, he wanted to. "But we can still see each other. I can come visit. Stay here just like I did at Thanksgiving. I'm sorry about your grandmother, truly I am, but it doesn't mean it's the end of us."

"No," she said, though her voice sounded tentative.

"What?" he asked, pulling back. "There's something you're not telling me."

"You won't be able to stay here at Gram's house."

"Why not?"

"It just won't work."

"Are you saying she disapproves of us? Of me? Of our relationship?"

"No. Of course not."

"Then I'll stay in a motel. Surely you can be away from her for a few hours."

"Guthrie, sweetheart, you've got to give me some time to get things straightened out here."

"What needs straightening out?"

"Organized. I need to figure out what needs to be done. What my role will be."

There was a subtext in her words, something he didn't understand. She wasn't giving him the full story.

"Don't be angry," said Kira, touching his face. "We'll work it out. This has been a hard few days. I'm feeling overwhelmed. Gram's in a bad way and if you were here, my attention would be divided. It would stress Gram—and it would stress me. Please, Guthrie. Don't push. Give me the space I need. This won't last forever."

Of course it wouldn't. Why would she even need to say that? The fact that she had made him uneasy. The entire situation continued to set off alarm bells deep within him. "Maybe I should go in, tell Evangeline how sorry I am. That if there's anything I can do—"

"No, you can't. I mean, this wouldn't be a good time."

She'd said the words so quickly, with such vehemence, that Guthrie was once again left with the sense that she was hiding something.

"I better get back inside," she said, starting to pull away.

"No," he pleaded, holding her, refusing to let go. "Not yet. There's so much I need to tell you." It was the wrong time and he knew it, and yet he couldn't help himself. Maybe if she understood what her family had done she might not be so willing to devote herself so totally to such a deceptive old woman.

Gazing into her eyes, searching for the right words, an idea struck him. Did she already know the truth? Is that why she felt overwhelmed? Had these last few days been about more than just Evangeline's illness?

"They told you, didn't they?" he said. The words came out matter-of-factly, though that wasn't how he felt.

"Told me what?" she asked. Fear flooded her eyes.

"About your mother. That someone in your family *was* responsible for her death."

She blinked. Then blinked again. "That's ridiculous. It was just a dream I had, Guthrie. A nightmare. It doesn't mean anything."

"What if I told you I'd found proof?"

"I'd say it's not possible."

"Someone sent me photos of the crime scene—your mother in the ravine. If you look closely, you can see strangulation marks around her neck."

As her eyes locked on him, they both jumped at the sound of a rap on the window. Guthrie had to crack the door to see who it was because the windows were covered by the steam from their breath.

"Hi again," said Father Mike. "Kira? I think you better get back inside. Your grandmother's looking for you. It's time to open presents."

"Kira, no," said Guthrie.

"I have to go," she said, kissing him, looking into his eyes ever so briefly with an unreadable expression, then opening her door and climbing out.

"Good to meet you, son," said Father Mike, slipping his arm around Kira's shoulders and walking her back toward the front porch.

Guthrie felt like he was in a tug of war with Kira's family.

"Merry Christmas," called Father Mike.

"Screw you," Guthrie shouted after him. "And screw Christmas. This isn't over."

19

I know I have no right to be here," said Guthrie, sitting at Jane's kitchen table the next afternoon. "I'm ruining your Christmas."

Jane had been in her living room, playing charades with her family and friends, when she'd heard someone bang on the front door. Cordelia had been standing in front of the fireplace, flapping her arms wildly and hopping up and down off a footstool. They were doing *movie titles.* Jane had guessed it was Alfred Hitchcock's *The Birds,* but since she wasn't on Cordelia's team, she kept her mouth shut. Ducking under Bolger's arm, she'd gone to the door and found Guthrie outside looking frantic.

Leading him back to the kitchen, she'd closed the door. Everyone continued to shout in the living room, so she figured she wouldn't be missed, at least not immediately.

"I'm sorry to interrupt your Christmas," said Guthrie, wringing his hands. "You've already spent two days in New Dresden. I can't pay you what you probably charge, and even if I could, you've made it abundantly clear that you don't have the time to work on any of this. But I'm desperate. I don't know where else to turn.

I need someone to figure out what's really going on with Kira. I know it has something to do with her mother's murder."

Over the next few minutes, it all tumbled out. His second trip in five days to see Kira last night, his feeling that she was keeping something from him—a secret that could, if he wasn't able to get her to open up about it, eventually break them apart. "It's like her family has closed ranks around her. Like they're sucking her into something she may only vaguely understand. I liked Evangeline so much when I first met her, but now I'm beginning to see a different side to her. She's manipulative. I'm not sure she has Kira's best interests at heart. Maybe I'm wrong, but I think she's using the secrets surrounding Delia's death to bind Kira to her. The more information Kira is given, the more danger she's in if she ever decides to break free and leave." Dropping his head in his hands, he said, "I don't even know if I believe Evangeline has cancer. It could be a ruse. I don't trust any of them."

Jane had been naive to think she'd seen the last of Guthrie Hewitt. Still, to help him—and she found that she did want to help—she needed to sort fact from feelings.

"Will you go back?" asked Guthrie. "We don't have a minute to waste."

Cordelia bustled into the kitchen, waving air into her face. "They *finally* got it."

"*The Birds?*" said Jane.

"Heavens, no. Birds tweet. Flap. They don't galumph their arms like I was doing."

"Then?"

"*Rodan,*" she said triumphantly. "Hey, my man Guthrie. How's tricks?" She marched over to the refrigerator and removed a can of black cherry soda. After swigging half of it down, she smiled, then frowned. "Did I interrupt something?"

"I'm going back to New Dresden," said Jane, not realizing she'd made a decision until the words left her mouth.

"Tonight?" asked Cordelia.

She had to clean a few projects off her desk before she could head out of town. "Probably can't go until late tomorrow afternoon."

"But, wait now. Wait now," said Cordelia. "I can't possibly go back to New Dresden with you this week. I have meetings, work that needs to get done before New Year's."

"That's okay," said Jane. "Might be better if I go back by myself."

"Without *moi*?"

"Jane, thank you, thank you," said Guthrie. "You're saving my life."

"Who's going to save *hers* if I'm not there?" asked Cordelia.

"I doubt it will come to that," said Jane. "Here's what I need you to do." She turned to Guthrie. "Does Kira have any family photos?"

"Yeah, I think she has an album somewhere."

"Find a picture of her dad, her mom, her grandmother, and anyone else you think might be important for me to know about. Label the back of each photo with the person's name and their relationship to Kira and to each other. I need you to bring the pictures over ASAP. Tomorrow morning at the latest. If I'm not here, slip them through the mail slot."

"Will do," said Guthrie, tapping his fingers on the table. "When you get to New Dresden, you might want to contact a man I met last night. He was over at Evangeline's house for Christmas Eve.

Older guy. Name's Michael Franchetti. Calls himself Father Mike."

"He's a priest?" asked Cordelia.

"The Adlers are Catholic. Who knows? He might be able to help. He's known the family for years. I mean, if you can't trust a priest, who can you trust?"

Cordelia lowered her glasses. "You've *got* to be kidding."

"I'll look him up," said Jane.

"Great," said Guthrie. "And I promise, I may not be able to pay you every penny your time is worth, but I'll make it up to you. Someway."

20

Father Mike often had breakfast with Evangeline on weekdays. On this bright, sunny morning after Christmas, he stood at the kitchen sink in the old farmhouse, Evangeline's apron tied around his waist, and finished up the dishes. He liked to do his part, especially when Evangeline made his favorite: a cinnamon-and-walnut coffee cake with a drizzle of maple frosting. At sixty-one, he understood the struggle to keep fit and not gain weight. Walking from St. Andrew's to the Adler's farm was part of his regimen, though this morning the frigid temperature had urged caution, so he'd driven instead of hoofing it.

Turning around at the sound of creaking floors, he offered an amused smile as Kira came into the kitchen. Not even the wonderful aromas emanating from her grandmother's stove had been enough to draw her downstairs for breakfast. How well fed we were these days, he thought, when bacon and fresh-brewed coffee didn't create a stampede.

Kira had slept in, but was now dressed in jeans and a gray wool sweater. She held car keys. She looked tired. Of all the members of the Adler family, Kira was the one Mike knew the least. She'd rarely come to church with her dad when she was young. Evangeline insisted she attend mass on major holidays, but Mike couldn't remember a time when she'd ever come to confession. He didn't hold it against her, any more than he did with Kevin or Doug. Religion wasn't for everyone. Perhaps he was too modern for the priesthood. He'd always believed that God understood a person's heart and that's what mattered most.

"Morning," mumbled Kira. She poured herself a cup of coffee and stood across the room from him, hip pressed against the counter, both hands wrapped around the mug.

"Are you hungry?" Mike asked.

"I'm not much of a breakfast person," she said. "Where's Gram?"

"Out in the hayloft, I think." It was what they called the barn's second floor, though it had been entirely remade as a kind of small apartment. He closed up the dishwasher and turned it on. Sitting back down at the kitchen table with a glass of orange juice, he motioned for her to join him.

She seemed hesitant, but eventually curled her thin frame into one of the ancient bentwood chairs, setting the mug on the oilcloth-covered table and turning it around in her hands. "Can I ask you something?"

"Anything."

"First, can we keep this conversation just between you and me?"

"If that's what you want."

"I do." She raised the mug to her lips, but set it down again without taking a sip.

"Are you angry at your family?" He had to ask.

"How could I not be?"

"Have you talked to your father about your feelings?"

"I can't talk to anyone until I work through everything and figure out what they are." She hesitated, then asked, "Did you know my mother?"

Of all the subjects she might have brought up, this was the most difficult. "Of course I knew her."

"I was only five when she died. I remember she made cupcakes once with pink frosting. They were for Gracie's birthday, but Gracie got to them before the party and ate all the frosting off. Mom totally lost it."

Father Mike smiled. "Sounds like the little Grace I remember."

"Gracie and I used to go into Mom's makeup drawer when she was out and try on all the lipstick, the eye shadow. Gracie drew these heavy, dark eyebrows on me once. I thought I looked like a movie star until Dad made me wash them off."

"So you remember your childhood."

"The thing is, I don't. Not as well as I'd like."

"I'm sure your family has talked to you about your mom."

She gave a noncommittal shrug. "Gram never liked her."

"Why would you say that?"

"Come on. Tell me I'm wrong."

He couldn't exactly argue the point. "You know, Kira, when I came to St. Andrew's, the first people I met were Evangeline and Henry. They became, in every way that counts, the parents I never had. Your father and Doug were like my younger brothers. Hannah, like a sister."

She drew closer to the table. "That's why I thought you'd be the right person to talk to."

"Then I'm glad you came to me. I think we have more in common than you realize."

She gave him a skeptical look. "In what way?"

"Well, my childhood was difficult, too, though in different ways than yours. I never knew my dad. He left my mother before I was born." He stopped, then asked, "Would you like to hear the short version of my story?"

"Sure. I suppose."

It wasn't a ringing assertion of interest, but he went ahead anyway. "My mom died when I was two years old. I don't remember her at all. Nobody ever gave me the details, but from what I could piece together, I think she died of a drug overdose. I lived with my grandmother until I was seven, and then was sent away to stay with Aunt Bette, in Lima, Ohio. That's where I graduated from high school. My aunt was a single parent with three children of her own, so I was kind of lost in the shuffle. I was a very angry kid. Very self-conscious about the fact that I was shorter than all the other boys. I don't know what would have happened to me if my tenth-grade algebra teacher hadn't taken an interest. He was a deeply religious man. He took me hunting and fishing, got me out into the woods and taught me how to take care of myself. Taught me to box. Helped me get involved with the wrestling team at my school. I thought the world of him. I see now that I entered the priesthood not because it was something I wanted, but in order to please—and perhaps impress—him."

"Are you sorry you became a priest?"

"No," he said. "Not anymore. Early on, it was a struggle. I went through the motions, but between you and me, I felt like a fraud. I fell into a relationship with a woman—not physical, but emotional—and I almost left."

"What stopped you?"

He gazed into her quick sparrow eyes, so much like

Evangeline's. "Your grandmother. She saved my life, Kira. You don't get many second chances, but she gave me mine."

"How——"

"She listened. Didn't judge or condemn. She helped me find my way back to my faith." It was clear that Kira wasn't all that interested in his crisis of faith. She wanted to talk about her mother. She had no idea that the two subjects were, at least for a time, interwoven.

"You said you knew my mother. What did you think of her? What was she like?"

"She was . . . strong-willed. Very beautiful. And very troubled."

"She drank too much. I remember that. I remember my parents arguing a lot, how scared it made me."

"They both loved you, Kira. There was never any doubt about that."

"But did they love Grace?"

His jaw tightened.

"Dad may have. But Mom——I think she hated her."

"Unfortunately, if that's true, then the feelings were mutual." He regretted saying the words as soon as they were out of his mouth.

Kira bent her head. "Yeah, you're right. I never understood what really happened the day Mom died until I came for a family meeting a few days ago."

"What did your family tell you?" He needed to know.

"Have you talked to them about it?" asked Kira.

"I've heard some of the story. I doubt I know it all."

Folding her arms around her stomach, she said, "Gracie didn't go to school the day Mom died. For some reason she stayed home.

Mom promised my dad that she wouldn't smoke in the house. She'd always go out on the deck, even in the winter. That morning, Gracie locked the door after her. It was bitterly cold. I assume Mom must have yelled for Gracie to open up. If there'd been any furniture on the deck she might have been able to break the window and get inside, but Dad had dumped all our old stuff. He was planning to buy a new table and chairs in the spring. When Gracie wouldn't let her in, Mom must have panicked. Gram figures she climbed over the rail and tried to drop onto this narrow strip of snow that ran along the edge of the backyard fence next to the ravine. Instead, she fell wide of it."

"Such a tragedy," said Mike.

Kira's gaze jerked away.

"Can you forgive your sister for what she did?"

"I remember the way Mom treated her when we were little. Those are my most vivid memories. I never talk about them, not to anybody."

"But you understand now why your family needed to cover up the truth."

"I guess. It's just—"

"Just what, Kira?"

"I have a hard time believing Gracie would do something like that."

"You think your family is lying to you?"

"They've lied to me before."

"But they explained all that. Told you everything."

"Have they?"

He was confused by her response. "Yes."

Pushing her coffee mug away, she got up. "Let Gram know that I'm going for a drive."

"Please tell me you trust your family to be truthful."

She didn't answer right away. "Sure. You're right. I'm being silly. Again, please keep this conversation between the two of us, okay? It's just . . . I'm having a hard time taking all of this in."

"Of course you are. No worries. And if you need to talk again, remember, I'm always here for you."

She offered him an unsmiling nod and left the room.

When he heard the front door click shut, he collapsed against the back of his chair. He sat like that, immobile, his stomach roiling, until Evangeline entered through the kitchen door a few minutes later.

"Oh, my, you did the dishes," she said, walking over to pour herself a cup of coffee. "You didn't have to do that." When she turned and saw his face, she said, "What's wrong?"

"Kira left."

She let out a frustrated sigh. "Oh, that girl. She doesn't understand yet. She will. It's simply going to take some time."

Forcing himself to smile, he said, "I have to get back to the church."

"You better take off that apron."

He laughed. "Not a very priestly look?"

"You're my dear, dear friend. What would I do without you?"

21

Jane had hoped to get out of town Wednesday afternoon, but it was early evening before she was able to leave for New Dresden. During the time that she and Cordelia had spent in town, she'd noticed a HELP WANTED sign in the window of Kevin Adler's Sportsman's Tavern. If he ever needed someone to help him, it would be this week. Like so many other small-bar owners, Kevin undoubtedly understood the psychological nature of the week between Christmas and New Year's. Family gatherings might be fun and festive, but as the clock ticked away and one person became annoyed at Uncle Bill's politics and another got outright pissed at Aunt Beverly's snarky remarks, a good thing could turn sour. Now that all the presents had been opened and the hit each person's bank balance had taken began to sink in, the neighborhood bar started looking like the place to spend a little quality time.

Following a couple of women inside, Jane immediately noticed a sign that said: LAST OPPORTUNITY TO BUY TICKETS FOR NEW YEAR'S EVE STEAK RAFFLE. ONE TICKET PER CUSTOMER. She figured it might be one reason the place was so packed. People stood three and four deep waiting for their drink orders, talking, laughing, even dancing. Kevin was doing his best to handle the orders. An older woman was helping him, alternating between ringing up the sales and working as a bar back. The mood was boisterous, the TV tuned to a replay of an old Wisconsin Badgers game.

Stepping to the side so that she could get a closer look at the bar setup, Jane was glad to see that there were two jockey boxes. Kevin was only using one, though both had been prepped. The pour spouts on the liquor bottles were all needle noses, which Jane preferred. The glasses were generic sizes. Nothing silly. Four beers on tap. Favorite call liquors directly behind the box. Two blenders on the back bar. Freezer below holding the chilled beer glasses. Small refrigerator. All the necessary juices in a row next to the ice. A couple muddlers next to that. Shakers and strainers, all cleaned, organized, and ready to go. Everything looked straightforward.

Hearing Kevin curse as he knocked over a bottle of gin, Jane moved around him to the open jockey box and slapped a napkin on the counter. Customers began to line up in front of her.

"One Manhattan on the rocks," said an older woman. "And one vodka tonic."

When Jane looked over at Kevin, she found him staring at her.

"You know what you're doing?" he called.

"I better," she called back. "Just need the portions."

"Ounce and a quarter, mixed. Ounce and three-quarters up or rocks."

"Got it." She smiled at the woman in front of her and began pouring. It had been a while since she'd worked a bar this busy, but it all came back to her, the moves, filling the glasses with ice, then slapping them on the counter, counting out the pour, using both hands, hitting the glass with the liquor and the mix gun at the same time. It took a few minutes to get the speed rail arranged the way she liked. As she worked, she laughed, talked, and mixed it up with the crowd. Every now and then, Kevin would glance her way and nod. She was saving his ass and they both knew it.

The crowd didn't start thinning out until close to one-thirty. After pulling himself a beer, Kevin moved over to Jane, stuck out his hand, and introduced himself. "You looking for a job? If you are, you got one."

"I don't know," said Jane, spraying soda water on the bar mop and wiping down the lacquered wood counter. "I'm kind of, you know, in between at the moment. I've got some friends in Duluth. They invited me to stay with them over New Year's, so that's where I'm headed."

"Is your plan set in stone?"

"Not really."

"You from Wisconsin?"

"I've lived all over the country. I don't seem to stay in any one place very long. Could be I'm searching for home."

His gaze roamed the room. "From one fellow traveler to another, I hope you find it. You got a license to pour?"

"In Minnesota."

"Good enough." He spoke with his hands in his pockets, never taking one out except to hoist the beer glass to his mouth. Nodding to a group of men as they passed on their way to the door, he continued, "Even if you only stay a week, two weeks, a month, you could really help me. I've got a lot on my plate right now. Would be nice if someone who knew the business could handle the place for me. I'd pay you extra."

"You mean, like, take over? Open and close."

"I'd close up every night, set up the bank for the next day. I've got a guy who can open, work the early part of the afternoon. But yeah, if you could do the rest—sweep, clean up, prep the garnishes and set up the boxes, then stay until I can get here, that would save my life. What do you say? You interested?"

This was perfect, thought Jane. She needed a way into the Adler family. She'd been hoping that the HELP WANTED sign would be her ticket to ride. "Let me think about it." She didn't want to seem too eager.

"You got anything better to do? Who knows? You might even decide that New Dresden is heaven on earth." His grin was infectious—a genuine smile, crooked and friendly.

Jane found herself smiling back. "Okay. You found yourself a bartender." Folding the bar rag, she asked, "Do you mostly work alone?"

He took a few swallows of beer. "In the nineties, when I first took over, times were good. We did a great business, especially in the summers. I always had a second bartender working with me on weekends. But when the economy tanked in the mid two thousands, nobody had a dime to spend, so I ended up doing pretty much everything by myself. Eight months ago, I hired a Michigan State grad. He had a degree in finance, but before he started his real work life in earnest, he wanted to relax a little. He said he'd been in school for so long that he couldn't stand the idea of sliding right into a nine-to-five. He wanted to travel. He was here for six months. I trained him. After he left, I gave the job to my sister-in-law. I trained her, too. She worked part time, then up and quit two weeks ago. Really left me in a bad place, especially with Christmas and New Year's coming on."

"I guess I showed up at the right time," said Jane.

"Where are you staying?"

"At the moment, nowhere. Figured I'd find a motel room for the night."

"My apartment is upstairs. There's also a separate room, has a separate entrance around the back of the building. The college kid stayed there when he worked for me. I charged him rent. I'd be happy to let you use it free of charge for however long you need or want. It's not much, but it's clean. There's a good lock on the door. A single bed. One of those tiny refrigerators. A small microwave. An old TV that still works. The bathroom is down the hall. I don't use it, so it would be yours exclusively. What do you say? You interested?"

"I can hardly turn that down."

"Great. This must be my lucky day. So what do I call you?"

"Jane. Jane Lawless."

"Had a friend in the army named Frank Lawless. You any relation?"

"Not that I know of."

"So, Jane. Plain Jane. Except you're not plain. Doesn't hurt to have an attractive bartender behind the counter."

"Are you flirting with me?"

"Not much good at that anymore. No, no flirting. No hitting on employees." He lifted his beer glass. "Here's to a mutually productive relationship, for however long you decide to stick around. Please, God, let it at least be until after New Year's."

22

Laurie opened the front door of her mobile home and stepped out onto a deck barely large enough to hold two small chairs. It was a crisp December morning, just the kind of day she loved. With Doug still inside, however, sitting mutely at the breakfast table, finishing his cereal and his third beer, it was hard to achieve any sort of Zen. Normally, he was gone by the time she went outside to the mailbox. He'd overslept this morning, most likely because he'd had too much to drink last night. He'd phoned the lumberyard and lied to his boss, telling him he was having car problems and would be late. It was an excuse he'd used before. One of these days, his boss was going to call him on it. And then what? Would he get fired?

Walking out to the mailbox, still dressed in her bathrobe and slippers, Laurie pulled the front cover down and found that her neighbor, Tanya Simpson, the woman who lived in the double-wide across the street, had stuffed yesterday's copy of the *Basaw County Independent*, the newspaper that was published twice a week over in Union, into the mailbox.

Laurie adored newspapers. It was one of the reasons she'd been so drawn to Doug in high school. These days, the over-fifty crowd—people like her—were the only ones keeping old-fashioned newspapers alive. Her morning ritual was pretty simple: She would brew a pot of tea, cut a sliver of lemon, make herself two slices of buttered toast, and then sit down at the breakfast table to read. It was also the way she kept in touch with what was happening locally. The *Independent* had a dedicated page of news for the five largest towns in the small county. Doug, of course, hated the paper on general principles because it was still going strong when his newspaper had tanked a decade ago. Laurie always hid the paper from him, and tossed it into the garbage, shoving it way down into the bottom of the plastic bag, when she was done.

When she came back inside this morning she simply wasn't able muster the energy to protect his tender feelings anymore. Working at Kevin's bar had become a turning point for her. As usual, nobody in the family had noticed. She was a known quantity—the quiet one, the workhorse, the good girl. She didn't make waves. She might lose her temper occasionally, though as an adult, she'd learned how to hide the worst of it. Her time at the Sportsman, however, had become her "road to Damascus" moment. Like Saul of Tarsus, soon to become Paul the Apostle, the scales had finally fallen from her eyes and she began to see clearly what she had to do. Habit had ruled her existence for al-most as long as she could remember. The fact that Hannah was pushing for change at the farmhouse gave Laurie the strength to push for her own kind of change. If she actually did leave Doug, she would face even more difficult questions. Nothing was going to be easy.

She flapped the paper in front of her as she sat down at the table.

"What's the hell do you have there?" demanded Doug, finishing his beer.

"The *Basaw County Independent*."

"Where'd you get it? If you paid money for that rag—"

"Tanya puts it in our mailbox. It's a kindness, Doug. I asked her to pass it on when she's done with it."

"I will not have that trash in my house."

"It's mine and I'm going to read it." She got up to pour herself a cup of coffee, then sat back down and turned to page five—the New Dresden news page. She did her best to ignore her husband as he stomped out of the kitchen. As she skimmed a piece about a local man who was turning field grass into an alternate fuel source, Doug, who was acting like a nasty four-year-old with a bad hangover, returned to the kitchen, yanked open a cupboard, stuffed his cereal box back inside, and banged the door shut.

"Don't you want to hear about a new form of fuel some local guy's developed? They think it will really boost the economy around here."

"Laurie, if you buy into the bullshit that paper pushes, you're as ignorant and terminally gullible as the rest of the people in this town."

"You think they're making the story up?"

"For once in your life, use the brains natural selection gave you. Crap like that sells papers. The *Independent*," said Doug as he made himself his usual three peanut butter-and-jelly sandwiches for his afternoon snack, "prints fake stories all the time—and liberal garbage. Lies that support their political agenda."

"I'm *not* talking politics with you, Doug."

"Well maybe you should. You might learn something."

He spoke the words with such venom that she twisted around to look at him. "You get so worked up that I'm afraid you're going to have a coronary."

"Just what you'd love, right?" He pointed the knife at her. "If I died, you'd be free."

"Doug, please." This was a new low.

He came closer, the knife still in his hand.

"You're scaring me."

"Good. You should be scared." He stood staring down at her, his fingers working at the wooden handle. "People hide, Laurie. Behind their job title. Behind their religion. Behind their good looks. They use words to obscure their real feelings. You do that all the time. Hell if I ever know what you're thinking."

Instinct told her to defuse the situation. Fast. In all their married life together he'd never hit her—not technically. His preferred method of control was to hold her down in bed, making it impossible for her to get up. A few times he'd thrown her against a wall and then used his weight to keep her there, all the while spewing venom into her ear. Afterwards, he was always contrite, begging her to understand the pressures on him, saying that he loved her and nobody else. She told herself that this wasn't the same thing as domestic abuse. "I want to be honest with you, Doug, but when I try, you twist what I say into something I don't mean."

His eyes dropped to the knife in his hand. "*You* do this to me. I'm never angry like this when you're not around."

"Then maybe I should leave."

"We always get back to that, don't we. One way or another."

"What do you want from me? I never quit on us, never stopped trying. Can you say the same?"

Turning back to the kitchen counter, he mumbled, "You have no idea how much I hate myself sometimes."

"You do?" That was news to her.

Running a hand over his balding head, he said, "I don't want to be like this."

The comment should have reassured her, but it was too late. She'd spent her life feeling sorry for him, making excuses for him, soothing his feelings, pumping up his sagging ego, trying to ignore or rationalize away his growing bitterness, and always, every moment they were together, doing everything in her power to avoid setting off his anger.

"Look, I'll rent a movie in town," he said. "Bring home a pizza and a six-pack after work. Maybe we can, you know, just try to have a nice evening." He slapped the peanut butter-and-jelly sandwiches together, dropped them in a plastic sack, and kissed her cheek before grabbing his coat and keys.

Laurie listened to his car roar to life. After he'd driven off, she propped her elbows on the kitchen table, dropped her head in her hands, and cried.

23

After cruising around town looking for a place to have breakfast, Jane settled on a cafe two doors down from the Sportsman's
Tavern. Millie's Kitchen was small but clean, with red gingham
curtains and old-fashioned gray formica-covered tables. A lunch
counter ran across the right side of the room, which was where
most of the customers were seated. After ordering coffee and the
breakfast special—two eggs over medium, three slices of bacon
and two blueberry hotcakes—she settled in with her coffee, ready
to think about the day ahead.

The small room Kevin had given her, especially the bed, had
been surprisingly comfortable. The only downside was the lack
of Wi-Fi. Even her cell phone would register a few bars, only to
lose them a second later. After breakfast, her first order of business was to drive around the area and see if she could find a spot
where her electronics connected, assuming there was a tower
somewhere in the vicinity.

When the food arrived, Jane took out a notebook and, while
she ate, went over the notes she'd made. There were three

columns: What she knew; what she suspected; what she needed to find out.

"I see you discovered my favorite cafe."

Jane looked up to find Kevin smiling his crooked smile down at her.

"Mind if I join you?" he asked.

"Have a seat." She closed the notebook.

The waitress came over with a mug and the coffee pot. "Same as usual?" she asked, pouring him a cup.

"Thanks, Peg." Taking a sip and then holding his large, calloused hands around the mug, he watched Jane for a few seconds, then asked, "How'd you sleep?"

"Great."

"And the food?" He nodded to her plate.

"It's good."

"It's the best place in town, which I suppose isn't saying much."

"I love small-town cafes. You never know what you're going to find." Breakfast was her favorite meal when she was on the road because a cook had to be uniquely incompetent to screw up eggs, bacon, and toast.

"Listen, I was wondering: I'm heading over to my mother's house after I'm done here. She makes up batches of seasoned popcorn for the bar. Cheese flavored, and sour cream-and-onion flavored. It's real salty, you know? Makes people thirsty."

"That's a great idea."

"And sometimes, if I'm real lucky, she bakes me a few pies. They go like crazy. I suppose if I figured out a way to serve more food, I could add to my bottom line. I'm not much of a cook, so that's probably never going to happen. But anyway, thought maybe you'd like to come along, help me load the food into my van. I could use an extra pair of hands. And also—I suppose this is the real reason—if you're there, I won't get stuck talking to my mother for an hour."

"I'd be happy to," said Jane, amazed again at her good luck.

"You'll also get to meet my daughter, Kira. She staying with my mom for a few months to help out."

"Does your whole family live in New Dresden?" asked Jane.

"Pretty much. My grandfather began the local paper, which he passed on to my dad, and my dad passed on to my older brother."

"You didn't have any interest in it?"

"Wasn't really an option. Doug got the paper and I got the bar. Worked for me. 'Course, I've still got the bar and he had to shut down the paper. He was a good journalist—really enjoyed re-searching stories, writing opinion pieces. He's a talented writer and photographer. He used to always travel with a camera, took most of the pictures for the paper. I love my brother, but . . . when it comes to managing people, he's hopeless. No business sense at all. My dad never saw that. Or maybe he did. Who knows? Doug ran that newspaper into the ground. Kept losing his best people because they didn't like the way he treated them. He works at Vaughn's Lumber now."

"I would imagine the job base around here isn't that strong."

Turning the salt shaker around in his hand, he said, "You got that right. Once upon a time, his wife, Laurie, had a great job. Taught English at the middle school. But when they shut it down in 2007 and started busing our local kids to the middle school in Pine River, she lost her position. Couldn't find another one—too many teachers out of work"

"Last night you mentioned that she'd been bartending for you. Why'd she stop?"

"Oh, you know. This and that. The next few months are some of my busiest. It's cabin fever. People get sick of being cooped up at home because of the cold, so they brave the weather and go out to a bar." He leaned back as the waitress set a big stack of hotcakes and a side of hash browns in front of him. "Looks perfect, Peg," he said. "Thanks." He smeared butter around the top cake and then poured syrup all over it. "You married?" he asked.

"Nope. You?"

"Once."

"Divorced?"

"She died."

"I'm sorry."

He shrugged. "We were headed for divorce court. We'd been having problems for years. This may sound cold, but I was always kind of grateful that I never had to fight her for custody of the kids."

Jane wondered if he'd just given her the motive for Delia's murder. "How'd she die?"

"Fell off a second-floor deck."

"Yikes."

"We lived next to a ravine. That's where she was found."

"How awful."

"She was a big drinker—even in the mornings."

"Is that why she fell?"

"Probably. I wasn't there, so I'll never know for sure. Years ago, a buddy of mine and I started a construction company. My dad hired us to create an office for him by closing off the hayloft in the old barn. High gambrel roof, open rafters. As a kid, I remember playing in there and feeling like I was in an old Gothic church. When he died in '94, Mom needed something to take her mind off his passing. She decided to go back to raising Airedales. She wanted to use the bottom half of the barn for that, so I had to clean it out, insulate it, and figure out a way to tie the heat in from upstairs. That's what I was doing the morning Delia died. I didn't realize what had happened until I got home that afternoon."

"Who found her?"

He blew out a breath. "I did."

He was a likable guy, came across as open and honest, giving her no reason to doubt him. Nobody would suspect, unless they knew the truth, as Jane did, that he'd just lied to her—easily, casually, without missing a beat. It was something she needed to keep in the forefront of her mind. "Look, we don't have to talk about this."

"Yeah, it's not a good memory."

He worked at his hotcakes while Jane finished up her meal. After paying their bills, they headed out to Kevin's van. He switched on some music as they sped along, a Steve Earle CD, and began humming as they turned onto a county road. A few minutes later, he veered off onto a gravel path and pulled in next to an old wood-frame farmhouse. "When I was a kid, this was way out in the country. Not anymore."

"Great old house," said Jane, pushing out of the front seat, her boots hitting the snowy ground.

"And that's the barn I worked on," said Kevin, pointing, a note of pride in his voice. "I used to think I'd make a career out of transforming old barns into usable living space, but when the great recession came along, I was glad I had the bar. I still do an occasional construction job. Between that and the bar, I'm able to make a decent living."

Before they reached the base of the porch steps, the front door opened. Evangeline Adler stepped out into the chill morning to hug and kiss her son. If she was ill, she didn't look it. On the other hand, cancer was that kind of disease, especially in the early stages. "This must be Jane," she said, squeezing Jane's hand. "Welcome."

She led them back to the kitchen, where a pot of soup was simmering on the stove. Carrots, celery, parsnips, turnips, and a big yellow onion lay on the cutting board, waiting to be chopped. The two kitchen windows facing the back of the property were blurred by condensation. Jane liked the old-fashioned feel. The tall, painted cupboards were original, the appliances immaculate specimens from the 1950s, she guessed. No stainless steel or granite in this woman's kitchen. Jane thought it was a breath of fresh air.

"Where's Kira?" asked Kevin.

"Out in the barn tending to Foxy."

"She have her litter yet?"

"I expect she will by the new year."

Easing onto a stool, Evangeline picked up her knife and began working on the carrots. "Sit down," she said, motioning to the kitchen table. "You can stay for a few minutes, can't you?"

Kevin cupped his hands together in front of him. "Actually, we can't. I have to break Jane in this morning, show her what has to be done before we open the bar at noon. So, I'm afraid we need to pack up the food and get going."

Evangeline checked her watch. When she looked up, her gaze fastened on Jane. Those old eyes didn't miss a trick, thought Jane.

She felt thoroughly evaluated, placed in a box and labeled. What she wasn't able to read in Evangeline's expression were the words on that label.

"It's only ten o'clock, Kevin. My car's been giving me some trouble. Wouldn't take more than five minutes for you to look at it."

"I guess," he said, zipping his suede jacket back up.

"Jane, why don't you stay here and keep warm. The coffee's on, so go ahead and help yourself. Kev, I'll get my keys."

Jane sensed that Evangeline wanted to talk to her son and didn't want Jane listening in. As they bustled out the door, she took a moment to stir the soup. It was chicken noodle. She found a spoon and gave it a taste. The woman certainly knew how to make chicken stock.

This family, so tightly knit, was a fascination to Jane. On the outside, they seemed like such decent people. Perhaps they were, with the exception of one self-serving moment when they'd all banded together to save one of their number from a homicide charge. Thanks to the fact that Evangeline had so many connections in this small town, they'd succeeded in covering up a murder. So why were they still having secret family meetings twenty years after the fact?

The only conclusion Jane could draw was that Evangeline, the one who appeared to be the prime mover in the family, had decided it was time to explain to Kira what had gone down all those years ago. Jane wasn't sure why Kira needed that information. She could live her entire life without it and be a much happier woman. Still, if Jane had guessed right, Kira would require time to deal with the news, to process her feelings, to ask questions, so sticking around New Dresden for a while made sense. But

Guthrie had said she intended to stay for months. The reason given was Evangeline's cancer—her chemotherapy appointments. With so much family in town, with her friends and her church connections, one would think there would be plenty of people to give Evangeline a helping hand. Why put Kira's education on hold? Why take her away from the man she loved? After staying at the house on Thanksgiving, Guthrie hadn't even been allowed to come in on Christmas Eve. Something didn't add up.

Drifting into the living room, Jane examined all the photographs. Some dotted the top of the piano, others hung on the walls. The mantel held dozens of small, framed baby pictures. Clearly, Evangeline's family was the center of her world—with the exception of one person: Delia. There were no pictures of Kevin's wife anywhere.

Walking across the hall to the dining room, Jane found a lovely, bright space dominated by a built-in breakfront filled with fine china and glassware. As she was about to move over to examine the contents more closely, the small hairs on the back of her neck began to prickle. She had a strong sense of being watched. Turning around, she scanned the room, and then moved back across the hall into the living room. The feeling didn't go away. If anything, it became stronger. She stepped over to the stairway leading up to the second floor and was about to start up when she heard the back door open. She immediately gave up her search and returned to the kitchen.

"Kevin said it may take him a few minutes to work out what's wrong with my car," said Evangeline. She removed her coat, hung it on a hook by the door, then retied her apron. "Did you get yourself some coffee?"

"If I drink any more I'll start flying around the room," said

Jane. She sat back down at the kitchen table as Evangeline returned to her stool to continue cutting up vegetables.

"Kevin tells me you're a terrific bartender."

"It's a good skill to have, especially if you like to travel. You can pretty much always count on finding a job somewhere."

"Where are you from?"

"My father's family is from Illinois. My mother was English."

"Was?"

"She died when I was in my early teens."

"Your father?"

"He's still alive. And I have a younger brother. He's married and they have one daughter."

"And you?"

"Never been married. No children."

Evangeline regarded Jane with her sharp eyes. "I don't mean to pry, but that sounds like a very lonely life."

"It can be. I'd like to think I'll find the right person one day."

"You will," said Evangeline. "Don't give up." She worked slowly, almost meditatively on the carrots. "I've lived a good, long life. I've been blessed and I know it. Worries, needs, circumstances within and outside of your control, they weigh on you. But in my time, I've discovered only one bottom line." Looking up, she said, "Family."

Kevin pushed through the back door. "Look who I found," he said, smiling broadly. Putting his arm around a willowy young woman with hair the color of winter wheat, he kissed her forehead. "Jane, this is my daughter, Kira."

"Hi," said Kira, looking a little embarrassed. "Nice to meet you."

"She gets her good looks from me."

"*Dad.*"

"Just stating the obvious."

Turning to her grandmother, Kira said, "You need to come out to the barn and take a look at Foxy."

"Is she all right?" asked Evangeline.

"I'm not sure. I never helped a dog give birth before."

"Likely she won't need our help.

"I think you have a bad alternator," said Kevin, popping a piece of raw carrot into his mouth.

"Can you fix it?"

"Yeah, but not this morning. I'll come by later."

"Thank you, dear boy," said Evangeline, removing her apron. "Any pies today?"

"Six. They're on the shelf in the pantry."

"What kind?"

"Apple, pumpkin, and lemon meringue."

"Score," said Kevin, pumping his arm as he turned around and winked at Jane. "We better get crackin' "

24

No more than a dozen people stopped into the bar that afternoon, all of them regulars. Jane made sure she talked to each person, serving them their favorite poison along with a heaping basket of Evangeline's popcorn. She preferred being busy to being bored, and bored was exactly how she felt as the day wore on.

Like so many small town bars, the interior of the Sportsman felt like being locked in a dingy, overheated closet. With light slanting in through the narrow, clerestory windows, she could actually see dust motes floating in the air. At least Wisconsin had voted through a smoking ban. She wouldn't leave smelling like an ashtray.

If a customer was used to the cramped shadows, the interior probably felt cozy, even comforting. The walls were covered with sports memorabilia, a moose head or two, and lots of framed photos of men and a few women holding up fish or standing next to strung-up dead deer. Hanging lantern lights over the tables helped patrons see well enough to play one of the many board games Kevin made available. Jane was glad she didn't have problems with claustrophobia.

The after-work crowd began trickling in around four, eager to order beers and munch on popcorn. It was easy enough for one person to handle. Nothing like the evening crowd at the Lyme House Pub, where two bartenders were always busy until closing.

After switching channels on the TV to the Milwaukee Bucks/ Detroit Pistons game shortly after eight, Jane retreated to a stool under the glow of one of the back-bar lights. She'd brought the latest *New Yorker* with her in case she had some time on her hands. She'd just finished reading through a long article and was paging through the magazine looking for any cartoons she might have missed when a familiar face came through the front door.

Jane was glad Guthrie had been able to drop off pictures of the Adler family before she left the Twin Cities. Hannah Adler, Kevin's older sister, was an unusual-looking woman, though that didn't mean she was unattractive. She was expensively dressed in a belted, camel wool coat and striped wool scarf. Her thick, shoulder-length bob was likely a dye job, strawberry blond, heavy on the strawberry, but her jewelry was tasteful, as was her makeup. Her most prominent feature was an unusually large mouth.

Stopping directly in front of Jane, Hannah said, "Where's Kevin?"

Not exactly the friendliest woman Jane had ever met. "Not here."

"When will he be back?"

"Around eleven."

The comment created a sour look. Pulling off her tight leather gloves, one finger at a time, Hannah dropped them and her purse on the counter. Unbelting her coat, she sat down. "I'm Kevin's sister. And you are?"

"The new bartender." Since Hannah hadn't offered her name, Jane didn't offer hers. It was petty, of course, but then, with so little of interest going on inside the Sportsman's, Jane felt a little power struggle might spice up the evening.

Much like Evangeline, Hannah's gaze was not only probing, it was thorough. The difference was that while Evangeline's assessment had come with a smile, Hannah's was heavy and direct.

"Can I get you something to drink?" asked Jane, easing off the stool. She closed the magazine and set it on the bar next to Hannah. She wanted her to see what she'd been reading. Jane was amused to watch the older woman's eyes widen ever so slightly. Jane was, after all, the hired help.

"A Rob Roy, up, with a twist," said Hannah, removing her coat and placing it on the stool next to her.

Jane wondered if this was a test. No one else, at least so far—and that included last night—had ordered a Rob Roy or a twist. Then again, Hannah probably wasn't a bump and a beer kind of gal.

"Do you need instructions?" asked Hannah.

"I think I can manage it," said Jane. "You have a scotch preference?"

"Johnny Walker Black Label is fine."

Jane packed the shaker and the glass with ice and set them on the bar, poured an extra-generous two ounces of scotch into the shaker along with the Italian vermouth and bitters. After shaking the drink, she dumped the ice out of the now chilled glass and strained the alcohol into it. Looking around for a whole lemon, she found one next to the well. She used a paring knife to cut an extra thin strip and twisted it once over the drink, dropping it directly on top. "Here you go," she said, slapping a cocktail napkin on the bar and setting the drink on top of it.

"You've been doing this a while," said Hannah, almost, but not quite, impressed.

"Cheese popcorn?"

Her face puckered with distaste. "I know it's my mother's recipe, but it's vile stuff. So, where are you from?"

"I've lived all over the country."

"No place to call home?"

"Nothing stands out."

Hannah pulled her drink closer, settling in for a conversation. "What do you do for a living?" asked Jane.

"I'm a doctor. My practice is in Eau Claire."

"What kind of doctor?"

"Gastroenterologist."

"You like it?"

With that one question, Hannah was off to the races. As she continued on to her second even stronger Rob Roy, she rambled through her childhood, her college days, talked about her extreme need for privacy and solitude. She hated the politics at her hospital, the petty jealousies. Doctors could be *so* spiteful, especially when it came to turf wars. HR was staffed by imbeciles with morbid power needs. People—especially her mother—were always pressing her about when she would get married. She was never getting married. She believed in monogamy, the serial kind that didn't come with legalities and which left her with an easy exit clause. Did that make her a three-headed monster? A freak of nature? She liked sex as much as the next person, but as for living with one man for the rest of her life—it was a ludicrous idea. At the moment, she was between relationships and that was fine with her. She kept coming back to her mother, how deeply her mom misunderstood her.

"I'm not a bad person," she said, pointing to a filled basket of her mother's popcorn behind the bar. When Jane set it in front of her, she began to pick at it. "But there's no way I can make my mother happy. Nothing I do is ever enough."

"That's hard," said Jane.

Into her third Rob Roy, Hannah admitted she'd been fighting a low-grade depression for years. Her past was riddled with bad decisions. One in particular wouldn't leave her alone. Was she being selfish, she asked, her eyes beginning to tear. She'd never be happy if she couldn't live life on her own terms. She seemed to sincerely need Jane's validation. The fact that she had no real idea who Jane was didn't seem to matter.

"You know," said Jane, "since you brought up the subject, I met your mother this morning. Kevin asked me to help him load some food into his van."

Hannah raised the drink to her lips, studied Jane over the rim. "And what did you think of the old farmstead?"

"Seemed comfortable. Unpretentious. A lot like your mom."

Hannah sipped her drink and didn't respond.

"She asked Kevin to take a look at her car. Something wasn't running right. While they were outside, I had a chance to look at all the family photos in the living room. I was curious about Kevin's wife, the one who died in that accident. He told me about her at breakfast."

"Delia? She's generally the last person he wants to talk about. Curious about what?"

Jane gave a noncommittal shrug. "Kevin's a good-looking man. I wondered what Delia looked like."

"You won't find any photos of Delia at my mom's house. No love lost between those two."

"Sorry to hear it."

"Delia was spunky, I'll give her that. My mother doesn't deal well with spunky women—I'm living proof. But none of us liked Delia or her scummy friends."

"Did she have a lot of friends in town?"

"A few. Her best friend, Macy Hendrickson, OD'd a few years back. Can't recall what her drug of choice was. Macy and Delia waitressed together. They liked working the evening shift at Big D's Steakhouse so they could go out afterward and get ripped. Her other good friend, Riley Garrow, runs the beauty parlor—the Cut & Curl—now. She graduated from high school the same year as Kevin and my sister-in-law, Laurie. She was a slut then, and as I understand it, still is."

"Small towns are small worlds."

"You got that right."

Jane made a mental note of the names. It wasn't smart to hit the subject of Delia too hard because it might set off warning bells. Shifting gears, she said, "I met Kevin's daughter. Can't remember her name."

"Kira."

A man wearing a blue FedEx uniform stepped up to the counter and ordered another pitcher of beer for his table. Jane pulled it for him and slid it across the counter top with a fresh basket of popcorn. She added the pitcher to his tab, then returned to Hannah, who, amazingly, had finished her third drink. "Another?"

"Why not?"

While Jane worked, Hannah said, "You say you had breakfast this morning with my brother?"

"We ran into each other at Millie's Kitchen."

"That right. He offer to let you stay upstairs?"

"As a matter of fact, he did. I thought it was very generous."

"Uh-huh."

"Are you saying he's planning to hit on me?"

"He's not like that. On the other hand, it doesn't mean you aren't planning to hit on him. Happens a lot. In case you didn't know, that sort of thing goes on in bars."

"You're kidding."

"Nope. God's honest truth."

"Well, not to worry. I won't be hitting on your brother."

"No? Just an FYI: He's at a very vulnerable point in his life. For many reasons. This wouldn't be a good time for him to get involved."

"I'm gay."

Hannah raised an eyebrow, studying Jane with new interest. "You say that so easily. Does my brother know?"

"Never came up. Is it a problem?"

"Not for Kevin. Just don't announce it to the customers."

Jane set the fourth Rob Roy in front of Hannah. She wasn't drunk, but she was moving steadily in that direction, thanks to Jane's heavy hand with the Johnny Walker. Jane figured this was her chance to ask a few leading questions. "I like your brother. He's easy to talk to. But boy, he's had a lot of loss in his life. Those three deaths right in a row. Your father, his wife, and then his little girl. What was her name?"

Hannah folded her hands around her drink. "Grace. Gracie."

"You expect your parents will go before you. Maybe even your spouse. But a child? That's brutal."

"It was a terrible time."

"How did it happen?" It was a nosey, intrusive question. Then again, it was a bar, and bar conversations, stirred together with alcohol, often tended to cross normal lines of discourse.

Taking a couple of delicate sips, Hannah eased a little closer to the counter. "Can't imagine why you'd want to hear about this."

"I'm interested," said Jane.

"You mean you're bored."

"That too."

Hannah twisted the glass around, thought about it for a few seconds, then plunged in. "After Delia died, Kevin and I got to talking. The kids were so down, so sad, that we thought we should take them somewhere to get their minds off . . . what had just happened. You know, a little trip. Mom thought it was a good idea, too. We decided on Disney World in Orlando. I called and set up the flight and the hotel, and Kevin took care of the various park tickets. He'd been there once before so he knew more about that than I did."

"And? How did it go?"

"The girls were on a real high. The last afternoon we were there, Kevin and Kira said they were beat. They wanted to go back to the resort, take a swim, and then maybe catch a nap before dinner. Gracie, as always, wanted to keep going. She was like that. A real buzz saw of energy. Since we only had one car, we had to drive Kira and Kevin back. Then Gracie and I headed to a mall, where we could do some shopping, maybe get an ice cream. On the way there, as I was going through an intersection on a green light, a guy broadsided our rental with his truck."

"The passenger's side?" asked Jane.

Hannah nodded. "I was pulled from the vehicle by paramedics and taken to a local hospital. I was in shock, had a badly bruised shoulder and hip. I walked away from it, but Gracie didn't. She died instantly."

"God, I'm really sorry."

"I never saw that truck coming. We were just sailing along." She jerked her eyes to Jane. "It was my fault. We were talking, laughing. I wasn't paying attention the way I should have been."

Jane wondered if this was the bad decision Hannah had referred to, the one that still haunted her. "I'd say it was the truck driver's fault."

"Kevin was devastated. The whole family was. I felt like crawling in a hole and never coming out." She drained the last half of her drink. "I don't want to talk about it anymore."

"Of course," said Jane. She folded a cloth and began wiping down the counter.

"Another," said Hannah, pushing the empty glass away. While she waited, she began to shred the cocktail napkin. "I just can't win. On Christmas, my mother called me self-centered and disloyal."

"Why would she say that?"

"Because I am. I made a promise and now I want to break it."

Beneath the self-loathing, Jane was beginning to glimpse a hard crust of anger. "Maybe you're neither of those things."

She fingered the pearls at her throat. "Yeah, maybe."

Kevin finally returned to the bar shortly after eleven, found his sister hammered, and helped her off the stool, saying he wouldn't let her drive and that she should come upstairs and spend the night in Kira's old bedroom. He was very kind to her, never showing any annoyance at her condition. From the way he handled her, Jane got the impression that it had happened before.

Kevin gave Jane an apologetic look as he scooped up Hannah's gloves and purse. "I'll be back down in a few minutes."

"Take your time," said Jane.

He tossed Hannah's coat over his shoulder, then gently placed his arm around her waist and guided her through the swinging door into the kitchen.

Jane resumed her stool, impressed and a little touched by the concern Kevin had shown his sister. She recalled Nolan's comment—that in the case of a murdered wife, the husband would be the number-one suspect. She had a hard time picturing Kevin that way, not that people weren't a crazy mixture of good and bad. The truth, as someone once said, was rarely pure—and never simple. She wondered at the cracks that could develop inside a human life, how deep they could run, and in the end, how devastating the consequences of those fault lines could be.

25

After tossing and turning for two solid hours, unable to stop obsessing about Kira and what might be happening in New Dresden, Guthrie threw off the covers, yanked on his robe, and went into the living room to dismantle the tree. Christmas had been a disaster. He didn't need anything around to remind him of it.

As he reached for the angel at the top of the tree, his cell phone rang. He rushed back to the bedroom and grabbed it off the nightstand. "Hello?"

"Hi, Guthrie."

"Kira. God, I'm so glad you called." He glanced at the alarm clock next to an empty bottle of Corona Extra. The blue numbers read 2:09 AM. "I'm sorry about Christmas Eve. I know I'm pushing too hard. But it's because I love you and I miss you."

"Guthrie?"

"Yes?"

"About those photos you said you have? You really think they're real?"

"I'm sorry, sweetheart, but I do. I had a private investigator look at them. They're not official police photos. Technically, what I have is proof that your mother was murdered, but no indication who did it."

"But you could see marks on her neck?"

"You have to use an enlarging loupe, but when you do, yes, you can clearly see them. It's not just a shadow or a trick of the light."

"But . . . my grandmother told me the chief of police was at our house that day. So was my great-uncle Brian, and my uncle Doug. They all saw her and said the death was accidental."

"They covered it up. All of them. There's no other explanation. Why would they do that unless they were protecting someone they loved?"

Kira was silent for almost a minute.

"Are you still there?" asked Guthrie.

"Yeah."

"Honey, I'm not trying to hurt you. I'd give anything to make this go away." He waited a few seconds then said, "What are you thinking?"

"If what you say is true, I'm angry. *Really* angry. And I'm confused."

"It's just, when you combine the photos, the note—"

"What note?"

He'd forgotten that he hadn't had time to tell her about it on Christmas Eve. "The photos were sent directly to me—the postmark was Henderson, Wisconsin."

"That's not far from here."

"I know. The packet included a note. It said, 'Proof Delia Adler was murdered. Stay out of it or the same thing will happen to you.'"

"Oh my God. Are you kidding me? Someone threatened you?"

"This is serious. It's why I'm frightened for you, why I want you to come back."

"I can't, Guthrie. Not yet."

"Then you've got to promise me you won't say anything to your family until we've had more time to talk, to figure out what to do."

"Why?"

"Just to be on the safe side."

"They'd never hurt me, if that's what you're suggesting."

He had to tread carefully. If it seemed as if he was criticizing them, she'd be forced to their defense. What she refused to see was that, when survival was at stake, when people felt pushed to the wall and saw no good way out, normal behavior went into the garbage with the rest of the trash. "No, of course not. I'm just saying that, since we don't know all the facts, it might be best to wait, not to talk about it until we do."

"And how would we find out those facts?"

"I'm working on it."

"Meaning what?"

"I've hired someone."

"Who?"

"A private investigator."

"Oh Lord. This just gets worse and worse. I need you to listen to me. Are you listening?"

"Yeah."

"Call that person off. Stop snooping into my family's business."

"Kira—"

"I get the impression that you think I'm some sort of passive victim. Have we met, Guthrie? Do you have any idea who I am? I'm *nobody's* victim."

"I'm just trying to help."

"You're not helping. Call off your dog. If you want to ruin our relationship, this is the way to do it."

He was stunned. He'd never considered that she'd have such a reaction.

"I don't want anyone looking into my family. Are we clear on that?"

"Okay. Yeah, we're clear."

"I've got to go."

"Not when you're so angry."

"I need time, Guthrie. To work this out. I've said that before but you never seem to get it. Don't call me again. When I want to talk to you, I'll call you. I'll be fine. There's no need to worry."

"Right," he said, knowing there was no point in arguing. If she didn't see that she was in danger after what he'd just told her, nothing was going to change her mind. "I love you."

"And I love you."

He held the phone in his hand until he saw that she'd ended the call. Falling backward onto the bed, he pounded the mattress and let loose with every swear word he'd ever heard.

It didn't help.

Jane left the Sportsman's that night and drove around town, looking for a spot where her phone could connect to a cell phone tower. She needed to check her voice mail messages and texts, and she also wanted to call Cordelia. Ten minutes into her search, holding her phone open in her hand and heading for the south side of town, she realized she should have asked Kevin what he did when he needed to use his cell. It would have saved her a lot of time. On the other hand, after being inside all day, she felt like breathing some fresh air. She pulled up next to a grain elevator, got out and leaned against the rear bumper of her SUV, and for a few minutes, gazed up at the night sky. This far away from the lights of a big city, the stars were the best show in town.

A while later, on the east end of town, two bars began to appear on the cell phone screen, though once again, as quickly as the phone connected, it lost the signal. She wasn't far from the Adlers' farmhouse, so she continued on toward the county highway. She would have missed the narrow dirt-and-gravel road Kevin had turned onto earlier in the day except for the glow of lights from the Adlers' barn. In contrast, the farmhouse, with the exception of a single lamp burning in what was probably an upstairs bedroom, was dark.

Not wanting to upset the quiet of the farmstead by pulling into the drive, Jane stopped by the side of the graveled road and let the CR-V idle as she checked her cell again. Amazingly, three bars held steady in the screen's top-left corner. A flood of texts, messages and e-mails began to download. Instead of reading them, she tapped in Cordelia's number.

Three rings later: "Where have you been?" demanded Cordelia's voice, all but hyperventilating. "I was worried sick."

"Why?"

"Because you left without me."

"You said you couldn't come."

"Exactly."

"You're saying you're the only thing that stands between me and total disaster?"

"Good. I'm glad you finally admit it."

Once again, Jane's eyes rose to the stars. "I'm fine. In fact, I got a part-time job bartending at Kevin Adler's tavern."

"Heavens. How loathsome. Why?"

"Where are you?"

"It was poker night at the castle. Merriman and I are just doing a little cleaning up."

"Am I interrupting?"

"If you will bear with me. I'm sashaying over to this over-stuffed couch and draping myself—decoratively—across it."

Jane could hear some grunting.

"There. Now, spill."

Jane briefed her on the high points. "I want to spend the next couple of days focusing on Delia, on what her life was like before she died. If I can shine a spotlight on that, I'll know far more about who might have done it."

"The husband did it."

"Maybe. Maybe not."

"Who else could have?"

"You and I both know things aren't always what they seem."

"Meaning what?"

"Meaning—I never expected to like Kevin."

"You're saying that murderers are never likable?"

"Seems like they shouldn't be."

"But you'll be back for my New Year's Eve bash on Monday night, right?"

"Yes, Cordelia. I'll be back."

"By the way, Guthrie is driving me nuts."

"Why's that?"

"He's like a bloodhound. Wherever I am, he finds me. And then he sits around, moping, until I throw him out. He's been as crazed by not hearing from you as I was."

"I've only been gone a little more than a day."

"Exactly. With no updates."

"Cell phone reception is lousy here."

"I know that. Why, oh why, did we give up on carrier pigeons?"

"It's no longer the Middle Ages."

"It is in my castle."

"Right. Look——" At the sound of a rap on the driver's window next to her, Jane jumped. A strong beam of light hit her square in the eyes.

"Janey? Are you there? What's going on?"

When the light swung away, Jane could see that Kevin was outside. She glanced up at the rearview mirror looking for his van, but saw nothing. It was as if he'd appeared out of nowhere. She rolled down the window.

"What are you doing here?" he said, an edge in his voice.

Jane held up her phone. "Give me one minute," she said. Returning to Cordelia, she said, "I've got to go."

"No you don't. Not until you tell me whose voice that was."

"Love to everyone," said Jane, keeping her tone cheerful as she smiled at Kevin. Cordelia continued to sputter in her ear. "Yes, no worries. I'm well. Employed. Even have a nice place to stay. Maybe I'll get down your way in the spring. Okay, then. Good to hear from you. Bye." She cut the line and quickly turned off the phone. Cordelia would be sure to call back within milliseconds. "Hey, Kevin. What's up?"

"What are you doing out here?"

The coldness in his voice startled her. "I've been driving around, looking for a place to find cell phone service. It's not easy in this town."

He watched her stonily, suspicion radiating off his stiff posture. Debating for a few seconds, he leaned closer and said, "You're right. A lot of dead spots. The best place to catch a signal is over by the courthouse. You been past there? Know where it is?"

"I'll find it."

"Best not to come out here. Cars and such, especially late at night, can spook my mom."

"Oh, sure," said Jane. "I didn't think about that."

"Okay, so . . . you just get on back to town," he said, slapping the hood and standing back.

"See you tomorrow," said Jane.

He didn't smile. " 'Night."

As she put the car in gear, she glanced over her shoulder. A light had come on in the farmhouse's first-floor living room. One of the drapes looked as if it had been pulled back. Had Evangeline seen the Honda's headlights and called her son to come check it out? Were they *that* afraid someone might be watching them?

This was the first time since coming to New Dresden that Jane had felt any sense of danger. It wasn't surprising, she supposed, that it had come from Kevin. If nothing else, it served as a good reminder that she needed to be careful.

26

I'd kill to have hair like yours," said Riley Garrow, standing behind the reception counter at the Cut & Curl on Friday morning. "What are you thinking? A new look for New Year's Eve? We could try bangs—or something shorter?"

"Just a trim," said Jane. "I've got some split ends."

"Not many," said the tall, slender brunette, leading Jane back to the first of three work stations. Another stylist, a tall, skinny man in a lime green silk shirt and black leather pants, worked in the next station, blow-drying a young woman's long curls.

The main reason Jane had come had nothing to do with her hair. She wanted a chance to talk with Riley, Delia's one-time friend. Sitting down in front of a mirrored wall, she surveyed the room, taking in the sleek, white, modern interior, the bright-red accents, the white leather couch and two matching chairs that greeted customers when they first arrived, a place to sit and read a magazine while they waited for a stylist There was a coffee bar, a manicure/pedicure station, and along the back wall, three white recliners in front of the washing station

As Riley tossed a red drape over Jane, she asked, "How do you usually wear your hair?"

"Mostly up," said Jane. "A simple chignon or a French braid."

"Ever tried a short cut?"

"Once. I liked it, but it was so much more work that I let it grow out."

"If you're game, I think you'd look fabulous with some blond highlights."

"For now, just a trim."

"I suppose your hair grows fast. It's so healthy. And you've got a lot of natural curl." She combed Jane's long chestnut hair, moving it this way and that.

"Heredity," said Jane. "My younger brother's hair is just like mine."

"Heredity can have a lot to do with it, but you also have to care for it. I see people in here all the time that don't spend any time at all maintaining one of their most important assets."

"Have you owned the salon long?"

"Twelve years," said Riley.

"Did you always like working with hair?"

"Yeah, I did, although I never thought about it as a career. After high school, I was headed nowhere. Working mostly minimum-wage jobs. I was never interested in college, but a friend eventually persuaded me to attend a professional beauty school. My husband and I found this property and hired a local guy to do the interior. I knew the look I wanted so I designed it."

"It's a great space."

"Best salon in the area."

"Are you from New Dresden?"

"I grew up near Egg Harbor. We moved here when I was eight.

What about you?" Riley opened a drawer and removed a metal comb and scissors.

"I've lived all over the country, never very good at settling in one place for very long. I was coming through town on my way to Duluth the other night when I stopped in at the Sportsman's. The place was really rocking. The bartender looked like he could use some help, so I pitched in. Turns out he was the owner. He offered me a job."

"Did you take it?"

"I did. I understand you know Kevin Adler."

"Who told you that?"

"His sister, Hannah. She said you and Kevin's wife, Delia, used to be great friends."

Riley moved around Jane, combing and examining. "That was a long time ago."

"Must have been hard for you when she died."

"It hurt."

"Yeah, Kevin, too. He's talked about her a little. He really seems like a great guy."

Shrugging, Riley said, "He's cute enough, I suppose, if you like the brooding, silent type."

"He seems talkative to me."

"I'd keep my distance."

"Why?"

"Just things Delia told me. The way he treated her."

"Like how?"

Riley began to divide Jane's hair, using clips to fasten back each section. "Oh, I don't know. Like . . . when he wasn't being a doormat, he could get mean."

"Physically?"

She shrugged.

"What about Delia? What was she like?"

Riley stopped and looked at Jane in the mirror. "How come you're so interested?"

"I don't know. I'm just curious."

"You're hot for Kevin, right?"

"No. Maybe."

Resuming her combing, she said, "I'll admit, Delia could be a real pain in the ass. She had a weird sense of humor, maybe she was even a little crazy, but a lot of fun. You knew if you stuck close, if you didn't let her buck you off, you'd be in for one hell of a ride. She was, oh, maybe six years older than me. We both liked to party, to chase guys."

"But she was married."

"She wasn't happy. She said all Kevin did was work. He was trying to make a go of his own construction company back then. I'd heard she was seeing a counselor. A priest, I think. She didn't tell me that, someone else did. She wasn't religious, so I never quite understood the choice."

"Did she get along with the family?"

"Yeah. More or less. Family stuff can be so complicated."

"For instance?"

"Well, she was sure Laurie—that's Doug's wife—had a thing for Kevin. Delia said Laurie would stare daggers at her whenever she and Kevin got into it—like Delia was never supposed to dis-agree with her saintly husband. And, for sure, Hannah never liked her. I think they were too much alike. Both had a wild streak."

"I met Hannah last night. Seemed nice enough."

"She was a real hellion when she was in high school. She's a lot older then me, but I remember the rumors." Riley stepped over to a drawer and began to look through it. "Apparently she was sleeping with—get this—the mayor. It happened during her senior year. He was an older guy, married, with a bunch of kids. Really sleazy. For someone with her past, she sure has a self-righteous streak. She's another one I'd keep my distance from."

"Not a fan of the Adlers."

"Not much. Except for Evangeline. She was always so kind to me—and to Delia and Kevin's kids. I mean, Delia loved her girls. That oldest one, though. Gracie. She was a handful."

"In what way?"

"The kid could be a terror." Riley began to trim. "She'd lie. Steal. She was seven years old, but she threw tantrums like a two-year-old. Delia would tell her to do something and Grace just ignored her. Absolute defiance."

"Sounds pretty tough," said Jane.

"Delia told me the kid never stopped crying when she was a baby. Drove her nuts. Gracie didn't like to be touched. Just strange all around. She was pretty—small, delicate, curly copper-colored hair, little turned up nose. I thought she was adorable, though I never wanted to spend any time with her. Delia asked me to babysit once. I made up some excuse. Five minutes with that kid and I wanted to strangle her. I know Delia kept working, even when Kevin said she didn't need to, just to get away from the house. She'd bring the kids over to Evangeline's place and dump them. Let Kevin pick them up and bring them home after work and put them to bed. It was an awful situation. Raising a kid like Grace must have put a terrible stress on their marriage."

"What about the other little girl? Kira?"

"Nice kid. Gracie tormented her. She'd steal her toys. Pick

fights. It was constant drama in that house. Seemed like Delia was always yelling at Gracie about something. Like . . . I mean, I remember this one time when Delia told Grace that she didn't want her riding her bike in the street. She explained that it was dangerous, said all the appropriate parental stuff. Next day, she came home to find Grace two blocks away . . . you guessed it: Riding her bike in the street. Like I said, total defiance. Only thing that seemed to settle Gracie down was TV. She'd sit in front of the thing like a zombie. Not that I blame Delia for the amount of time she let that kid watch it. Thing is, I always felt like the younger one got lost in the shuffle. Gracie was such a holy terror that nobody paid much attention to Kira."

This was all news to Jane. She had no idea if it was connected in any way to Delia's murder, but this was exactly the kind of information she'd been hoping to find about Delia's life in the days before her death. "And then Delia died."

Riley shook her head. "I mean, think about it. How do you fall off a deck? She was alone. Explain to me how that happens."

"You think it was suicide?"

"No way. Delia wasn't depressed. And one other thing: It never made any sense to me that she was out there when it was so cold out. Of course, Kevin said she'd been drinking, so I suppose that could explain it."

"Did she often drink in the morning?"

"Not that I ever knew. The day she died was her day off. She told me she was planning to do some last-minute Christmas shopping. She loved Christmas. She was all excited about it. Kevin always got Kira up and took her to kindergarten. Gracie didn't have to be to school until later, so she'd take the bus. The only free time Delia would've had that day was from nine until three.

So why start drinking? Sure, Delia liked a few cocktails, but not like that. She drank to add fuel to a good time. She didn't drink just to drink."

"Are you saying you don't believe her death was an accident?"

Moving around to the front of Jane, Riley said, "I wasn't there, so how could I know? It's just——" She stopped working and looked away. "The one thing Delia was terrified of more than anything else was fire. She was in a house fire when she was a kid and it left some major emotional scars. She would never——and I mean never——have wanted to be cremated. And yet that's what Kevin said she'd asked for. Nope, I don't believe that, not for a minute. The family didn't even give her a funeral. It was all private. I mean, the woman had friends. People who cared about her. What a crock." She returned to Jane's hair. "I shouldn't get so hot and bothered about something that happened so long ago."

"But you cared about her."

"Yeah. She had her flaws, but who doesn't? Look, don't tell Kevin we had this conversation, okay?"

"Sure. It's none of my business."

"I don't think he'd be happy to hear people were talking about his personal life."

"Are you saying you're afraid of him?"

"Of course not. Just, you know . . . best to let sleeping dogs lie."

27

That afternoon, the tavern's customers seemed to be sliding toward the spirit of New Year's Eve, even though it was a few days off. After the lunch crowd had cleared out, people kept coming in—some in pairs, sometimes as a group ready to mix and mingle. They didn't just order one beer either; they would, over the course of an hour, order two or three. The laughter skidded from merriment toward raucous and back again.

An older man kept feeding the jukebox in the corner of the room, and because of his age, all the tunes that came through the speakers were oldies, the songs Jane thought of as Vietnam War-era music. Kevin obviously knew his customers and had selected a mix of recent pop, a few country classics, all mixed together with a heavy dose of pop/rock nostalgia. *Angel of the Morning* had been the first selection, replaced by *Honky Tonk Women*, then *Love Her Madly*.

As Creedence Clearwater Revival's *The Midnight Special* began to play, Jane noticed another woman she recognized from Guthrie's photographs come through the door. Laurie Adler, Doug's wife, looked older than she had in the snapshot. Her once-dark brown hair was shot through with gray. Rimless glasses couldn't hide the wrinkles at the corners of her eyes, and yet she was still an attractive woman, one who stood erect and carried herself with the ease of an athlete.

Stepping up to the bar, Laurie asked, "Kevin around?"

"Sorry," said Jane.

"Do you have any idea when he'll be back?"

"He's closing up, so I'd think by midnight."

Laurie nodded as she scanned the room.

"Can I get you something to drink? A beer? A soda? Something to eat?"

"You're Kevin's new hire."

"Jane. And you are?" She didn't want to advertise her prior knowledge.

"Laurie Adler. His sister-in-law."

"Oh, yeah. The one who worked here before me."

"He tell you about that?"

"Just that you quit. So what do you say? Can I pull you a beer?"

Laurie had the kind of eyes that seemed to be asking something—a question she could never quite bring herself to say out loud. She dug out her wallet and looked inside. "It sure smells good in here."

"It's my new lunch special. Grilled cheese and ham. Since he's got a flat top out here, I thought I'd put it to use."

"I should probably pass."

She was either really frugal, didn't have much cash on her, or she was broke. Jane bet on the latter.

"You like to cook?" asked Laurie.

"Guilty," said Jane, stepping over to the grill and tossing one of the already-prepped sandwiches on top. As it fried, she pulled Laurie a beer. "Put your money away. It's on the house."

"I'm not sure Kevin would like that."

Jane gave her a conspiratorial wink. "Kevin's not here. I'm not going to tell him. You gonna tell him?"

Laurie smiled. "Thanks."

Making sure the cheese was perfectly melted and the bread was browned and crisp, Jane grabbed a paper plate and dished it up.

Biting into the grilled cheese, Laurie closed her eyes. "This is wonderful. I didn't have much for breakfast."

"A little garlic salt does wonders."

"What's in the pot on the grill?"

"I found a few number-ten cans of tomato soup in the back pantry."

"Oh, yeah, someone brought those over last summer. They came from a restaurant that was going out of business. Kevin wasn't sure what to do with them, so he just shelved them."

"I've used the product before. It doesn't taste very good, but if you sauté up some onions, celery, and carrots, toss in a few herbs, and then add some whipping cream to the mix, you get a pretty decent result. And soup, even with those few additions, is almost pure profit. I think there's enough left for a small bowl. Want to try it?"

"Sure," said Laurie.

Jane tipped the kettle and ladled out the dregs. Setting the bowl in front of Laurie, she said, "I'm not trying to turn the tavern into a restaurant, but I thought a couple of lunch choices might spice things up a little."

"This soup is great," said Laurie. "Kevin got lucky when he

found you." She wiped her mouth on a napkin. "I suppose you're curious why I quit."

"Nope. That's your business."

"It was personal stuff. I sure do miss the money though. Come the new year, I'll have to look for something else."

"Kevin said you used to be a teacher."

"English. I taught at the middle school until it closed. It was in bad shape, would have cost the town a ton of money to repair it. It was easier to close it down and bus the kids to another middle school. Honestly, that was my dream job. I loved working with kids."

"You have kids of your own?"

Fingering her wedding ring, Laurie said, "No. I wanted them. Just wasn't in the cards."

"I'm sorry."

"Yeah. Thanks."

"What kind of job will you go looking for?" asked Jane.

"Not much to choose from. Trying to make a decent living from the available jobs in the area is an exercise in futility."

"Did you ever think about moving?" asked Jane. "I'm sure you could find another teaching position."

"Doug—that's my husband—his family lives here. Neither of us wants to leave them." Finishing the soup, she added, more than a little bitterly, "So we live in a trailer and try to make ends meet. Another losing battle."

Jane was puzzled by the response.

"I know what you're thinking." She drained a good third of her beer. "You think his family should have encouraged us to leave, to make a better life for ourselves somewhere else."

"The thought did occur."

"Never going to happen."

"Why?"

"I mean, I get it. I do. Everyone has sacrificed to stay together. How can you not love people who are so, basically . . . decent?"

Decent was hardly the first word that leapt to Jane's mind.

"It's one of the reasons Kevin is gone from the bar so much when he can find a backup bartender. I don't know this for a fact, but I'll bet that right now he's out working a construction job somewhere. He can make more as a builder than he can on weekday afternoons standing where you are. He needs both the construction work and the bar to survive, so he burns the candle at both ends. He's tired all the time. It's not fair. Not for any of us." Realizing she might have said too much, she cracked a smile. "I don't really mean that. I had a fight with my husband this morning. Nothing new in that, but it kind of set a negative tone for the day."

"Sure," said Jane. Before she could probe the subject a bit more, the front door flew open. "Oh, no," she groaned. "No, no, no."

"What?" asked Laurie, turning around to see what had caused the reaction.

There, framed in the doorway, stood Cordelia. Her heavy, six-foot frame was covered by a black shirt and fringed leather vest, a red bandana at her neck, cowboy boots that added another two inches to her height, and a black ten-gallon hat that added maybe four more. The finishing touch? Leather chaps. Her thumbs were curled around a wide leather belt and her stance fairly shrieked gunslinger—minus, of course, the guns. As she assessed the interior, her eyes narrowed and glinted.

Jane watched every eye in the place turn and stare. She might have pointed out that one of this odd woman's core beliefs was that clothing and costume were essentially the same thing. Thus, the concept of "normal attire" didn't apply. But because that fact was already obvious, and Jane had no desire to call any more attention to Cordelia than Cordelia had already done herself, she let it slide.

"Who on earth is that?" asked Laurie.

"Sheriff Matt Dillon looking for Miss Kitty, I expect," said Jane.

"Excuse me?"

Cordelia sidled on up to the bar. "Afternoon, ladies," she said, touching the brim of her hat. Her gaze locked on Jane. "I suppose you're wondering what brung me to these-here parts."

"I'm wondering," said Jane, "if you've lost your mind."

"Ah don't darken the doors of many saloons these days, darlin'. Thought it only proper to dress the part."

"Can you lose the Texas drawl?"

"You're no fun at all, Miss Jane. No damn fun *at all.*"

"Would you excuse us for a few seconds?" Jane said to Laurie.

"Sure," she said, looking up at Cordelia with nothing short of awe.

Motioning for Cordelia to follow her, Jane headed back to the small kitchen behind the bar.

"Now, before you go getting all pissy," said Cordelia, fingering a container of green olives on the counter, "let me speak my piece."

"Yes, please do that."

"You need ma help."

"You said you couldn't get away from the theater."

"I cancelled a few meetings, had a few moved until after the new year. I am here," she said, lightly slapping Jane's cheeks, "until the stagecoach leaves midday tomorrow. So, give me an assignment. I'm all yours."

Jane needed to sit. Sometimes Cordelia had that effect on her. Pulling up a chair, she drew a finger through the fringe on her friend's vest. "Where did you find this . . . this getup?"

"Actually, I had everything in my closet—except for the bandana, which I found at Target on the way out of town. You like?" She twirled slowly so that Jane could see her from every angle.

"Investigators usually try for anonymity, Cordelia. They don't like to call attention to themselves."

"Not part of my personal idiom."

"You prefer the flashing-neon-sign form of research."

"You're durn tootin' I do."

"Cordelia?"

"Yes, ma'am?"

"Can you talk normally?"

"You are one boring filly, you know that?"

"*Cordelia?*"

"Oh, all right." She removed her hat, which allowed her long, curly auburn tresses to fall to her shoulders. Shaking them out, she said, "You never called me back last night. You can't do that, just leave me hanging."

"As I told you, it's hard to get a cell phone connection around here. Tell me, you do have other clothes with you, right?"

"My parka's in the car."

The mention of a parka gave Jane an idea. "As I think about it, I do have something you could help me with." Hearing a knock on the door, she turned to find Laurie poking her head inside.

"You've got some customers out here who need help."

"Would you mind taking over for me? I won't be long."

"Sure thing," said Laurie. "Happy to. Only thing is, I need to get over to the family farmhouse by five—"

"This will only take a couple of minutes."

"Great. No problem then."

Once she'd gone, Jane returned to Cordelia. "Here's the deal: Take the rest of the afternoon and go find yourself some dark-colored cold-weather gear. Fleece jacket. Thermal underwear. Maybe some Polartec bib overalls. Thinsulate gloves. A balaclava—or ski mask. Hand warmers. Anything and everything you think you'll need so you can stay out in the cold for several hours."

"Heavens, Jane. Why would I do that?"

"I need eyes on the Adler farmhouse tonight. I can't be there myself because I'm working here. I may be wrong, but I get the sense that something's going on out there—something the family doesn't want anyone to know about."

"Such as?"

"That's your assignment. You'll need to park your . . . um, horse . . . a distance from the house and then find a place, as close to the farmhouse as possible, where you can hide and watch who comes and goes. I've got binoculars and a digital thirty-five-millimeter camera out in my car. And night-vision goggles. You'll need all of that. Buy yourself a gym bag to carry it in." Looking around, she grabbed a napkin and a pen and began drawing Cordelia a map.

"What time should I get there?"

"By nine. Stay at least through midnight. Don't approach anyone. Just stay out of sight and observe."

"Got it."

"Do you? It's imperative that you don't get caught. On that one-in-a-million chance that you do, you better have a good cover story. I trust you can come up with that yourself. But whatever you say, don't mention me. Where are you spending the night?"

"The Timber Lodge, same place we stayed before."

"Good. We won't be able use our cell phones to communicate with each other." A fact that made Jane more than a little nervous. "When I'm done with work, which should be between twelve and one, I'll meet you at the motel and we can debrief."

"Bring a blowtorch."

"Why?"

"Because you'll need to melt the ice block around me before I'll be able to speak."

"I'll bring a bottle of bourbon."

"That's your preferred form of heat. Mine is a gallon of hot chocolate and a spray can of whipped cream."

"Be careful."

"Not to worry, dearheart. The game's afoot and Cordelia M. Thorn and her amazing gray cells are *on the case*."

28

That night, Cordelia quickly concluded that there was a major flaw in Jane's advice to buy dark clothing for the evening's surveillance. While dark clothing might work in most nighttime environments, when surrounded by a landscape of snow, that choice became the equivalent of Jane's charming little quip about neon-sign research.

Standing by her car, which she'd parked off the highway next to a stand of pine a good hundred yards from the farmhouse, Cordelia began to wonder if she—or Jane—had ever actually surveilled in the snow before. She couldn't come up with one instance in which they had. As long as she stayed in the center of the county highway—which, lucky for her, appeared to be as devoid of traffic as the planet Mars—she would probably be fairly inconspicuous.

Before creeping away from her car, Cordelia tried on the night-vision goggles. In an instant, the world around her turned vivid, although monochromatically green. As she began to walk down the center of the highway, she realized that the thermal underwear she'd bought at a Ben Franklin store in Willow River tugged in all the wrong places. The wool socks itched. The gloves, the only really warm ones she could find, were too large. The boots might afford her reasonable purchase in the snow, but because they were stiff and uncomfortably heavy, they slid much too easily on patches of ice.

"I'm getting too old for this crap," she grumbled. That saying about age being nothing more than a state of mind must have been conceived in the brain of an ignorant twenty-year-old with empathy issues.

Trudging along, carrying the sack containing the camera, the binoculars, a package of Oreos and two cans of black-cherry soda, Cordelia kept her eyes peeled for movement of any kind, something that would alert her that her presence had been detected. If the Adlers had something to hide, they might have posted a sentry. She had to be careful.

Approaching the farmhouse, she ducked behind one of the many trees on the property and counted three cars in the drive directly outside an old two-stall garage. Across an expanse of yard was a large barn with a high gambrel roof. It looked newer than the other two buildings. Lights were on in what appeared to be a living quarters on the second floor. Cordelia figured that if she could creep over to it, she could crouch down and hide next to the side that faced away from the house. She wanted to get as close to the action as possible without being observed. What she really wanted was total invisibility. That way, she could go inside, take off the wretched clothing that might be keeping her from freezing to death but had failed miserably to keep her warm, find a cozy, overstuffed chair, break open the cookies and the soda, and listen in comfort to the conversation.

Mumbling that imagination was a curse, she scuttled as fast as her legs, clad in tight, knit thermal underwear, would carry her across the open ground, flinging herself at last against the dark, stained-wood barn wall. As she stood there, catching her breath, she thought to herself, "In these clothes, I am a true vision of loveliness." With all the layers, she figured she looked like she weighed four hundred pounds. "Polar explorer," she muttered. "Sign. Me. Up."

Adrenaline flooded every synapse as she hunkered down. She'd made it. Of course she had. She was Cordelia M. Thorn. Thankful now that the man behind the counter at the Ben Franklin had urged her to buy a watch with a lighted dial, she pressed the side button to check the time. Ten after nine. Perfect. She settled in to wait for something significant to happen. Five minutes. Fifteen. At the twenty-minute mark, she opened the package of cookies, congratulating herself on her restraint. She allowed herself five, but upped it to eight when she thought about how cold it was. An hour later, with fifteen cookies missing in action and her fingers mere inches from another, the back door opened. Using the binoculars to enlarge the faces of two people who came out, she first zeroed in on the taller of the two. She went through a mental list of the photos Guthrie had supplied.

"Kevin," she whispered. "Check." The shorter, stockier, bald guy was Doug Adler, Kevin's older brother.

They walked quickly away from the house. Kevin glanced over his shoulder, back at the door, but Doug charged ahead, heedless of whoever might be watching. Cordelia was more than a little alarmed when they stopped mere feet from where she was hiding. Her body went rigid as she eased her fingers out of the cookie package, trying not to rattle the cellophane.

"Who was on the phone?" demanded Kevin.

"Katie Olsen."

"Crap, man. Your breath. You smell like a still."

"You smell like you stepped in dog shit. Makes us even."

"So what did Katie want?"

"It's Walt. He apparently had a stroke a few days ago."

"You're kidding," said Kevin. "Why didn't she call us before this?"

"She said the docs thought there was a good chance he'd recover. She didn't want to worry us for no reason. But he took a turn for the worse tonight."

"Jeez. With everything else happening right now, this is going to hit Mom hard."

"But we have to tell her," said Doug. "I mean, don't we?"

"I suppose we could ask Father Mike to do it."

"Not tonight. In the morning."

"What if Walt doesn't make it that long?"

"I refuse to drop this on her tonight. We wait, Kevin. If he dies, he dies."

"I need to see him. Right now. I'm not waiting."

"Katie said he's at the community hospital over in Henderson."

"Is she there right now?"

"No idea. Look, I'll ask Mike to come by after Mass in the morning. I can take Mom over to the hospital, if that's what she wants."

As they walked back to the house, Kevin put his arm around Doug's shoulder. A few minutes after they'd reentered the house, Kevin came back out, got in his van, and took off.

A heartwarming little piece of theater, thought Cordelia. Feeling that her little gray cells needed more sustenance, she reached for another cookie. She pulled a wooden crate over to sit on. It was going to be a long night.

As lights began to go off in the farmhouse, Doug appeared again, this time walking a dark-haired young woman out to the barn. He was smoking a pipe, acting very avuncular. Cordelia had never met Kira, but could see why Guthrie was attracted to her. As more lights went on inside the second floor of the barn, Cordelia began to wonder if Kira was sleeping out there. She'd been on her own for many years. Perhaps living in such close quarters with her grandmother wasn't giving her enough freedom, enough space. Doug returned to the house a while later. Two cars remained in the driveway. Cordelia deduced that one was probably Kira's, and the other Doug's. She was crack hand at deduction.

Bored, cold, and sick of Oreos, Cordelia whiled away the next hour and a half by making a mental list of her favorite plays, dividing them into comedies and dramas. When that was accomplished, she began a list of her favorite foods. But that made her hungry, so she was forced to stop, switching to favorite movies instead. She was determined to leave at midnight, even though she would have little to report to Jane. She wasn't sure what Jane had hoped she'd unearth. Zombies? Werewolves? Vampires looking for a light snack?

As fog began to settle over the farmland, Cordelia took off her night-vision goggles and rubbed her eyes. Okay, so she wasn't, strictly speaking, doing aggressive surveillance, but nothing was happening, unless you counted the owl that kept hooting and giving her the creeps.

She was packing up her cookies a short while later when she

heard a door creak open. The sound was so loud it seemed to be right next to her. Hearing the crunch of boots on snow, she picked up the binoculars and trained them on the back of the farmhouse, but saw nothing. Before she could aim them at the front door, a beam of light burst across the snow, then a figure wearing a dark jacket and carrying a flashlight lantern walked right past her. If he'd wanted to, he could have reached out and touched her.

Cordelia flattened herself against the barn wall as he headed straight across the property out to the gravel road. She waited until the man—she was pretty sure it was a man—reached the edge of the highway, far enough away so that he couldn't hear the crunch of her boots, then grabbed her sack and crept silently after him. She wasn't sure why she was following him, it just seemed like the thing to do.

The man wasn't dressed as warmly as she was. As he walked along, with Cordelia following at an appropriately safe distance, he pulled his scarf up over his nose and mouth. The lantern he carried, so bright when he'd come past her by the barn, seemed to be all but swallowed up by the darkness.

Another couple of city blocks—which was the best way she could think of to measure distance—and they would hit the outskirts of New Dresden. Then what? What was the plan? She supposed she wanted to catch a glimpse of the man's face, though she had no desire to walk for miles on such a forbidding night.

And then it happened. The figure stopped. Just stopped and stood there and didn't move.

Cordelia froze.

Turning around, a man's voice called, "Is someone there?" He lifted the flashlight lantern and squinted into the darkness. "Hello?" he called, moving the lantern around until the light fell on Cordelia. "Who are you? Why are you following me?"

She swallowed hard. Time for Plan B.

29

Before Cordelia was willing to talk to Jane about her evening of surveillance, she closed the door to the motel's bathroom and turned on the shower. Emerging half an hour later, her hair wrapped in a towel, her skin now flushed a deep pink, she searched out every blanket in the room. After piling them on one of the double beds, she donned her parka and crawled under the covers.

Jane had commandeered the other double bed, biding her time by watching an old movie on TV. "Feel better?" she asked.

"I am now able to communicate. Where's my hot chocolate?"

"This is the best I could do," said Jane, pulling a quart of chocolate milk out of a sack. "The last room had a microwave. This one doesn't."

"Did you bring brandy?"

"Bourbon."

"Think I'd rather have a few fingers of that. It must be ten below out there."

"It's twenty. Above."

"Wow. Balmy. Let's go find ourselves a hammock."

Jane walked over to the table where she'd set the bottle of Maker's Mark. After breaking the red wax seal, she poured the liquid into one of the clear plastic cups provided by the motel. She grabbed the quart of chocolate milk for herself, handed the bourbon to Cordelia, then returned to the bed.

"You're actually going to drink that?" asked Cordelia. "Jane Lawless? The original food snob?"

"I'm not a food snob. I merely believe in eating well. I didn't have much for dinner. Don't want to drink bourbon on an empty stomach."

"Want a few Oreos to go with the milk?"

"Thanks, but no thanks."

"Too bad I left my bucket of kale at home. Kale and chocolate milk. Yummy."

"Let's cut to the chase. Tell me what was going on at the farmhouse."

"Nothing much. Just two things of note. I'll start with the last one first. As I was packing to leave, this man came out a door in the barn right near where I was hiding. He set off across the yard and headed toward town. Well, of course, me, being the awesome sleuth that I am, I scrambled after him. I wanted to get a look at his face because I knew you'd ask me who he was. He had a flashlight—one of those big lantern types."

"That was dangerous, Cordelia. What if he'd caught you?"

"Actually, he did."

Jane lowered the quart of milk from her lips. "What?"

"He must have heard me creeping along behind him. I mean,

I thought I was being exceedingly stealthy." She took a sip of the bourbon. "Close your mouth, Janey. I handled it."

"How?"

"Well," she said, shifting to her hip, "I could tell by what he said that he couldn't see me very well. It was so insanely dark out there. No moon. No starlight. I figured all he could see was a big dark mound. Me."

"And?"

"An idea occurred: What other big dark mounds are out running around at that time of night?"

"Are you asking me a question?"

"A bear, Janey. So I raised my arms—you know, like a bear would do—" She gave a demonstration, clawing at the air with her fingers. "—and made this threatening low growl."

Jane closed her eyes. "Oh God."

"Yeah. Didn't work. Not many bears out in the wild wearing night-vision goggles. He called, 'Hey, friend, didn't hear what you said.' I think he was a little scared. I dropped the bear act and moved a little closer. My face was so well covered that I figured he'd never recognize me again, so I felt free to improvise."

Jane took several sustaining gulps of the milk.

"I told him I was in training. That I was planning to join a National Geographic expedition cruise to the antarctic. Wanted to get in a little practice in a similar habitat before I left. I explained that I was into polar surfboarding. Antarctic wines and cheeses. It's a perfectly plausible story, so wipe that look off your face."

"Did he ask your name?"

"Called myself Stella Nelson."

"And who was he?"

"Michael Franchetti. You know, *Father Mike?*" She bugged out her eyes. "The guy Guthrie told us about. The Catholic priest? I thought, hell, he asked me what I was doing out there in the middle of the night, so I asked him what he was doing."

"And he said?"

"Visiting Evangeline Adler. I already assumed as much. He said his church wasn't far."

"I wonder what he was doing in the barn," said Jane.

"That's what I'd like to know. But since I couldn't figure a way to ask the question without giving away the fact that I'd been trespassing on the Adler's property, I told him I needed to get back to exploring."

"So, what else did you learn?"

"Actually, there was a conversation I overheard between Doug and Kevin. Seems some old guy named Walt, a close friend of Evangeline's, had a stroke a few days ago. He's not doing too well."

"Walt?" repeated Jane. "Walt Olsen?"

"Does he have a daughter named Katie Olsen?"

Jane moved to the edge of the bed. "He was the police chief in New Dresden when Delia died. You remember? I told you all about him."

"Oh, yeah. Sure. You went to interview him while I was back here trying to convince my new marketing director not to jump off the roof."

"You say the stroke was recent?"

"That's what Doug said."

Jane had gone to visit Walt Olsen last Sunday afternoon. It must have happened sometime after she left. Were the two events related? How could they not be? At the time, she remembered thinking that she'd been too aggressive. Too rough. "Unreal," she said under her breath.

"Apparently Katie called the farmhouse tonight to tell them about her dad. The doctors thought he'd recover, but he's taken a turn for the worse."

Rising from the bed, Jane walked straight to the table and grabbed the bottle of Maker's Mark. She didn't bother with a glass.

"Hey, girlfriend, slow down," said Cordelia.

Jane began to pace. "I'm the one who caused his stroke."

"And you think *I'm* the queen of melodrama?"

"It's the truth. Simple cause and effect. I was too hard on him. He was a sick old man and I came on way too strong."

Cordelia sat up in bed. "If he lied about what he saw all those years ago, if it weighed on his conscience, that's not on you, it's on him."

Jane shook her head. Taking another swallow from the bottle, she said, "No."

"Yes."

She kept shaking her head, trying to force the sense of guilt away. Walter Olsen had made a mistake. He'd put personal ties ahead of justice. Jane had done that herself. One time in particular stood out: Jane had protected her brother at the expense of her own sense of right and wrong. She'd lied, covered up what he'd done. She knew intimately what that sort of decision had cost her. What right did she have to sweep in like some avenging angel and demand that Walt Olsen atone for his sins by telling her the truth?

"I think you better sleep here tonight," said Cordelia.

"Can't. You own all the pillows and blankets." Dropping down on the bed, she fell onto her back. "What hospital is he at?"

"The one in Henderson. That's all I know."

Jane had to go see him. First thing in the morning. She had to make amends. In fact, this whole business with the Adler family— it was beginning to feel wrong. Jane the Righteous, Jane the Good, was attempting to destroy Kevin and the rest of his nearest and dearest by linking them to a murder. As hard as she tried, she couldn't wrap her mind around the fact that some ambitious Wisconsin prosecutor would say that yes, prison was the price they all had to pay.

"It's nearly two in the morning," said Cordelia. "I don't know about you, but a hard night of espionage has truly tired me out. I think we should turn in."

Jane felt a pillow hit her stomach. A second later, a blanket descended. "Thanks."

"Think nothing of it."

Turning on her side, Jane pulled her knees up to her chest. As she closed her eyes, she heard the TV snap off, then the lamp. She supposed she could lay there and be still. But good, deep, restful sleep, the kind that would allow her to feel refreshed come morning? That had been in short supply lately. She doubted tonight would be any different.

30

Sunday morning dawned gray and raw, with bitter, twenty-five-mile-an-hour wind gusts blowing in an unwelcome change in the weather. Shortly after eleven-thirty, with a sleepy Cordelia dragging her luggage behind her, Jane led the way out to the parking lot. She'd been up for hours, had made herself coffee in the room and watched CNN while she listened to Cordelia snore.

Before Cordelia set out on the road back to Minneapolis, she wanted a full breakfast with "all the trimmings," as she put it, so they stopped at a cafe along the highway. As Jane picked at her omelet and Cordelia devoured her steak and eggs, they discussed the food for tomorrow night's New Year's Eve bash at the castle. Having slept only fitfully, Jane tuned in and out of the conversation, unable to fully concentrate. Thankfully, mercifully, Cordelia was so excited by the topic that she didn't seem to notice.

Returning to their cars, Cordelia gave Jane one of her bone-crushing hugs, meant to suggest affection, not the desire to send the recipient to the hospital. "Promise me again that you'll make it home in time for the party tomorrow night."

"Scout's honor," said Jane, raising a hand. "You drive safely."

"Always, dearheart. I'll crank up the tunes and boogie."

As soon as Cordelia had driven off, Jane jumped into her Honda and headed for the hospital in Henderson. She felt wired because of way too much caffeine, but also, strangely, like she was running on a weird sort of autopilot. After parking in a lot next to the hospital's main entrance, she stopped by the reception desk, where a woman was gazing with unblinking, zombielike eyes at a computer screen. The autopilot thing seemed to going around.

"Could you tell me what room Walt Olsen is in?" Jane asked.

"Are you a family member?" the woman replied without looking up.

"Yes."

She checked a clipboard. "He's in ICU. Room 211."

"How's he doing?"

"I don't have that information. You'll need to speak with his doctor. Also, talk to the charge nurse before you go in. He may not be allowed visitors." She explained where to find the ICU and the ICU waiting room, then offered a practiced spiel about the location of the cafeteria and the gift shop.

Jane took the elevator up to the second floor. Halfway down the hall, she came to closed double doors. The rooms beyond were glass fronted, dimly lit, and much larger. Finding the nurses station empty, she continued on, noting the room numbers.

Just before she reached 211, a thought struck her and stopped her cold. Why hadn't this occurred to her before? Would appearing at Walt Olsen's bedside, out of the blue, just as she had at the nursing home, have a negative impact on the old man's health? Hurting him was the last thing she wanted. Maybe, she thought, silently castigating herself for such a serious lapse in judgement, she ought to spend a moment examining her motives.

As Jane stood there, hands sunk in the pockets of her jacket, she was appalled at what she'd been about to do. This was all about her guilt, not Walt Olsen's welfare. Moving a little closer to the room, she saw that Kevin and a priest were inside. Kevin was holding Walt's hand, bending over the bed and talking to him. Jane watched for a few seconds, then turned and headed back the way she'd come.

Before she reached the nursing station, the ICU doors opened and Evangeline Adler and her son, Doug, came through. Jane quickly ducked into an empty room and crouched low. She held her breath and prayed they hadn't seen her. As they passed by, Doug had his arm around his mother's shoulders. Evangeline was crying, dabbing a tissue to her eyes. Once they were out of sight, Jane waited a full minute and then straightened up and peeked into the hall to make sure they'd entered Walt's room. Walking as fast as she dared toward the doors, she raced down the hallway outside the ICU to the elevators. The last thing she wanted was to run into someone who might recognize her.

When the elevator doors opened on the first floor, she came face to face with Todd Carmody, the brother of Steven Carmody, the funeral director she and Cordelia had talked with last weekend about Delia's cremation. Steven would surely have recognized her, but because she'd only met Todd briefly, she hoped that the baseball cap and glasses she'd been wearing at the time had disguised her appearance well enough that her face wouldn't ring any bells for him now. Still, when he looked at her just a moment too long, Jane ducked her head and threaded her way through a group waiting by the reception desk.

Damn, she thought, bursting out the front door. She rushed out to her car and climbed in, slamming her fist against the steering wheel. This decision to visit Walt Olsen's bedside had been wrongheaded for so many reasons. Sitting in the bitter cold with her breath swirling around her, Jane wondered if there wasn't some way she could salvage something positive out of an otherwise miserable day. She had a little more than twenty-four hours left in New Dresden. She'd been hoping for an opportunity to talk to Kira alone. At this very moment, most of the Adler family was inside that hospital. There might never be a better chance.

Jane backed her car out of the lot and burned rubber back to New Dresden.

After taking the porch steps two at a time, Jane stamped her feet to keep them warm as she waited for someone to answer the bell. She wished now that she'd thought to wear her much warmer sheepskin jacket last night when she'd set off for the motel. It was going on two in the afternoon, but the temperature wasn't much higher than it had been earlier. Thankfully, the bar didn't open on Sundays until four, so she had a little extra time before she had to get back to do her prep work.

For the last few days, Jane had been leaving text messages for Guthrie whenever she found that she had cell phone service. She wanted to keep him abreast of what she'd been learning. He'd sent back the occasional encouraging comment along with his always effusive thanks. He hadn't said anything about Kira, and yet, because she had more or less receded from view into the farmhouse, and this disappearing act had been a big part of why Guthrie had wanted Jane to go to New Dresden in the first place, making this visit to the farm seemed not only important, but imperative.

Jane rang the bell a second time. And then a third. When it seemed likely that nobody was going to answer, she trotted down the porch steps and walked out into the snowy yard to look around. There were lots of footprints going back and forth to the barn and the garage. Catching movement out of the corner of her eye, Jane looked up at a window on the barn's top floor just as a shade was pulled.

"Kira?" Jane called.

Inside the barn, dogs began to bark.

"Kira, please. It's important. I need to talk to you." It seemed apparent that she'd been seen. Hearing her cell phone trill, she fished it out of her pocket. She was so unused to hearing it ring that it startled her. But, of course, the farmhouse was one of the few places in town where she could get a good signal. Walking away from the barking dogs, Jane said hello.

"Is this Jane Lawless?" came a man's voice.

"Yes."

"It's Steven Carmody. Remember me?"

"Of course I do," said Jane, pressing a hand to her free ear.

"Listen, I thought I should call and tell you something. It's kind of strange. I'm not sure what to do."

Jane wondered if it had anything to do with running into Steven's brother at the hospital. Looking up at the gunmetal sky, she held her breath.

"When you were here, we were talking about Delia Adler's cremains."

"Right."

"The thing is, I was in the basement of our funeral home last night. We have this closet, where we keep the boxes of cremains of people that . . . well . . . that were left here. Nobody ever came to pick them up. I know that sounds cold, but it does happen. There aren't that many. In the last fifty years, maybe a few dozen." He paused. "So it really surprised me when I went in there to look around and I found Delia Adler's ashes."

"You did?" said Jane. Returning her gaze to the top floor of the barn, she was startled to see a ghostly visage standing at one of the windows. The face was there and it wasn't. Watery. Indistinct. Before she could register any of the features, it disappeared.

"Honestly, I was shocked," continued Steven. "I can't imagine why the family just left them with us. That can't be what they wanted. I'm wondering if I should call Kevin . . . or Evangeline."

"I think I'd leave it alone," said Jane.

"Yeah, maybe you're right."

"Have you mentioned it to your brother?"

"Sure, I told him."

"What did he think?"

"He didn't say much."

Jane wondered about Todd's nonreaction. Perhaps he knew something his brother didn't.

"Maybe it was an oversight—although I'm not sure how forgetting a loved one's ashes could be put in that category."

"I agree with you about it being strange," said Jane.

"Yeah. Makes me wonder . . . I mean, did they knowingly leave the cremains with us?"

"Hard to say what's in people's minds and hearts. But I do thank you for the information."

"No problem. Hey, if you ever see Cordelia—"

"I see her all the time. Don't worry. Her word is good. She'll send you those comps for her first production."

"It was really great meeting her—and, um, you," he added as an afterthought.

Jane smiled, thanked him again, and then, as she tucked her phone back into her jacket pocket, she walked closer to the barn, continuing to gaze up at the windows. Kira had been watching her. Surely she must have heard Jane shout her name, but for her own reasons, she didn't want to engage in a conversation with her father's backup bartender. Kira was an Adler. Guthrie would have to come to terms with that. Whatever secrets the family had hidden from the world all these years had now, for good or ill, become Kira's legacy as well.

31

Coming through the back door into the tavern's small kitchen, Jane found Kevin standing at the work table with various bar condiments—lemons, limes, oranges—spread out in front of him. Jane assumed that she would be the one doing today's prep. She was a little surprised that he'd shown up. Then again, he didn't appear to be working, just staring at the wall.

Turning to her as she took off her coat, he said, "You look like shit."

"Thanks. Didn't get much sleep last night. You don't look so great yourself."

He scratched the scruff on his cheeks. "Guess this is the home of the walking wounded today."

Jane hung her coat on a peg and then pulled up a stool. "I thought I was doing that." She nodded to the fruit.

He seemed spacey, only vaguely tuned in to his surroundings. "Huh? Oh, well. I was free. Sometimes it's good to be busy, you know?"

"You okay?"

He picked up the lemon, squeezed it, then rolled it against the cutting board. "A friend of mine is dying. He's old. My dad's best friend. Our families were close when I was growing up. It wasn't unexpected, but even so . . ." He let the end of the sentence trail off. "I just came from the hospital."

"You really have had a hard day."

"Mom's taking it the hardest." He pinched the bridge of his nose as if trying to fight back tears. "Can't help but think she's next. I don't believe I told you: She has cancer."

"I'm so sorry."

"Yup. Not good news." He straightened the knives on the cutting board.

"Cancer's not always a death sentence anymore."

"From your lips to God's ears." He scraped at his eyes. "I've been visiting Walter—that's my friend—in the nursing home at least once a week ever since he moved in there. I hated to think of him in that drafty old building all alone. I mean, I know there are people around him, but in every way that counts, he's on his own. Seems like a rotten way to treat a guy who helped so many people during his life. He's one of the best men I've ever known."

Was it a self-serving comment or the truth? Jane felt certain it was a little of both.

"It's kind of odd, you know? He was doing well. And then he up and has a stroke. Of course, I guess that's the way it happens."

"I guess," said Jane, shifting uncomfortably on her stool.

"I was watching my mom with him this morning," he said, resting his elbows on the counter. "I know when she sees him, she sees her future. We'll all be there one day, I suppose. It hurts to watch, to be so helpless. But the thing is, what's been eating at me lately . . . I mean, seeing Walter there in that bed today,

220

knowing him the way I do . . . it just helped me realize how out of control my own life has become."

"Yeah, perspective. It's a precious commodity. I've struggled to find that in my life, too. I guess everybody does."

"I don't know. I think about my brother. He's been anesthetizing himself with booze and politics for so many years that I don't think he has the capacity for self-analysis anymore. It's sad. Sadder still for the woman he married." He picked up the orange and examined it. "Have you ever felt like . . . like everything is in flux? That things are changing fast—and not for the good?"

"You mean your mother's illness?"

"That's part of it. Maybe it's the catalyst. See, I've done things in my life I'm not proud of, but I always understood my reasons. For good or ill, I was clear about it in my own mind. Now, the clarity is gone. It's all become so tangled."

"Life as Gordian knot."

"Exactly. If I could just find a sword to cut through it." Kevin wiped his hands on a towel, then began to slice up the lemon.

Jane was happy to let him talk. He was looking for perspective about his life—she was looking for perspective about him and the entire Adler family. "Your mom seemed pretty religious to me when we talked the other day. That must offer her some solace."

"Have you met Father Mike?"

She shook her head.

"He's a Catholic priest, one of her best friends. Yes, she is deeply religious. She's attended St. Andrews' Catholic church her entire life. Mike likes to think he's part of our family."

"You don't agree?"

He pulled over the condiment holder and began to fill it. "He's

221

not a hard-line sort of priest. It's just . . . he never had much of a family life growing up. He came to New Dresden when I was a sophomore in high school. Right away, he started coming over to the house for dinner at least once a week. My mom and dad felt sorry for him. He was so obviously lonely. After a while, he started acting like he was my older brother. Same with Doug and Hannah. I never liked it. I still don't."

"Because?"

"He idealized my family, which was kind of a joke. We were hardly the picture of familial perfection. He started preaching about how important family life was, as if he was some kind of expert. It was one of his pet subjects. How it was the foundation of a person's future success. It wasn't just idealization, either— he idolized my mom and dad. That blinded him. It was clear to me that, even with a good foundation, kids could still screw up in a big way. Family wasn't a holy institution, it was entirely human. It just made him seem naive when he wanted to appear older and wiser."

"He wanted what he'd never had?"

"Yeah, I guess. I've gotten used to the fact that he's always around."

"Still?

"Oh, yeah. He and mom are closer than ever. He helps out at the farmhouse, and for that I'm grateful. He's just . . . kind of a mixed bag." After finishing up the last of the fruit, Kevin wiped his hands again. "And that, as they say, is about all the self-analysis I can stand for one day. Your turn."

Jane smiled.

"Look, it's gonna be crazy here the next two nights."

"Don't I know it."

"I think the two of us can handle it this evening. I've got Tammy Dimitch coming in to help tomorrow—late afternoon. Have you met her?"

"I don't think so."

"She's an older gal. Knows her way around a bar. She's not interested in a steady job, but she's pretty good about helping out when I need her. As long as you don't say anything bad about the Green Bay Packers, you'll be fine. So, here's the deal. Why don't you go upstairs and catch a a few Zs. Then go get yourself an early dinner. Once it gets dark and people start arriving, it's gonna be nonstop."

"You're sure? You don't need my help with the prep?"

"Just be back by five."

A nap sounded like a godsend to Jane. "Okay, then."

"Hey," said Kevin. "Come here." He stretched out his arms and gave her a hug. "You're a good listener. I mean that. I'm happy to return the favor anytime. Now go. Sweet dreams."

32

Late Sunday night, Father Mike entered the sanctuary at St. Andrew's. He wanted to make sure the building had been securely locked before he headed back to the hospital, where he planned to spend the night at Walter Olsen's bedside. The amber light suffusing the sanctuary soothed him as he faced the altar to offer a silent prayer. He closed his eyes and bowed his head, and when he was done and had turned around, he noticed that a woman was sitting in a pew in the dimness at the back of the church.

Walking down the aisle toward her, Father Mike said, "Laurie?"

"I know it's late. I didn't want to bother you at the rectory. I thought I'd just slip in and sit here for a few minutes."

"Is everything all right?"

She bit her lip, shook her head.

"Can I help?"

"I'm not sure anyone can."

He sat down in the pew in front of her and hooked his arm across the back. Laurie rarely came to church these days. Mike saw her regularly at the farmhouse, and thus felt he knew her well. She'd converted to Catholicism before marrying Doug. Not that Doug had cared, but Evangeline and Henry had applied some discreet pressure and Laurie, who'd been raised a nominal Presbyterian, had complied.

"Maybe it would help to talk," said Mike.

"It's been years since I last came to confession."

"It's never too late."

Laurie pressed her hands into the pockets of her wool jacket. "Do you ever question your beliefs, Father? Is that too personal a question?"

"No, it's not too personal. There was a time in my life when I had a lot of self-doubt—never about God or the church, but about what my proper role should be. I'm not a perfect priest, Laurie, but I do believe I'm on the right path. My faith is stronger now than the day I took my vows."

"That's good. I'm happy for you." She hesitated. "Could you not be a priest for a few minutes? Could you just be my friend?"

Puzzled, Mike said, "I think I can handle that."

She removed her hands from her pockets and folded them in her lap. "I keep a lot of things inside me, you know?"

"Do you?"

"Everyone has secrets. I'm no exception. I think people—my family, especially—see me as generally kind and giving. I believe that, most of the time, I am that person. I'm quiet and respectful. I do what's expected of me. I'm not a complainer. Wouldn't you agree with that?"

"I would."

She wiped a tear from her cheek. "It's partly Walt. Seeing him this afternoon, it got me to thinking . . . about, you know, Delia."

Delia had been on Father Mike's mind, too—all day. "What about her?"

"I hated her."

"You weren't alone in that."

"But I hated her for different reasons. She was Kevin's wife. He married her, wanted to make a life with her. She had his children and she treated them like dirt."

"I don't see the difference."

"*I* should have been Kevin's wife, not Delia. I could have been, too, but I chose Doug. Kevin was the one I loved, but I was a coward—and I was greedy."

"I never knew."

"Doug was going places, had a great career path all set out for himself. He was treated with respect in the local community and I absolutely ate that up. I grew up poor, Mike. My dad scraped together a living, but he never had a plan for his life. Kevin might have been golden. Handsome. Fun and gentle. But he liked to play more than he liked to work. He was a jock and preferred partying to studying. He had no plans for his future. I thought he'd always be that way. I couldn't stand to live like that another minute, not when I had a way out."

"Kevin never once let on, never said a word to me about his feelings for you."

"He wouldn't. He's not the kind of guy to kiss and tell. And he didn't want to hurt his brother. Remember, I got engaged to Doug toward the end of my senior year. Doug was off at college— in his junior year in journalism school. Kevin and I were at a party one night at this friend's house out on Birch Lake. We were both drinking. We ended up walking down to the beach together. We sat there and looked up at the stars. It was one of those magical moments. Almost against our will, we told each other the truth that night. We were in love. We'd felt the connection all year, but never acted on it. Mainly, Kevin stayed away from me because Doug had more or less claimed me. I stayed away from Kevin because I couldn't see a future with him. But that night, none of it mattered."

"You slept together."

"And the next day, I regretted it. That reaction cut Kevin to the core. He stuck around town long enough to be the best man at his brother's wedding, and then he left, joined the army. He would never have met and married Delia if it hadn't been for the way I treated him. I was the one who doomed him to a life with that vile woman."

"You can't blame yourself for his decisions."

"I not only wrecked Kevin's life, I wrecked Doug's. I was never able to love him the way he deserved. He knows something's been missing from our relationship. How could I tell him the truth? I tried with him, Mike. I really did. I wanted to be a good wife. But then Doug and I learned we'd never have children. Doug called it his 'lousy sperm.'"

"Was that the official diagnosis?"

Laurie allowed herself a rueful smile. "Funny. No. I don't remember the specifics. The thing is, Doug blamed himself. I told him it wasn't his fault, but of course, deep down, I did blame him, even though I didn't want to. We talked about adoption, but it was expensive and by then, I wasn't sure I wanted to bring children into our relationship. I was reeling from all that when Kevin returned to New Dresden with Delia and his two beautiful little girls. It was almost more than I could take. She had everything I should have had. Did she value it? Nobody in this family hated Delia the way I did."

"I can see that," whispered Father Mike.

"She deserved what—"

"Laurie, you mustn't say such things. This is God's house."

She looked down, closed her eyes. "I want a divorce. How do you suppose Evangeline is going to take that news?"

She was right to worry about Evangeline. "But you're Catholic. Doug's Catholic, even though he's estranged. The church doesn't allow—"

"I know that and I don't care."

"Have you and Doug talked about this?"

"No. And when I do, he's not going to take it well."

"Does Kevin know?"

"Kevin and I have repaired our relationship. We're not close, not the way we once were, but at least we can say we're friends. That's all we'll ever be. I don't blame him. And no, he doesn't know that I want to divorce his brother. I have no idea how he'll react to it. But his reaction is the least of my worries."

"Meaning?"

"Doug's an alcoholic. The rest of the family may turn a blind eye to his drinking, but I can't. His bitterness has become toxic. He's falling apart, Mike. His temper is out of control. He approached me yesterday with a knife in his hand."

"Laurie, you have to get away from that house."

"If I can just get through New Year's, then I can make some plans. I want Doug to know that I do care about him. That I'll be there for him if he ever decides to get help for his alcoholism. But my question is, if I'm the one who needs help, would you be there for me?"

"I can't condone divorce, but if you need a place to feel safe, come to the rectory."

She reached her hand toward his. "Thank you."

He had the sense that she hadn't told him everything. As a priest, he was used to being the repository of secrets. He even had a few of his own. And yet this time around, he was glad she hadn't come to air out every last skeleton in her closet.

33

Bright winter light pouring in through the window woke Jane on Monday morning. Checking the clock next to her on the nightstand, she saw that it was going on seven. She'd only been asleep for a few hours. She'd stayed up late, talking and laughing with Kevin down in the bar after closing.

Muttering deprecations, she slipped out from under the covers to yank the cheap shade all the way down, then jumped back in bed and pulled the blankets over her head.

The thought of working another shift from hell made her groan as she tried to get comfortable. It would be New Year's Eve tonight. The bar wouldn't open until five. It took a moment for her to realize that today was the day she would put New Dresden and all the Adler family secrets in her rearview mirror for good. She would leave without the proof she'd come looking for—no smoking gun pointing at any specific person in the Adler family. The failure rankled, though the idea of returning home, getting back to her normal life, pretty much outweighed any real sense of defeat.

Leaving today would, of course, put Kevin in a bind, but she was sure he could handle New Year's Eve without her, especially with Tammy's help. She hadn't quite worked out the excuse she would give him for taking off so suddenly, but she still had time to devise something plausible. Maybe she'd help clean up from last night and get the bar ready for another big evening before she gave him the news.

Stop thinking, she ordered herself, turning over and punching her pillow. But when she heard a noise out in the hall—and then the sound of voices—her curiosity got the better of her. Throwing on her robe, she ran a hand through her long, tangled hair as she made her way, barefooted, toward the bathroom.

Kevin stood next to his door, fumbling with his keys. Hannah waited behind him, yawning as she brushed snow off the front of her belted camel coat.

"Jane, hi," said Kevin, looking up as she came toward them.

Jane stopped by the bathroom door and flipped on the light. "What are you two doing up?" She tried to make the question sound light, even humorous.

"It's our friend, Walt Olsen," said Kevin. "I'm afraid he died about an hour ago."

"I'm so sorry." She leaned heavily against the door frame.

"Our mother called us, told us we should come to the hospital," said Hannah. "That he didn't have much time left. Kevin swung by my place and picked me up."

"My brother offered to take Mom, Kira, and Katie over to the funeral home in Union."

Of course, thought Jane. Carmody & Sons would handle the burial.

Hannah poked Kevin's chest. "If they're all off dealing with the funeral, who's covering the farmhouse?"

"Laurie," said Kevin. "She'll stay until Mom gets home."

"Oh, yeah. Forgot about her."

"We've got to get some shut-eye," said Kevin, finally finding the right key and pressing it into the lock. "I'll see you later down in the bar."

"Right," said Jane. As she stepped into the bathroom, she repeated Hannah's comment. *Who's "covering" the farmhouse?* What the hell did that mean?

By one, Jane was seated at the cafe down the street, finishing her omelet and her fourth cup of coffee. She'd thought about getting started on cleaning up the Sportsman's, but because Kevin and Hannah were still asleep up in Kevin's apartment, she didn't want to wake them. She opted for lunch instead.

After paying the bill, Jane went back to her room, packed up her things, and carried her suitcase out to her car. With some free time on her hands, she decided to drive over to St. Andrew's. She'd heard Father Mike's name often enough. Since it was Monday, she assumed he might have some free time.

The church was located along the same county highway as the Adler's farm, approximately half a mile away. Jane parked her car in the empty lot next to the church. The coffee had helped, but she still felt sleep deprived, not entirely focused. She hoped her decision-making abilities would be better today than they had been yesterday.

The white clapboard building was old and picturesque, with a tall spire topped by an ornate metal cross. The front of the church was dominated by lovely recessed and arched double front doors. Jane made her way down the sidewalk next to the building. As she walked along, she admired the row of narrow stained-glass windows that undoubtedly brought light into the sanctuary. Behind the church was a modest-looking two-story brick house. A sign above the front door announced that it was the rectory. If Father Mike wasn't inside, she would try the church next.

She rang the doorbell. Less than a minute later the door was drawn back by a short, plump man with an amused look and a clerical collar. "Can I help you?" he asked, peering at her over his reading glasses.

"My name's Jane. I'm working at Kevin Adler's bar. Both he and his mother said that, if I had some time, I should come by and meet you, maybe see the church."

"Lovely. May I ask . . . are you Catholic?"

"I'm . . . looking."

"Of course. Well, you might as well do your . . . looking . . . here."

"Is this a bad time?"

"No, absolutely not. Come in." He turned away and coughed into the crook of his elbow. "You must forgive me. I seem to have contracted my first winter cold."

The interior surprised Jane by being more than a little messy. Books, papers, and magazines were scattered on top of every flat surface. A plate with a half-eaten sandwich rested on an upholstered footstool in front of the TV.

"I'm interrupting your lunch."

"Not at all. Can I offer you something? I just made a fresh pot of Earl Grey."

"That would be wonderful."

"I'll just be a minute."

As he crossed into the kitchen, Jane drifted around the living room. She examined the books in his bookcase, then moved over to his desk, where a photo album was open to a five-by-seven close-up of Delia Adler. She stopped and turned the page, only to find more photos of Delia. Hearing the clink of glasses in the kitchen, she pushed a pile of magazines to the side and sat down on the couch. Father Mike reappeared a few moments later.

"Here we go," he said, setting a tea tray on the coffee table. "I think you'll find everything you need. Lemon. Milk. Sugar." He stepped over to his desk to retrieve the desk chair. As he eased it out, he shut the album, then turned to Jane and smiled.

"I've always loved tea," said Jane. "My mother was English. I actually grew up there."

"Really? What part?"

"In and around Lyme Regis. We came back to the states when I was nine. I guess I've always considered myself half English."

"With all the Emerald Isle descendants around these parts, I wouldn't say that too loudly."

Jane laughed. "You must love art." She glanced around at all the framed photos, drawings, and paintings. "Are you the artist?"

"I took some of the photos. Photography has always been a hobby of mine."

"Really." Doug wasn't the only photographer in the Adler universe. "And the drawings?"

"My drawing skills are at the level of stick figures, so no, I can't claim anything else." He poured some milk into his tea. "You said you've been . . . looking. For a spiritual home?"

"Yes," said Jane. "I suppose you could say that."

"Have you attended other churches?"

"A few."

"Nothing interested you?"

"Not really. The last church I attended, the minister had a rather bland delivery. The entire service seemed flat and uninspired."

"Here's something I've always believed but rarely stated: If you want to be a minister, you better be a good storyteller. You better have the skills of an entertainer. Otherwise, people tune out." At the sound of the doorbell, he groaned. "Will you excuse me? I need to get that."

While Jane waited, she turned around to look at the large painting on the wall behind her—three compelling images of the same horse. The style was part modern, part primitive, full of motion and intense color. As she stood to study it more closely, Father Mike returned to the room followed by Evangeline Adler, who was carrying a blue Le Creuset pot, holding the handles with hot pads.

"You shouldn't have brought that over today," said Father Mike.

"I'd already made it. You've got a cold. This will help." She smiled at Jane. "Nice to see you again."

"You've met?" said Father Mike.

"We have," said Jane. Evangeline looked exhausted, her skin exceptionally pale, her fine white hair pulled haphazardly back into a bun.

"I'm sorry to interrupt your tea," she said, her smile uncertain, "but I need a couple minutes of your time, Father. It's about Walt's funeral."

"I should probably get back to the bar anyway," said Jane, setting her cup down on the tea tray. She'd wanted to ask him about Delia, but that wasn't going to happen now. "Tell me one thing before I go. This painting, it's wonderful. Where did you find it? Who's the artist?"

"Her name's Nina Careg Darel. She's a Wisconsin woman. I love to visit art galleries when I have the time. I found that one at a gallery in Milwaukee."

"She's popular around the Midwest," said Evangeline. "I've always admired the painting, too—and, of course, Father's photographs."

It was small talk. Evangeline was trying to be polite, but she couldn't hide the strain in her voice.

"I'll stop by another time," said Jane.

"Tuesday, Wednesday, and Friday mornings are reserved for confession. Afternoons are best."

Jane smiled. "Thanks again for the tea."

As he walked her to the door, he said, "Don't stop looking." His amused expression had returned.

"I won't."

Once outside, Jane returned to the parking lot. As she was about to get into her car, she spotted Evangeline's Jeep. Inside, behind the wheel, sat Kira. This was likely the last chance Jane would have to talk to her. Trotting over, she stood next to the driver's door until Kira lowered the window.

"Hi," said Jane. "Do you remember me?"

"You work for my dad. At his bar."

Jane figured she didn't have much time. "Look, what you don't know is that I'm a private investigator. Guthrie hired me to look into your mother's death."

Kira slouched forward and groaned, her head resting against the steering wheel. "I told him to call you off. He said he would.

Now I find out you're still here?" She looked up sharply. "I don't need your help. I don't want it."

"Kira, you've got to listen. We have photos of your mother in the ravine behind your parents' house. You can clearly see strangulation marks on her neck."

"Where'd you get those pictures? Who sent them?"

"I don't know." It was the wrong answer and it only made Kira angrier. "I think you might be in danger," said Jane, all but pleading for her to listen.

"From who? My dad? My grandmother? That's crap and you know it."

"What's going on inside that farmhouse?"

Kira was taken aback by the question. "What?"

"Why does someone always have to be there?"

"That's nonsense. And besides, it's none of your business. Go back to Minneapolis and tell Guthrie I'm fine. See?" She held up her arms. "Completely intact. Nobody's torturing me, making me stay here against my will. I love that guy, but boy, he's really trying my patience. So are you."

"You're telling me your family loved your mom."

"There were issues. But yes, they loved her."

Jane had only one card left to play. If this didn't knock Kira off balance, nothing would. "If your family loved her, why didn't anyone ever pick up her ashes from the funeral home?"

Kira blinked. "What?"

"Call Steve Carmody. Ask him if your mother's ashes are still there."

"No," she said, shaking her head. "No way."

Out of the corner of her eye, Jane saw Evangeline come around the corner from the rectory and walk toward the parking lot. She was the last person Jane wanted to talk to right now. Before she turned to run back to her car, she pointed at Kira and said, "Make that phone call. You deserve the truth."

34

Hannah and Tammy were cleaning up the front room of the bar when Jane returned shortly after four.

"Is Kevin in the kitchen doing the garnish prep?" she asked, unzipping her jacket.

"He's not here," said Hannah, blowing a wisp of hair away from her face. "He was hoping you'd do it."

"Sure. Not a problem." She needed something to occupy her until he got back. "Will Kevin be gone long?" She still had to deliver her story about her dear mother on her deathbed. She would do her best to make it sound less hokey than that.

"He didn't say," said Tammy.

Shrugging, Jane headed into the back room, where she put on an apron and washed her hands. And then she got down to work. Both of the blender jars needed to be washed, as did the muddlers and the strainers. Someone had already put several loads of glasses through the dishwasher. The back bar would need to be restocked.

A while later, as Jane was coming out of the kitchen with the last condiment box, she noticed that Kevin had arrived. He was standing next to the Adler brother Jane hadn't managed to meet: Doug. He was seated at the bar, drinking from a rocks glass. They appeared to be deep in conversation.

Catching Kevin's eye, Jane smiled. Kevin's response was a hard stare, two or three beats too long. He finished talking to Doug, then moved behind the bar and stood next to her.

She felt an odd electricity coming off him. "Everything okay?"

"Rough day."

"Hannah still here?"

"She left."

"I probably prepped too much fruit."

"Better to be on the safe side." He popped a cherry into his mouth.

Jane was about to feed him her sob story, why she needed to leave right away, when Todd Carmody, the man she'd run into yesterday at the hospital, entered the bar. Doug turned around and motioned for him to sit down next to him.

Todd nodded to Kevin and then glanced at Jane. Again, the glance lasted just a hair too long. When he returned his gaze to Kevin, something passed between them. Jane wasn't sure, but she thought she saw Todd give a barely perceptible nod.

"I've got a few things left to do in the kitchen," said Jane.

"Fine," said Kevin. "Go do them."

It took all her willpower not to run. As soon as she was inside the kitchen, she grabbed her leather jacket and made straight for the back door. When she was halfway out, Kevin and Doug were on her.

"What are you doing?" she demanded as each man grabbed

one of her arms and dragged her into the alley. "Kevin? What's going on?"

"Shut up," snarled Doug. "We need a little quality time with you."

"What's that mean?"

"We need to talk," said Kevin.

"Fine. Let's talk."

"Not here," said Kevin.

"We know just the spot," said Doug.

She could smell liquor on his breath.

"Someplace quiet. Private."

"You really disappointed me," said Kevin. "I don't like being lied to."

Jane kicked and fought until Doug pulled out a hunting knife. "If you don't calm down, I'll knife you right here."

"Shut up, you idiot. Put that away."

"You think I won't use it?"

Kevin pulled Jane's arms behind her back and secured them with duct tape. Doug opened the trunk of his car. And then they picked her up and tossed her in.

"Kevin please," she pleaded. "You don't have to do this."

Doug shut the trunk and Jane's world went dark.

PART FOUR: MID-JANUARY

Sometimes there is absolutely no difference at all between salvation and damnation.

—STEPHEN KING
THE GREEN MILE

35

Everything looks good," said Julia Martinsen, shining a light in Jane's eyes. "Any more dizziness? Nausea? Headaches?"

"Slight headache," said Jane, who was seated on an examining table in Julia's downtown clinic. "Nothing terrible. And the pressure inside my head is finally gone."

Julia checked through the information on her clipboard. "All the neurology reports came back normal." Looking up, she added, "Sorry we had to meet here instead of the hospital. I've been out of town for the past week. I wanted to see you right away to do a checkup and give you the results."

Julia's clinic in Minneapolis was closed on Sundays. She'd made an exception for Jane, opening the doors just for her. Jane was grateful, but it also put her in Julia's debt, which was undoubtedly the intention.

"Your bruises seem to be healing nicely. Still feeling cold all the time?"

"Unless I'm in the bathtub," said Jane. "I can't exactly stay there all day." At the moment, she was wearing thermal underwear, a thick flannel shirt under a heavy wool sweater, flannel-lined winter jeans, and three pairs of socks, which made her hiking boots too tight. She figured that was the price she had to pay.

"You need to start eating more normally."

"I don't have much of an appetite."

Julia cocked her head. "Those are words I never thought I'd hear coming out of your mouth."

Jane forced a smile. "Yeah, not exactly me."

The brain fog that had surrounded her after her return from New Dresden had been lifting, little by little, each day. While most of her memory was back in place, parts of her last day in Wisconsin, as well as the night she was attacked, were still huge black holes.

Jane had spent the last couple of weeks sleeping, eating very little because of the dizziness and nausea, and generally hanging out at Cordelia's house, resting. Cordelia had insisted that Jane stay with her until she was "more herself." Since Jane wasn't exactly certain, at least initially, what that "self" looked like, she thought she'd let Cordelia be the judge. Jane's father had stopped by once a day to check up on her. They both appeared concerned about the concussion and the bruised ribs, but mostly Jane sensed that they were monitoring the low-grade depression that had settled over her, something that showed no signs of going away.

"Still no memory of the attack?" asked Julia.

"I get flickers. Flashes. Half-formed thoughts zip through my mind, but as soon as I try to catch one, it dissolves. Frustrating, you know?"

Jane's memory might have been damaged, but the one thing

she did remember about her life were her dogs. They'd always been her lifeline. On the day after New Year's, Cordelia had picked them up from Evelyn Bratrude's house, where Jane boarded them when she was away. Gimlet, her little black poodle, had always been a snuggler who preferred Jane's bed to her own, so when she dove under the bed covers, it felt right—like Jane had found a piece of home. Mouse, her chocolate lab, was not a cuddler. He preferred his comfortably stuffed bed on the floor. And yet after Jane turned out the lights the first night they were back together, she was a bit startled when she felt him climb up next to her and press his body against hers. It was so like Mouse to understand, to want to be there when she needed him. He was the most generous soul she'd ever known.

"And," said Julia, dragging out the word, "your memories of me? Have they returned?"

Jane raised an eyebrow. "Yes, they're back."

"I trust they're not all bad."

Clearing her throat, Jane said, "No. Not all of them."

"Well," said Julia, stepping back from the examining table, "I'd say you're fit to return to work—and to anything else you think might speed your recovery."

As usual, the innuendo was thick. "Thanks."

"How about dinner? You need to eat. I need to eat. We might as well pool our needs."

"Look, Julia—"

Julia held up her hand. "I withdraw the offer." She sat down at the small desk in the examination room and focused all her attention on the computer screen. "Do you have enough Vicodin?"

"More than enough."

247

"If you run out, just let me know." She punched a few keys, then turned and smiled. "I think we're done."

"I'm sorry," said Jane. "About dinner. I'm just not up to sparring with you."

"I wasn't suggesting that we spar, merely eat."

"I know what you were suggesting." She eased off the examining table.

"You should still try to take it easy," said Julia, opening the door out to the hallway.

As they entered the waiting room, Cordelia stood up and began to struggle into her calf-length faux fur coat. She'd offered to drive Jane to her appointment——and, more importantly, to run interference if needed.

"Are you actually wearing nylons with *seams*?" asked Julia, a hand rising to her hip.

"What?" said Cordelia, looking over her shoulder at her lifted leg. "Aren't they straight?"

"It's not 1940," said Julia.

"Sure it is. Somewhere. Read Einstein. Max Planck. Spacetime is relative."

"I thought you were a theater drudge, not a physics professor."

"I am universes within universes."

They were giving Jane's headache a headache. "Enough." Slipping her arm through Cordelia's and moving her out the door, she called, "Thanks."

"I'm always here for you," Julia called back.

On their way home to Cordelia's minifortress, Jane suggested that it was about time she packed up her dogs and went back to her house.

"Not yet," said Cordelia, giving her hair a good fluff. "Not until you're one hundred percent."

"I may not be one hundred percent for months," said Jane.

"Fine. Stay as long as you want. We could fit the Mormon Tabernacle Choir in that mansion and still have room."

Jane looked out the window as they passed the new Vikings stadium. "The point is, I think going home would help, not hurt me."

"Humor me. Just a couple more nights."

"Will you drop me off at the Lyme House? I'll walk up the hill to my place later and get my Mini out of the garage." Her CR-V was still back in New Dresden. A problem she had to resolve.

"Don't work too late."

"No, Mother, I won't."

Cordelia looked over and grinned. "It could be worse. At least I don't do bed checks."

This was only the second time Jane had been back to her restaurant during the two weeks she'd been recuperating. The first visit was to look around, to get her bearings, to fill in the gaps in her memory. It had been a weird sensation, retuning to a building she'd help design, a place she knew more intimately than any other spot on earth, and yet feeling as if she were coming upon parts of it for the first time. That sensation had dissolved after everything began to fall into place. Still, the stark realization that her mind could be such a fragile instrument had an impact.

During many strange, alienated moments, Jane had felt very far away from herself, and in many ways, even though most of her memory had returned, she still did. The cold, empty blankness of that last day in New Dresden had settled down inside her. She was positive it was the reason she felt so continually chilled. Clothing, blankets, and hot baths were no help with a cold that didn't come from without, but from within.

Jane spent a few minutes in the kitchen office being brought up to speed by her executive chef and assistant manager. Here again she realized that her concentration skills weren't normal. She took notes, did her best to appear on top of things, to absorb the information and ask good questions. It struck her that her absence had caused no particular problems for the restaurant, which was good, although it made her feel just a tad inessential, even though she knew that wasn't the case. She'd hired excellent people—something she was proud of. She drifted through the dining room, greeting guests, trying to get her old rhythm back. She thanked various members of her staff for their get-well cards and flowers.

Returning to her downstairs office with a carafe of hot coffee and the overwhelming need to hide, she turned up the heat in the room and then sat down behind her desk. She read through the list of phone calls she needed to return. Not today, she told herself. Maybe not even tomorrow. She switched on her computer. She picked up a pen. She felt overwhelmed.

Jane needed to get away from Cordelia's house and thought coming to the restaurant made the most sense. Now she wasn't so sure. She jumped when her intercom buzzed. Picking up the receiver, she said, "Hello? I mean, this is Jane."

It was Conor, the afternoon host. "You've got a visitor. Guthrie Hewitt. He says it's important."

Jane pressed a hand to her forehead. "All right. Send him down."

When he entered her office a few minutes later, she almost didn't recognize him. "You cut your hair?"

"I was sick of the ponytail thing," he said, sitting down in a chair opposite her desk. "No," he added, shaking his head, "that's not entirely true. I thought if I got rid of it, maybe I'd be more acceptable to Kira's family."

"Have you talked to Kira in the last couple of weeks?" Jane hadn't felt up to seeing him since she'd returned.

"Once," he said. "I told her what happened to you. She wouldn't even entertain the possibility that someone in her family was responsible. But she did say something interesting. Turns out nobody in her family ever picked up her mother's ashes from the funeral home. All these years and they were still there when Kira went to get them."

Jane recalled Steven Carmody delivering that piece of information to her. She couldn't imagine how Kira had found out unless Jane had told her, which must have come during the fog of her last day in New Dresden. "Didn't that shake her?"

"Actually, I think it did. But I still got the same refrain: You need to leave me alone until I figure things out. We text occasionally, but I haven't talked to her since that conversation. Speaking of people who are hard to get ahold of, I stopped by Cordelia's house a couple of times to talk to you. Both times she said you were asleep."

"I probably was."

"I called a couple of times, too."

"This hasn't been the best couple of weeks."

"I need to tell you how sorry I am for getting you mixed up with the Adlers. I should have kept my nose out of it."

"Really? You could have done that?"

"Well, no," he admitted. "But I could have left you out." He sucked in a breath. "I wish there was something we could do to jump-start your memory."

"Not sure what that would be."

"Have you given any thought to the few days you do remember?"

Jane leaned back in her chair. "Actually, I've thought about them a lot."

"Have you reached any conclusions?"

"I made some notes. I promise, I'll write them up for you."

"But tell me some of your conclusions now."

She glanced at the carafe of coffee, then folded her hands in her lap. "Okay, let's think this through out loud. The Adler family may seem close-knit, but there's a lot of friction under the surface—a lot of history—that makes them a volatile mix. As for who murdered Delia, with the exception of Evangeline, I think it could be any of them."

"Why not Evangeline?"

"Her age, for one."

"She was much younger when Delia died."

"I know, but I just can't envision her committing a murder. Maybe she did it. It's possible I have a blind spot when it comes to her. I can easily see her being the prime mover in covering up the facts of Delia's death. She loathed her daughter-in-law. And I think she would have done anything to protect a family member from going to prison for her murder.

"It's possible Doug—and even Father Mike—had a sexual relationship with Delia. Or maybe it was simply flirtatious. But if it did turn physical, and if it had come out, it could have been curtains for the priest's career, and would have created havoc in

Doug's personal and professional life. Doug still needed to impress his father back then. And after his dad died, if the good citizens of New Dresden had learned he was having an affair with his brother's wife, his standing in that conservative community would have crashed and burned.

"Hannah hated Delia on general principles. She may suffer from generalized Catholic guilt, but I don't think that's why she's so hard on herself. Maybe she thought her brother needed protecting from a wicked witch and did the unthinkable—the unforgivable. It's possible an argument got out of hand."

"And Aunt Laurie?" said Guthrie.

"Riley Garrow—one of Delia's friends—told me she had a thing for Kevin. She hated the way Delia treated him, would stare daggers at her. Not positive that rises to the level of motive, but I'm sure people have been murdered for far less. Katie Olsen said Laurie was the type to let things smolder until she couldn't hold her anger in any longer, and then she'd explode. That's a dangerous kind of personality."

"And Kevin? What about him?"

What about Kevin, thought Jane. "He probably had the strongest motivation of all. We had breakfast together right after I started working at his bar. He told me that he was glad he never had to fight Delia for custody of the kids. That's certainly a sufficient motive right there. Add to that the fact that Delia was staying out late drinking in bars, openly flirting with guys—and maybe even sleeping with them. That must have been humiliating. How could he not have been angry at her? The thing is, in the end, I still have no proof that any of them did it. If I could've stayed longer, dug deeper, maybe I would have found something. As it is . . ." She shook her head.

"Please don't apologize." He moved to the edge of his chair. "Jane? Don't take this the wrong way, but you seem so down. Are you sure you're okay to be back at work?"

It was a good question. The idea of going back to Cordelia's house felt like nothing short of total claustrophobia. She could walk up the hill to her house, another familiar place she hadn't explored since coming home. What if it felt weird? Just the idea of having to struggle again with a space that had once been so commonplace and comfortable but that now careened in and out of focus was more than she could stand. She was sick of feeling barely in control.

Looking up, she asked, "Could you give me a ride?"

"Sure. Where to?"

"New Dresden."

His eyes widened.

Just the thought gave Jane an unexpected jolt of energy. "What do you say?"

"Why on earth would you go back there?"

"To get my C-RV."

"Oh, yeah, I forgot. Can't exactly leave it there. How long would we be gone?"

She could see the wheels turning inside his mind. He wanted to go. She wouldn't need to push. "If we left right now, you could drop me off and be back later tonight. Then again, I can't go without telling Cordelia. She might want to come along. We'd have to stop at her place first."

"The more the merrier. It's not safe for you in that town. We could be your posse—protect you."

"Sounds good to me."

"Look, Kira texted me a while ago. Evangeline starts her

third round of chemo tomorrow, except Kira won't be driving her down to Eau Claire. Laurie will. Apparently Kira and Hannah have been working on some project together. Some family issue. Kira will be there alone tomorrow morning. Evangeline and Laurie won't get back until late in the day on Tuesday. What would you say about spending the night there—and then driving out to the farmhouse tomorrow morning with those photos of her mother in the ravine? It's about time she sees them for herself."

"You're sure you want to be the one to show them to her?"

"I have to, Jane. Sometimes I get the impression she thinks I'm making the whole thing up."

This was exactly what Jane needed. Simply making a decision to act, to face the dragon down, caused her spirits to rise. "Let's do it."

As Jane came through the front door of the mansion, she found Hattie thumping down the central stairs outside the great hall, otherwise known as the living room. Behind her trotted Mouse and Gimlet, both with bows from discarded Christmas wrapping stuck to their heads. When the dogs saw Jane, they raced ahead and charged across the fieldstone foyer to greet her. Hattie stood back and adjusted her gaudy crown, a Christmas present from her dear auntie. It was part red velvet, part fake white fur and fake jewels, and lots of fake gold—not exactly Hattie's taste, though Cordelia insisted it had been her niece's idea. She was holding another Christmas present, a world atlas that weighed almost as much as she did.

"Hey, where's your matching red velvet cape?" asked Jane.

"I got some peanut butter on it. Accidentally."

"Uh-oh."

"Yeah, Auntie C. was pretty pissed. But Bolger has this book called *One Hundred and One Household Hints*. It explains how to get peanut butter out of velvet. He's taking care of it."

"That's good."

"The cape's a little much. But the crown is cool."

"Very."

She held up the atlas. "You know where the Gobi desert is?"

Jane had to think. Before she could come up with an answer, a scream rang out. "Who was that?"

"Octavia."

"You mean your mother?"

"She came home a little while ago."

"Don't you call her 'Mom' anymore?"

"Doesn't feel right. I don't see her much. She feels more like Octavia to me."

"That okay with her?"

Hattie shrugged.

Another scream, this one more of an angry shriek.

"It's Auntie C. and Octavia," said Hattie, her expression bored. "They're fighting."

So what else was new?

"It's because of Ivan," said Hattie, plunking down on a bench.

Jane was afraid to ask. "Who's Ivan?"

"The guy who came home with Octavia. They came in a limo. Took forever to bring all their luggage inside."

"I'll bet."

"If I had a sister, would I argue with her as much as Auntie C. argues with Octavia?"

"Hard to answer a hypothetical. They are rather unusual people."

"Yeah," Hattie agreed, hopping off the bench. "I'm gonna go study my atlas. Come on, critters," she said, motioning for the dogs to follow her. Gimlet spun in circles and chased after her. Mouse held back, gazing at Jane with earnest eyes.

"You go, too," she said. She gave him a quick kiss on his muzzle and then watched him bound off.

"Oh," called Hattie, stopping before she disappeared into the great hall. "The Gobi desert is in China."

"Right," said Jane. "Thanks for the clarification."

"Anytime."

Once up in her bedroom, Jane tossed a few clean clothes into her backpack. She was zipping it up when Cordelia rushed in and slammed the door. "My sister's back."

"I heard."

"She has a new man with her."

"Boyfriend or fiancé?"

"You think she makes that sort of distinction? We start working on our first production in early February. She already has changes she wants to make."

"Good changes or bad changes?"

Cordelia leaned against the door and fanned air into her face. "She wants Damien Carroll to play the male lead opposite her."

"The movie star Damien Carroll?"

"They're friends."

"Wouldn't that be good for the theater—to have two major stars in the first production?"

"I suppose. It's just . . . I've heard he's a terror to direct." She glanced down at the backpack. "What are you doing?"

"I'm packing up a few things."

"I can see that. *For what reason?*"

"Guthrie's driving me back to New Dresden. I need to pick up my Honda. I thought maybe you'd like to go with us."

One eyebrow arched. "No more sleuthing, right?"

"We might go see Kira. She'll be alone at the farmhouse."

"But that's it. You'll both be back tomorrow."

"Yes, Cordelia. We'll be back. Why don't you come with us?"

"And leave Octavia here all alone to do God knows what? By tomorrow night, she could move a circus into the rose garden. Or get married to Ivan."

"He would be number fourteen?"

"Ten, but who's counting. Besides, Damien Carroll and his wife are arriving next week to look at the renovations we've done at the theater. Octavia offered to let them stay here at Chez Thorn. I have to get cleaning people in, find a temporary chef—"

"I can help you with that one."

"Yes . . . good, good. There's so much to do."

Jane could see that a road trip was definitely not in Cordelia's future. She'd moved on from the mystery in New Dresden. Jane, however, was still struggling to dig herself out. "You'll take care of my dogs while I'm away?"

"Of course," she said, sitting down on the edge of the bed, spreading her arms wide and falling backwards. "If they're not chasing Hattie, they're chasing the cats. What do you feed a movie star of his magnitude? His wife, Lena—she's a minor actress in comparison. You've probably never even heard of her."

"Lena LaMarr? Of course I have. She's hardly minor."

Cordelia eyed Jane thoughtfully. "Obviously, I follow the trades. I know she did some directing last year. What if she wants to horn in on my creative efforts? What if that's Octavia's plan?"

Within their new theatrical partnership, Octavia was the one with the money, which gave her the edge in the power game both sisters constantly played. Cordelia was the one with the expertise in running a theater, and the one with stellar directorial credentials. Jane sometimes wondered if the Thorn Lester Playhouse would ever get off the ground. As she was searching through the dresser drawer for the keys to her CR-V, the door burst open and Octavia entered, flapping a brochure in front of her.

Jane's first impression was that her nose looked different—more pointed. It was probably naive of Jane to think Cordelia's sister maintained her youthful beauty without the occasional nip and tuck. This particular nip wasn't an improvement.

Before launching into a tirade, Octavia nodded to Jane.

Jane nodded back. So much for human warmth.

"Who created this piece of crap?" demanded Octavia, flinging it at Cordelia. "Well?" she said, hands rising to the gold belt in her designer jeans.

"What's wrong with it?" said Cordelia, moving ominously off the bed, instantly prepared for battle.

"It was designed to trumpet the opening of our new theater?"

"It was."

"Could have fooled me."

"Meaning?"

"The thing looks like a mattress ad."

"I think that's my cue to duck out," said Jane, picking up her backpack. "I'm sure you can figure this out without me."

Cordelia turned her fuming eyes on Jane. "You'll be back tomorrow night, right?"

"You betcha." She smiled as she skirted Octavia and left without a backward glance.

36

The day had finally come. For the past couple of weeks, Laurie had been packing up the clothes she needed the most while Doug was away at work, selecting memorabilia from around the trailer house and putting them in grocery bags, loading up her Windstar in preparation. She couldn't take everything she wanted because she didn't want to alert Doug that she was leaving him. She doubted that, after she had delivered the news, he'd let her back in. Because she paid the monthly bills, she'd been able to squirrel away bits of money. It was partly the reason they were behind on so many of their payments. She'd also hid some of the tips she'd received while working at Kevin's bar. She supposed that, even though she couldn't admit it to herself, she'd been planning this move subconsciously for over a year. She had slightly more than a thousand dollars stashed away. It wouldn't last long, but it was enough to give her some breathing room without Doug's paycheck.

The final straw for Laurie had come on New Year's Eve, when she'd found Jane, Kevin's bartender, beaten up on the highway a few miles from town. In retrospect, everyone realized that she'd been asking a lot of questions about the family, though at the time, nobody assigned it much significance—not until Todd Carmody mentioned to Doug that he'd seen Jane at the funeral home a week or so before Christmas. She'd given a business card to his brother, Stephen, stating that she was a private investigator. Laurie only found this out after the fact—after she'd pushed Jane out Hannah's back door with nothing but a twenty-dollar bill and a bottle of pain pills in her coat pocket. The poor woman had been so confused. Laurie was still worried about her and hoped she somehow got home safely, wherever home was. She remembered Jane's kindness that afternoon at the bar, when Laurie had come in with little money and Jane had pulled her a beer and offered her a sandwich.

As usual, Doug refused to talk about what had happened that night. All Kevin would say was that Jane was a threat, something that he and Doug had handled. End of story. Except it wasn't. Family matters had reached a tipping point, with members lining up for or against the brutal action. Hannah, Kira, Laurie, and Father Mike felt a line had been crossed. Doug and Kevin defended themselves by saying they were only doing what was necessary. Evangeline was on the fence. With the beginning of her chemo, she had so much on her mind already that nobody wanted to push her for her opinion, and yet without it, they were at an impasse.

Gazing at her bedroom one last time, Laurie figured that she was supposed to experience something profound, and yet all she felt was drained. Closing the door behind her, she stepped out into the hallway and approached the living room. Doug was seated, as usual, in his recliner rocker, watching a game on TV and smoking his pipe. He wore work clothes all week, but on the weekends, without fail, he would shower and shave, put on a clean white shirt, a tie, and his only business suit or his one sport coat and pair of dress slacks. It was as if he was informing the world that he might have to do grunt work all week, but it wasn't who he was. The spectacle of him sitting there all dressed up, getting drunk slowly on beer, a sight she'd seen so many times before, seemed overwhelmingly sad to her now. He was a pitiful wreck of a man, beaten up by life and yet still maintaining a piece of himself through it all. She silently cheered him on, knowing in her heart that if he ever stopped dressing up on weekends, it would be the end of him.

She cleared her throat.

Doug pulled the pipe out of his mouth and turned to look at her. "You going to the farmhouse today?"

"Not until tomorrow. I'm driving your mother to her chemo appointment in Eau Claire. Giving Kira a break."

He nodded, looked back at the TV.

A six-pack of beer, minus four bottles, sat on the kitchen counter next to a half-filled bottle of tequila. "Doug?"

"Hmm?"

"I'm leaving."

"Just go already. You don't need my permission."

"I won't be back." There was no easy way to say it. "I want a divorce."

His body jerked. That was it. He gave no other outward sign that he'd heard her.

"If we can agree on terms, we can use one lawyer. It would be cheaper that way."

He returned the pipe to his mouth.

"We don't need to talk about it now." She waited. Digging in her pocket for her car keys, she finally said, "So, I guess this is good-bye. Doug? Please, at least say you heard me."

"I heard."

"Don't you have anything you want to say?"

With his eyes till on the TV, he half muttered, half slurred, "What's to say? You've already made up your mind. You made it up a long time ago."

She couldn't argue the point. Not anymore. "I'm sorry," she said softly. As she opened the front door, she heard him get up. Turning back to him, she saw that his face had flushed a deep red.

"I need you," he said, his eyes pleading.

"Doug—"

"I'm not as strong as you are. Isn't there something I can do to change your mind? Just name it. I'll do anything."

She hadn't expected this.

"Anything, Laurie. I can change. I'll be a better husband. I'll work on my temper, I swear."

"You're an alcoholic."

His eyes narrowed.

"Nobody ever says it out loud, but we all know it's true."

Wiping a hand across his mouth, his eyes bounced around the room. "Sure, I drink too much. Kevin drinks a lot, too. So does Hannah. Runs in the family."

"It's not the same. If you can't see that you have a problem, one that's wrecking your life, I don't know what's going to become of you. I'm afraid for you, Doug. Afraid that you'll get fired because you miss so much work. You give them these lame excuses, but your boss can see through that. And then what? How will you support yourself? I fear for your health, for your safety if I'm not here to look out for you. That time you fell in the snow—"

"Then stay."

"I can't. I refuse to watch you commit suicide by alcohol. You need to get into a treatment program and some kind of personal therapy."

"Therapy never helped anybody. It's utter bullshit. And besides, I could drink less if I wanted to. If that's what I need to do to convince you to stay, I'll do it." He snapped his fingers. "It's not a problem, Laurie. Just give me a chance and I'll show you."

"Stop drinking. Today. When you're clean for three months, we'll talk again." She would never go back to him. Still, if he thought it was the price he had to pay, maybe he'd get some help.

"*Three* months?" He spit the words at her.

"Father Mike said I could stay at the rectory. He's got an extra bedroom." She was frightened by the anger building in his eyes. "Please, Doug. Think about it." She rushed out to her car. As she started the engine, he stumbled out onto the tiny deck. Shaking his fist at her, he screamed, "You fucking bitch. You never loved me. You think you can leave? Just like that? I won't allow it. I won't *allow* it."

He was still standing there screaming, this time in her rearview mirror, as she pulled out onto the highway and sped away.

Laurie entered the Sportsman's shortly after four, readying herself for another difficult conversation. It was early for bargoers, so there were only two customers seated at the counter and none at the tables. Kevin was behind the bar watching the same basketball game Doug had been watching back at the trailer. When he heard the bell above the door jingle, he turned with a smile on his face.

"Laurie," he said, easing off his stool. "Is everything okay? You look upset."

She hadn't thought he could read her so well. "Could we talk?" she asked quietly, nodding to the empty tables in the back.

He seemed puzzled, but recovered quickly and said, "Sure. I'll pull us a couple beers."

She took off her coat and dropped it over the back of a chair, then sat down and fidgeted with the buttons on her cardigan, noticing that one was hanging by a thread. She pulled it off before it could fall off and slipped it into her pocket. A moment later, Kevin set a pint in front of her.

"What's up?" he asked, sitting down, drawing his own pint toward him.

She had steadfastly refused to plan out what she would say, preferring to let the conversation flow naturally. She had no expectations. She felt numb. "I've left Doug. I asked him for a divorce."

Kevin's eyebrows shot up.

"It's been coming for a long time. We haven't been happy for years."

"I have to say, I'm not all that surprised. But what will you do? Where will you live?"

She explained about Father Mike's offer, and that she'd saved a little money. She was temporarily okay, though it wouldn't last. "I need a job. That's why I'm here."

He frowned and looked away.

"Hire me back, Kev. I won't quit on you this time."

"I never understood why you quit last time."

She searched his face. She wasn't sure how far to go. "It was just too hard."

"Hard? Making drinks?"

"Working with you. Being around you. You like to wind down after the bar closes with a beer and conversation. You have no idea how much I looked forward to those talks. Doug and I haven't talked like that in twenty years. It made me remember——"

"We can't go there."

"I know. That's why I quit."

He spent a few seconds digesting her words. Turning the beer glass around in his hands, he asked, "Does Mom know?"

"That I planned to leave Doug? Yeah. I told her last week. She was surprisingly okay with it—as long as I don't ask for a divorce."

"But you did."

"He's an alcoholic, Kevin. I've said that to your mom before, but she always deflects it. Minimizes his drinking. But she doesn't have to live with it. I do. His temper is out of control."

"I know," said Kevin, looking down.

"He scares me."

His head snapped up. "Has he hurt you?"

"I'm not talking about that."

With his hands balled into fists, he said, "You should have told me."

"What would you have done? Beat him up? It would have only pissed him off more. I've been holding on, trying to make things work for the sake of this family. I just . . . I can't do it anymore."

He aimed his unblinking eyes at her. "God, what a mess we've made for ourselves."

"I made the mess, Kevin. I committed the original sin. I chose Doug instead of you." She wrapped her arms around her stomach and sat back in her seat, fighting the urge to cry. Looking up, she saw Kevin's face harden and a darkness creep into his eyes.

"You're hired," he said flatly. "You can start tomorrow."

"I promised to take Evangeline to Eau Claire for her chemo tomorrow. We won't be back until Tuesday afternoon."

"That's fine. I'm starting a construction job up in Glenham tomorrow. Tammy's helping me out right now, but she doesn't want steady work. You start when you want. Just let me know. And as far as staying at the rectory, that's up to you. You're welcome to the room I have upstairs. Free of charge. For as long as you want."

The tight ball in her stomach began to ease. "I'll take the job. But I can't stay here."

"Because?"

"Evangeline would say it doesn't look right."

"I don't give a rip about that. I want you here. I want to take care of you."

"You can't. Like you said, we can't go there. That's all in the past."

Pushing his beer away, Kevin stood. "Just think about it." Bending close to her ear, he whispered, "You weren't the only one who looked forward to those late-night conversations, Laurie."

37

Jane was chilled to the bone when she and Guthrie arrived at the Timber Lodge Motel just after eight that night. She blamed the car's heater. Even though Guthrie hadn't been bothered by the cold air coming out of the vents, Jane sure was. She borrowed his car blanket and wrapped that around her, though because it was thin, it hadn't helped much. Before heading off to their respective rooms, Jane asked Guthrie for his car keys. She was grateful that he didn't press her for why she needed them.

Lying down on the bed under a pile of blankets, Jane turned on the TV. She watched an old movie for a while, then set the alarm on the nightstand next to her for 3 A.M. With so much on her mind, she figured there was a good chance she wouldn't need the alarm, but set it anyway, just to be on the safe side.

By two, she was up, a blanket wrapped around her shoulders, looking out the window at the parking lot, itching to get her errand over with. Grabbing the car keys, she exchanged the blanket for her heavy sheepskin jacket, flipped the collar up, and left the room. As she drove through the dark, empty streets of New

Dresden, she felt as if she was in an alternate universe. The last thing she needed was to run into a police cruiser. The simple fact that she was out and about at such an hour in this tomb of a town would make her presence suspicious.

Parking at last a few doors down from Kevin's bar, she cut the headlights and the engine and then slipped out, looking both ways down the silent Main Street to make sure she wasn't being observed. The keys to her Honda were in her pocket. Approaching the small lot at the back of building, where she'd parked her car when she was living above the Sportsman's, she saw that the CR-V was buried in at least five inches of snow. Two other cars in the lot were free of snow, making hers stand out. Again, she didn't want to telegraph her presence, so she took her time, brushing off as little as possible to get the key into the lock. Carefully cracking open the door, she ducked inside and opened the glove box. Inside was a Smith & Wesson J-Frame, a .38 caliber revolver Nolan had urged her to buy and learn how to use. She loathed guns, but after listening to the case he made, she figured he was right. She traveled with it when she was on a job, but rarely took it out. She also removed a box of ammunition and a middle-of-the-back holster that she could thread through her belt. It made the weapon almost impossible to spot when she was wearing a jacket.

Closing and locking the door, she gazed up at Kevin's second-floor apartment for a few seconds. Lights were on behind the drawn shades, though she assumed he was still in the bar cleaning up. She would see him tomorrow—this time, on her terms.

The next morning, Jane found Guthrie seated on one of the couches in the front lobby. Before they got started, he passed her a small package filled with copies of the crime-scene photographs he'd been sent anonymously through the mail. They spoke little on the ride to the farmhouse. Jane was going over the potential outcomes of their encounter with Kira, and assumed Guthrie's mind was filled with the same issues.

As they pulled into the driveway behind Kira's Chevy Cobalt, Jane heard Guthrie give a sigh of relief.

"She's here."

As she opened her car door, she was immediately assaulted by the high-pitched yips and barks of dogs inside the barn.

A moment later, Kira came out of the back door of the house with an old black lab tagging along behind her. She was about to toss a stick when she saw them. The lab turned and ran at Jane. At the last minute, he changed directions and raced around the front of the car to greet Guthrie.

"Hey, Sammy," said Guthrie, reaching down to scratch the dog's ears. "Long time no see, fella." As he straightened up, Kira rushed into his arms.

"Oh, God, it's so great to see you," she said.

Jane took a moment to say hi to the old dog while the two young lovers embraced.

"But . . . what are you doing here?" she asked. She backed up a step and directed a hard look at Jane.

"We need to talk to you."

"I need to talk to you, too. But not with her hanging around and not right now."

"It's never a good time. We've traveled a long way, Kira. You can give us ten minutes."

"Hannah and Father Mike are coming for a meeting."

"Your family sure has a lot of meetings," he said with a grin.

Jane figured he'd meant it as a joke. Kira obviously took it as a criticism.

"Don't be mad," said Guthrie, reaching for her hand.

Sammy trotted back to the barn and sat by the door.

"What have you got inside there?" asked Jane.

"Our Airedale had a litter."

"How many puppies did Foxy have?" asked Guthrie.

"Eight."

"Evangeline raises them," Guthrie said to Jane.

"I'd love to meet them," said Jane, hoping a look at the pups might cause a thaw in Kira's general demeanor.

"Maybe later," said Kira, eying Jane uncertainly. She motioned for Sammy to come as she led them up to the front porch. As they entered, Kira and Guthrie removed their coats and hung them on a coat rack. Jane left hers on. They all sat down stiffly in the living room.

Kira spoke first. Looking pointedly at Jane, she said, "I suppose I should tell you: I checked out the funeral home like you suggested. You were right. Nobody in my family ever picked up my mother's ashes. So I went and got them. I'll scatter them myself. I asked my dad about it. He said he just couldn't do it. You may not understand his reasons, but I do."

Guthrie rose, moved hesitantly across the braided wool rug, and handed Kira the package of photos.

"What's this?"

"Take a look. You tell me what you think they are."

"It's not my mother. It can't be. Someone's trying to play a trick on you."

"Just look." As he sat back down, the front door opened. A moment later, Father Mike appeared, sans coat and shoes. He was carrying a pair of slippers. "Hannah's going to be a little late," he said. He stopped when he saw that Kira wasn't alone. "Oh. Hi. I wasn't expecting—"

"Neither was I," said Kira.

The priest gave Jane and Guthrie an easy, practiced smile. "Perhaps I should busy myself in the kitchen."

"No, stay," said Kira, nodding to the spot right next to her on the couch. "Father Mike is a friend. There are no secrets here."

Jane found the comment just short of ludicrous. She did, however, understand what Kira was doing—evening out the sides, two against two instead of Jane and Guthrie against her.

As he sat down, Father Mike said, "Nice to see you both again."

For some reason, the comment unsettled Jane. She'd gone to the rectory on her last day in town. She had very little memory of what they'd talked about, though she doubted she'd learned anything new. The image of the priest's desk floated into her mind. A photo album open to a large photo of Delia Adler. Why had he been looking at it?

Kira opened the envelope and flipped through the photos. "Oh God," she said, a hand flying to her mouth. "It is her."

"I had a couple of the shots enlarged," said Guthrie. "I'm sorry, sweetheart. I realize this is a brutal way to prove my point, but you can clearly see marks around your mother's neck. It was murder, Kira."

Father Mike stared hard at Guthrie. "Where did you get these?" he demanded.

"They were sent to me anonymously in the mail." Taking a paper out of his pocket, Guthrie opened it and passed it to Jane, who passed it to Kira. "That's the note I told you about."

Kira read it out loud: "Proof Delia Adler was murdered. Stay out of it or the same thing will happen to you."

The priest leaned over to look at it. He pressed a finger to his lips. "Oh, no."

"What?" said Kira.

"It's Doug's handwriting. He must have taken them and kept them all these years."

Kira paused to collect her thoughts. "But this makes no sense. We know what happened. We know exactly how my mother died and why the family covered it up."

Father Mike flicked his eyes to Jane and Guthrie. He took the photos from Kira to examine more closely.

"Maybe you'd like to explain it to me," said Guthrie. "Since there are no secrets here."

Kira shot him an angry look as she hunched back against the couch cushions, chewing at her lower lip.

"I think you owe me that much."

She thought about it a moment more, then said, "If I agree to tell you, it can't leave this room." Her gaze moved back and forth between Jane and Guthrie.

"I promise," said Guthrie. "As for Jane, a private investigator is bound by client confidentiality."

That was true, though Jane couldn't participate in anything illegal and still keep her license. A murder cover-up was an illegal act.

"My sister, Grace, and my mother never got along. The day my mom died, my sister stayed home from school. She was supposed to catch the bus in front of our house, but she never went. Mom apparently didn't check on her. That wasn't unusual.

"Dad didn't like my mom to smoke in the house, so she'd go

out on the deck, have a cigarette, and then come back in. That day, as a prank, Grace locked the door and my mom couldn't get back in. In attempting to drop from the deck into a section of snow next to the ravine, she missed and fell to her death. My father and grandmother made a knee-jerk decision to cover it up. Grace was a troubled child. They thought this might damage her even more."

"That is absolute crap," came a voice from the doorway into the front hall.

Jane looked over to see a petite, dark-haired young woman in jeans and a Milwaukee Brewers baseball jacket. A pair of horn-rimmed glasses dominated her face. She held a baseball mitt in one hand and a baseball in the other. More importantly, she looked thoroughly enraged. "I never did that. No way. Who told you that crap?"

Kira jumped to her feet. "What are you doing? You shouldn't be in here."

"Who's she?" asked Guthrie, adjusting his glasses as he rose up and stood next to Kira.

"Um," said Kira, rubbing her arms and looking around.

"I'm Grace," said the young woman, her eyes fierce. "You can't expect me to listen to lies and not call you on it. I never hurt Mom. I thought you knew what happened. We talked about it and you acted like you'd heard it all."

Kira's mouth opened, but she couldn't seem to find any words.

"That's your *sister*?" asked Guthrie, his eyes wide with surprise. "The one you said was . . . dead?"

Jane stood, too. Would the Adlers' secrets never end?

"You want the truth?" Grace searched the faces staring back at her. "Well, here it is."

"Grace, no," said Father Mike. "This isn't the place."

"I was there that day," said Gracie, ignoring him. "That part you got right. I was hiding behind the big brown chair in the living room. Dad rushed in and began shouting. Mom shouted back. They went into the kitchen and I could hear them talking. I thought maybe things were okay. I was about to go back to my room when Mom ran out on the deck to get away from Dad and he ran after her. That's where it happened. He had his hands up around her neck. I closed my eyes because they were scaring me. When he came back into the house, Mom was gone. He went in the kitchen and called Gram. I could hear him crying. I spent most of the day hiding in my closet. Dad eventually figured out I was home, and that I'd seen the fight. Don't you remember? After we were put to bed that night I crawled in with you and told you what happened, except I never said who did it."

"It was *Dad*?" said Kira, eyes fixed on her sister.

"Yeah, afraid so. Back then, all I knew for sure was that our mom was gone and she wasn't coming back. I didn't really understand death, not until years later. I wasn't sad. I wasn't sure where she'd gone, but I liked it better without her. And then I came to stay here with Gram and I didn't see you anymore, Kira. I loved being here, but I missed you. But now we're back together. It's all worked out."

"I don't understand any of this," said Guthrie, appearing completely confused.

Kira gazed at Father Mike with helpless eyes. "Did you know any of this?"

He shook his head. "They told me the same story they told you. Only thing is, I always knew it wasn't the entire story."

"They're liars! All of them. Why couldn't they tell us the truth?"

It seemed clear to Jane what the primary reason was for keeping Kira and Father Mike in the dark. The family didn't want to make them accomplices.

Father Mike moved in front of Kira and spoke to Grace. "Hey, kiddo, you want to toss that baseball around a little?"

"I guess," she said.

"Go on out to the barn. Find me a good mitt, okay? I'll be there in a sec."

Before she left, Grace said, "You're Kira's boyfriend aren't you? She showed me pictures."

Guthrie was still so stunned he could hardly speak. "Ah, yeah. I am."

The puzzle pieces were finally falling into place for Jane. From her very first visit to the farmhouse, she'd felt something strange was going on. The day she'd looked around the living room at the family photos, she'd felt a presence. It had to have been Grace. But more importantly, she now knew who'd murdered Delia, though Kevin's motive was still a mystery.

What struck Jane most was that, even with Gracie's admission, there was still no real proof that Kevin had murdered Delia. Certainly, the testimony of a seven-year-old child was a gap in the case large enough for a good defense lawyer to drive a semi through. Grace had a childhood memory, sure, but most of what she knew was what she'd been told. Memories could be shaped by a family determined for her to remember something in a specific way.

After Gracie had left the room, Father Mike and Kira sat back down on the couch. "Listen to me for a minute," he said gently, waiting for her to look at him. "I believe I know why your father told us that story. He didn't want to involve us in a cover-up. Covering up a murder is a felony, Kira. And—" He took hold of her hands, "Beyond that, I'm sure he was ashamed of what he'd done. Telling you—it would have been so incredibly painful."

"So he's a coward."

"Don't make any judgements right now. Give yourself some time to process this. Talk to your family. If you want, you can talk to me. All I know is, your dad loves you and Gracie more than anything in this world. You believe that, don't you?"

Kira lowered her head. "I suppose."

Jane felt her phone buzz inside the pocket of her jeans. She took it out and looked at the caller ID. "Katie Olsen." It took her a minute to remember who that was.

"I better get out to the barn," said the priest. "Gracie's as upset as you are. I need to talk to her, too. Are you okay?"

"I don't know," said Kira. "But go."

Jane excused herself along with Father Mike. Ducking into the kitchen, she answered the call. "This is Jane."

"Hi. Finally. Katie Olsen," came a clipped voice. "You remember me? My father was Walt Olsen. You came to my house to talk to me about Delia Adler—and about my dad. You went to see him, didn't you? You spoke to him about Delia."

There was an edge of anger in the woman's voice. Jane sat down at the kitchen table. "Yes, I did go see him."

"You know he had a stroke shortly after you two talked?"

"Yes, I'd heard." She assumed Katie had put it together and decided that Jane was the cause. There were undoubtedly many factors, yet she could hardly argue the point.

"He died. Right before the new year."

"I'm very sorry."

"I want to talk to you."

Jane closed her eyes. If this woman needed to scream at her, Jane figured she owed her a few good shots. "Okay."

"The business card you left me says Minneapolis. I could meet you in, say, Eau Claire. That's about halfway for both of us."

"Actually, I'm in New Dresden."

"My lucky day. What are you doing right now?"

"I'll . . . come over. Again, I'm really sorry about your dad."

There was no response, just dead air.

38

Kira wiped tears away from her eyes as she walked Guthrie out to the barn. In the aftermath of the revelations inside the farmhouse, his main concern was for her.

"Are you going to call your father?" he asked as they moved across the packed snow.

She shook her head. "He's out of town working a construction job today. Besides, I think Father Mike is right. I need some time. Right now, I'm angry. I feel betrayed. I need to understand why he did what he did. None of this is something I want to discuss on the phone."

"I'm glad I'm here."

She looked up at him. "Me too." Haltingly, she began to open up on what had happened to her since she'd left for that family meeting after Thanksgiving. "I want to show you where Grace has been living all these years." Pulling back the heavy barn door, Kira nodded for Guthrie to enter first.

Inside, he found a wide-open space lit by fluorescent lights. He judged it to be at least a hundred feet long, maybe a third as wide. "It's warm in here."

"The entire barn is heated and insulated. It used to be an old tie-stall dairy barn. Dad renovated it."

The barn floor appeared to be original, a kind of scraped, textured concrete. The rafters and walls were made of wide wood planks that had been stained and varnished. On the opposite side of the building was another, wider door. A chain-link fence cordoned off a hay-covered section. Inside were the cutest puppies Guthrie had ever seen. "Have they been adopted yet?"

"A few have," said Kira. "Gram's very careful about where they end up."

Father Mike and Gracie were tossing the baseball to each other at the other end of the barn. Next to them, attached to the wall, was a basketball hoop. Behind them, along one wall, were several weathered looking couches.

"There's a volleyball setup, too. Dad built it, I guess. The poles can be switched out for badminton. Gracie loves sports. Likes being busy all the time. Sometimes the entire family gets together to play."

If it wasn't so twisted, thought Guthrie, it sounded almost idyllic.

They trudged up a rustic wooden staircase to the second floor.

"Hey, Kira," called Gracie. "Close the door to my room. It's a mess."

Kira turned and gave her a thumbs-up.

"She's lived here since she was seven?" asked Guthrie. "All alone?"

"Never alone," said Kira.

The second floor, what had once probably been a hayloft, had been closed off to create another large, almost cathedral-like space. Along the far wall were a couple of bedrooms, and between them was a bathroom. A galley kitchen ran along the wall opposite the bedrooms. There was a long wooden table, big enough to seat at least twelve. Next to that was a living-room area centered around a shag rug, with a comfortably used-looking overstuffed couch, matching love seat and chairs, a flat-screen TV, and a battered oak coffee table. What struck Guthrie most was the artwork on the walls. Everywhere he looked he saw paintings—from eye level all the way up to the rafters. "Who did those?" he asked.

"Gracie. That's her passion. She's been creating art since she was a kid. Father Mike thought they were so good that he asked a friend of his, a guy who owns a gallery in Milwaukee, to try to sell some of them. It took a while, but she's actually making herself quite a name around the Midwest. She calls herself Nina Careg Darel. Nina is her middle name. Careg and Darel are both anagrams for Grace and Adler. She has a studio behind those sliding doors." She pointed.

"I don't understand all this," said Guthrie, looking around. "Is she trapped in here? Do they ever let her out?"

Kira sat down on the couch and motioned for Guthrie to join her. "When I came here for that first family meeting, that's what we talked about. I was absolutely stunned. I was angry, too. I never got to have a relationship with my sister. It was stolen from me. I had no idea any of this was going on—that she was alive. I'd been here at the farm hundreds of times and I never saw her."

"Are you still angry?" asked Guthrie.

"I don't expect that will ever go away."

He nodded.

"Years ago, my Grandpa Henry had my dad rehab the upper part of the barn, making the hayloft into an office for him. After he died, Gram asked Dad to make more extensive changes. She wanted to enlarge the space to include the entire upper story. It became her sanctuary. Gracie and I weren't allowed up here— ever. Right after Mom died, Hannah and my dad took Gracie and me on a trip to Disney World."

"Yeah, I know all about that."

"You do?"

"Hannah stopped into your dad's bar one night when Jane was bartending. After several drinks, Jane got her to tell the story."

"I'm surprised she'd talk about it. I thought my family's decisions were all about protecting Gracie. Turns out, they were protecting themselves."

He put his arm around her. Nothing was going to seem normal to Kira for a long time. "Do you have any memories of Disney World?"

"I remember the hotel pool and meeting Mickey Mouse. That's about it. I flew back with Dad. Hannah flew back with Gracie. And then I was told that Gracie had died in a car accident. I just remember my dad sitting on my bed one night, explaining that Gracie was in heaven with Mommy. We'd see them again one day, but not for a long time. I suppose I cried. I don't really recall."

"And they moved Grace in here," said Guthrie.

"It's actually more understandable if you realize that Gracie was having terrible trouble in school back then. She was picked on by other kids. The teachers thought she was a trouble-maker because she couldn't sit still in class. She never sat still— anywhere—unless the TV was on. She would have these sudden

283

outbursts—rages. She'd throw things or haul off and kick whoever was in the room. I got kicked a lot. She was very angry, *that* I remember. She and Mom fought all the time. Mom actually threw her across the room once. It was awful. I'm not sure my dad ever knew about it. Dad was the only one who could calm Gracie down. And Gram—well, I mean, Grace loved being at the farm almost more than anything. After Gracie moved in here, Gram told me she slept out here with her each night. Or sometimes Laurie would come, or Hannah. Uncle Doug and Father Mike were also around a lot. So were Walt Olsen and our uncle, Brian Carmody. And Dad—he was her constant support. The family closed ranks around her, became her playmates, her teachers and her companions. She always had people in her life. And for the first time, she began to thrive. I'm not saying that it was easy or that there weren't problems. I've spent the last month getting to know her again. It's been . . . amazing."

"But she's twenty-two, Kira. Doesn't she want a life of her own? Is she still confined to the barn?"

"She's never been completely confined to the barn. Gram has taken her on lots of trips. So has Hannah. Dad goes for walks with her after dark. When we were kids, she had long red hair. Laurie died it a dark brown and cut it short. She's got terrible eyesight, so the horn-rim glasses change her appearance some. Honestly, she's changed so much that I'm not sure I would have recognized her if Dad hadn't told me who she was."

"So the family trusts her now not to tell what happened to your mom?"

"Yes."

"Except, she just told the story to Jane and me."

Kira had to think about that. "She never would have if I

284

hadn't just given you an explanation she knew was a lie—and also blamed her. Gracie is very black and white. She reacts instantly to injustice. I mean, she's not retarded. She has a normal IQ, but she's . . . different. She can be impulsive. She has sensitivities to light and sound, to tags in clothing. She struggles, Guthrie. Things that you and I might find simple are hard for her."

"It just seems so crazy that nobody ever saw her. All those years."

"Right from the start, Gram came up with the idea of calling it 'The Hiding Game.' Gracie loved games. Before she could understand why she needed to stay out of sight, my family framed it that way. She had a wall for stickers and gold stars that were her rewards." Glancing at her watch, Kira added, "Hannah should be here soon."

That was another question Guthrie had. "Why are you and Father Mike meeting with her?"

Kira gave a somewhat muted groan. "When I first arrived, Hannah was in the process of a mutiny. She told Gram, in no uncertain terms, that she'd given enough time to raising Gracie. She wanted her life back. Gram was extremely unhappy about that. See, years ago, after Mom died, everyone in the family pledged to take care of Grace for as long as necessary. That's why nobody could ever move away. Gram even wanted Hannah to move back to New Dresden, but she refused. She kept a bungalow, but her main residence and her job is in Eau Claire."

"I don't blame her."

"Gram wants me to consider living full time at the farmhouse."

"No! Kira, you can't do that."

"She's afraid the cancer will take her life, Guthrie. Sooner rather than later. She's been under a huge amount of stress. Hannah's added to it by refusing to cooperate anymore."

"She has every right."

"I agree, but it's put Gram in a bad place. She's scared—about her health, and about what will happen to Grace. You have to understand. My family made these incremental decisions, for good or ill, that have taken on the power of immutable law. 'We've always treated Gracie this way and thus we need to continue to treat her that way.' Changing long-held attitudes and approaches is hard. Grace isn't a child anymore and, strange as it may seem, I'm not sure my family really sees it that way. She can't live totally on her own—I get that—but she needs far less supervision than most of the family insists on. The thing is, I found out yesterday that Laurie has left Doug. That may just be the solution we've all been looking for."

"She would move in here?"

"She says she wants to. Like I said, Grace is able to be far more independent that Gram or Dad give her credit for. The way things stand right now, it's not working. For anyone. It's complicated, but Hannah and I think we've come up with a compromise. Something that would allow Grace more freedom, and yet she could still live within the protection of the family. Very simply, she would become someone else—but also, someone she already is. Nina Darel. The artist. She'd come to town. Look around to rent a space, and settle on the barn at Evangeline Adler's farm."

"That's brilliant."

"There are some problems we'd have to work out, but nothing insurmountable. Believe it or not, she already has close to twenty-five thousand dollars in the bank. Father Mike has taken care of all that, made sure every dime was saved for her future.

She's earning her own living, Guthrie. It makes total sense. Hannah and Father Mike and me, we intend to present our idea to the family next weekend."

"And then you can come home, right? We can get on with our life together."

She moved in close and kissed him. "That's the plan. May take a few weeks, but I think we've found a solution."

He held her tight. "Do you think you can ever forgive your family?"

She leaned her head against his shoulder. "I hope so. But trust . . . I'm not so sure about that."

39

When Jane pulled up to Katie Olsen's house that morning, she found a FOR SALE sign stuck into the snowy front yard. Inside, all the furnishings were gone, replaced by a minimally staged living room and dining room—just the bare essentials. A few rugs. A table and chairs. Two love seats facing each other across a coffee table in the living room.

Katie ushered Jane in without speaking. She looked worn out and walked slowly. Jane sat down on one of the love seats. Katie took the other. A closed folder rested on the table in front of her.

"Again," said Jane, "I need to say how sorry I am about your father." She steeled herself, waited for Katie to lash out. Instead, the woman just sat there, her mouth twisting, her eyes unfocused. Jane decided to add, "I think it's possible that my conversation with him may have hastened his death."

"Yes," said Katie. "I think so, too. I was really furious at you for a while. I found your card and tacked it up on the bulletin board in the kitchen, intending to call after the funeral. But the truth is, my dad was miserable in that nursing home. He was a deeply lonely man after my mother died. Her loss just seemed to sap the life out of him. My brother is career military. He's been posted all over the world. When he gets back to the US, he wants to spend time with his wife and kids in California, not fly here. My daughter went to school out east and then stayed on to work at the college. She rarely makes it back. Most of Dad's friends have died. The ones who are still alive don't get out much. I went to see him almost every day. We'd play a game of cards or pull out the Scrabble board, but he never showed much interest. Evangeline Adler came by once a week. Kevin usually stopped by at least that often. And Father Mike always came to visit on Sunday afternoons. But it wasn't a life, not the kind he wanted."

"That's so sad," said Jane.

"Yeah. It is." She rubbed her ear. "I suppose you're wondering why I wanted to talk to you."

"I am."

Katie opened her mouth, then closed it. "I'm not sure where to begin." Clearing her throat, she tried again. "A couple of nights before Dad died, Doug Adler brought Evangeline over to the hospital. When Kevin arrived a few minutes later, I asked if they'd mind if I went down to the cafeteria to get myself a sandwich and a cup of coffee. They told me to go, to take as much time as I needed. When I got back maybe half an hour later, I found that Evangeline and Doug had gone. I didn't go in right away because Kevin was sitting by the bed holding my dad's hand. He was crying. Dad was crying, too. The only other time I ever saw my father cry was when my mother died. Kevin kept saying, over and over, how sorry he was. That he'd made a mess of everything. That he'd single-handedly wrecked the lives of all the people he loved most.

"Needless to say, I had no idea what he was talking about. He begged my dad for forgiveness. He was almost inconsolable. At one point my dad lifted his hand and put it on Kevin's head, smoothed his hair. Because of the stroke, that had to have been a real battle for him. The whole scene was heartbreaking. I backed away from the door and gave them some time. When I approached the room again, I made sure my shoes slapped hard against the tile so they'd know I was coming. Their eyes were red when I entered, but they'd mostly regained their composure. Kevin left almost immediately, saying he'd be back first thing in the morning."

"Did you ever find out what it was about?" asked Jane.

Katie rose and stepped over to the front window. Turning her back to Jane, she said, "Yes, I did. I assume you already know. That's why you went to the nursing home to see my dad. You wanted to find out if your suspicions were accurate."

"Did he tell you what happened?"

"It was difficult for him to find words, but his mind was still clear. Slowly, haltingly, he explained that he'd helped the Adler family cover up Delia's murder."

"That must have been hard to hear."

"Very."

"Did he tell you who committed the murder?"

"Kevin."

So there it was. A "dying declaration" in a criminal case didn't fall under the hearsay rule. Walt Olsen's statement would be permissible in court, if Katie was willing to testify. For Jane, it was one more nail in Kevin's coffin. "Have you talked to Kevin about it?"

"No. And I don't intend to." She sat back down on the love seat. "For years, I had the sense that my father had a secret, something that ate at him. I even talked to my mother about it once. She said she'd sensed it, too, but had no idea what it could be. That night, after Kevin left, Dad did his best to explain. He made it clear that covering up a murder was a crime—the single worst thing he'd ever done as a police officer. After that day, he said he never again felt like he deserved to wear the uniform. And then, opening his eyes and looking straight at me, he said that he'd do it again in a heartbeat. He said those last words perfectly. No hesitation."

"Did he tell you why he did it?"

"I didn't ask and he didn't say. He was exhausted by the admission. I wasn't about to push him for more detail."

"Of course."

"The next night, he motioned for me to bend down close to his mouth. He whispered, reminded me of the old wooden box in his room at the nursing home. He always kept personal papers inside. In his broken speech, he told me that there was a letter in there addressed to me—that I should go get it right away. He died in the wee hours of the following morning." She flipped open the folder. Inside was a typed letter. "Here," said Katie. "You might as well read it."

Jane took it and read silently. It started out, "To Whom it May Concern," and then detailed everything Walt Olsen had done on the day of Delia's murder. How Evangeline had called him to the scene. That Brian Carmody, Evangeline's younger brother, the owner of a funeral home in Union and the elected county coroner, had joined him. That Brian, Kevin, and Walt had carried

Delia's body out of the ravine. That Brian had pronounced the death a murder by manual strangulation, and that Kevin admitted to the crime. How Delia's body was whisked away in the coroner's van. And finally, that Brian's intention was to cover up the marks on Delia's neck and send the body to be cremated. The letter, amazingly enough, had been notarized. At the end of the letter, Walt had added a handwritten personal note:

My dearest Katie: There is no excuse for a police officer to act as I did. I deserved to be criminally prosecuted and sent to prison. Every day of my life I have lived with the shame of my actions. I am an old man now and there is no way to change any of this. I leave it to you to decide what should be done. Give the letter to the police, or burn it. My ultimate crime was putting love and loyalty above honor and duty. I will meet my Maker one day soon, and He will tell me if I did right or wrong. Perhaps I did both. In any event, I trust your judgment more than mine. I only ask that you remember me kindly as the loving father I always tried to be. Dad.

Jane looked up, tears in her eyes.

"He told me he wrote that last part the day before his stroke. If you hadn't gone to see him, I never would have received that. Knowing his thoughts mean the world to me."

Jane handed the page back.

"No, you keep it."

"Me?"

"I've thought about this and nothing else for weeks. I can't bring myself to turn my father in, and yet maybe that's what needs to be done."

Jane felt a sudden rush of adrenaline. This was exactly the piece of evidence she'd been looking for, and yet now she, too, had a dilemma.

"I pray that you'll be given the wisdom of Solomon," said Katie. Rising and looking down at Jane, she added, "With so many lives hanging in the balance, you're going to need it."

40

The vibe was mellow inside the Sportsman's Tavern when Jane entered just before closing time. Kevin was wiping down tables, singing along with the Righteous Brothers' *Unchained Melody* on the jukebox. Only one customer remained seated at the bar—an old guy with nothing better to do than nurse his last inch of beer.

When Kevin looked up to see who'd come in, his face brightened. He even looked a little relieved. But then the memory of what had gone down must have penetrated because the smile dissolved into a frown. He switched off the music, then called, "Hey, Burt, time to call it a night."

The old guy turned and nodded to Jane. "Evening," he said.

"Morning," she responded.

"I suppose you're right." He finished his drink in two sips. "I'll catch you tomorrow," he said, tossing a look at Kevin. As he shuffled to the door, he donned a fur-lined cap with earflaps. "Cold out there," he said to Jane with a wink. The bell above the door jingled as he trudged out.

As Jane glanced around, she unbuttoned her sheepskin jacket, making sure she had easy access to the holster clipped to the back of her belt.

"Surprised to see you here," said Kevin, moving behind the bar, tossing the white towel over his shoulder.

Jane kept her distance. "Have you talked to your daughters today?"

The question seemed to confuse him. "*Daughters?*"

"I met Grace this morning."

A silence followed her comment, brief but undeniably charged. "You just never quit, do you?"

"No, I don't."

"I thought I made it clear the last time we talked that you were to leave this town and never come back."

"Funny thing about that last *conversation*," said Jane. "I don't remember a word of it. It's called retrograde amnesia. Often happens after a traumatic injury. I'd say that the beating I took falls under that heading, wouldn't you?"

He pulled the rag off his shoulder, dropped his gaze to the bar.

"Why, Kevin? Why did you do it?"

His eyes inched up. "You really don't remember?"

"I vaguely recall dragging myself out to a highway, getting picked up by a van. I remember looking at myself in a mirror in a bathroom somewhere, seeing my face all bruised and bloody."

"Honestly, Jane, I'm glad you're here. I was worried and hoped you'd be okay. I've thought about you so many times."

"You should have been worried. I suppose, since I don't remember much, you could lie, tell me whatever you want, but I don't think you will. Some part of the man I met and got to know during the time I worked for you had to be real."

His eyes searched the row of glowing lanterns hanging above the tables. "I wasn't the one who hurt you."

"Right. It was your evil twin."

"Look, I just wanted to talk to you away from the bar. I had to find out how much you knew, and what you intended to do with that knowledge. Mostly, I needed to convince you to leave town, to get the hell away from me and my family and never come back. You lied to me about who you were, why you were in town."

"Yeah, lying sure is a mortal sin, isn't it? I mean, you'd know if anybody would."

"I thought we were friends."

"In another time and place, we might have been."

"My brother came along that night. He was the one who got rough with you."

"*Rough?*"

"I know," he said, eyes cast down again. "I know. I never intended any of that. When Doug gets drunk, he's hard to control. He slugged me in the stomach and shoved me into the snow, then he started in on you. I finally dragged him off and pulled him back to the car. I told you to wait for me, that I'd be back. I had to get Doug calmed down. It took longer than I'd expected. He eventually agreed to sit in the car while I ran to get you, but when I reached the clearing, I saw that you'd gone out to the road. Laurie's Windstar was parked there, so I knew she had you—that you were safe. But then I got to thinking that you might convince her to drive you straight to the police station. That you'd file an assault charge against us, maybe even tell them what you thought you'd found out. Doug and I drove over to the government center. The Windstar was nowhere around, so we got the idea of driving to Hannah's house, thinking that Laurie might have taken you there. Sure enough, the van was in the drive. We ran up and banged on the door." He stopped. "You don't remember any of this?"

"Nothing," said Jane.

"We demanded to be let in. Hannah came out on the front steps. She refused to let Doug into her house because he was so obviously angry—and hammered. She acted like she didn't know what we were talking about. She eventually let me in, but you weren't there. You must have told Laurie what had happened when she picked you up, but she refused to talk about it. At that point, since I assumed you'd heard what I said to you, I figured you were sufficiently frightened and that you'd taken off. Only thing is, when I got back to the bar, your SUV was still parked behind the building." Kneading the white towel, he added, "You may not believe me, but I'm sorry about what happened."

"Really? If Doug hadn't been there, and if I refused to do what you asked, how *rough* would you have gotten?"

He hesitated before answering. "I don't know." Approaching his next comment more warily, he said, "You said you met Gracie this morning. How——"

"Guthrie Hewitt and I came back here last night. We drove to the farmhouse this morning. Kira was in the process of feeding us this fake story about how her mother died when Grace appeared out of nowhere and said it wasn't true. She gave us the real story, which came as a complete surprise to Kira."

"Oh God," groaned Kevin, placing both hands flat on the counter to steady himself. "Can this get any worse?"

Jane moved up to the bar, removed the package of photographs from her pocket, and dropped them in front of him. "You said there was no proof that Delia was murdered. You might want to take a look at that."

"What is it?"

"Photographs of the crime scene. Strangulation marks are clearly visible on your wife's throat."

He pushed the package away. "I don't need to see them. I was there. Tell me how Guthrie got them?"

"They were sent to him in the mail along with a note that said, 'Proof Delia was murdered. Stay out of it or the same thing will happen to you.'"

Kevin seemed confused. "Who——"

"Father Mike looked at the handwriting and said it was Doug's."

His smile was bitter. "Ah, Dougie. I can always count on him to do the wrong thing, especially when he's had too much to drink."

"So you admit you murdered Delia?"

"Are you wearing a wire?"

The comment struck her as funny. "No, Kevin. No wires. No recording devices. Just you and me talking."

He considered that for a moment, then seemed to accept it. "Whatever I say means nothing without proof. That's critical to any investigation and you don't have any."

She shrugged.

"Those photos may show that my wife was murdered, but that says nothing about who did the deed. The death was ruled accidental. There's nothing out there that points to anything else."

"You've covered your tracks well," she agreed.

"Thank you."

"Still, I've managed to figure most of it out."

"If you say so."

"I know what happened. I know you did it. But I don't know why."

"Why would you care?"

It was a good question. The answer slipped out before she could stop herself. "Because I don't want to hate you."

The tightness in his face eased. "You think understanding why someone does something mitigates the action?"

"No."

"Then?"

"You had to have a reason."

"I had many reasons."

"So it wasn't just an impulse?"

"It was a total impulse. It was over before I even knew what I'd done. But that doesn't mean I was sorry. I wasn't. Not then. Oh, I was sorry enough for myself—for what it would mean for my life if I got caught. It's taken me years to realize how disastrous my actions were for everyone else—my family and all the people I love. Delia's death is the gift that keeps on giving, in more dreadful ways than I could ever have imagined."

"But you still haven't said why."

"Are you always like this? A dog with a bone?"

She sank her hands into the pockets of her jeans. "Yes, pretty much."

Pulling over a stool, he sat down, nodding for her to do the same. "It's been a long day."

She drew one of the bar stools away from the counter. She didn't want to sit too close to him.

"You don't trust me."

"No."

"But you don't want to hate me."

"What I want more than anything, Kevin, is to understand."

"Won't change anything."

"Why can't you just say it?"

Looking away, he said, "Because it's ugly. Deeply, irrevocably ugly." Pressing his hands together, he gave himself a moment. "Right from the start, Delia and I had a stormy relationship. It was one of the things I liked. She was a party girl. I thought I was a party guy. She came from a military family and I was in the army when we first met. But then, after we married and I left the military, I dragged her back to the middle of nowhere to raise two kids she didn't even like. She couldn't believe she'd ended up in rural Wisconsin. I think she thought of it as almost a fate worse than death. We began talking about divorce. The kids were miserable.

"I'd started a construction company with a friend of mine, so I was gone a lot. She couldn't stand being alone, so she dumped the kids at my mother's place and found various waitress jobs. Because the kids were spending so much time at the farmhouse, and because Hannah was often there to visit, she got to wondering about Gracie, why she was the way she was. She did some digging, had some tests done, talked to a few doctors she knew at a couple of university hospitals, and eventually came to the conclusion that Grace suffered from fetal alcohol syndrome. It wasn't talked about—or even understood well—back in the mid nineties, not like it is today. I was always after Delia to stop the wine and beer when she was pregnant with Grace, but I know she still drank. She held her liquor well for such a small woman.

Most people, if they didn't know her, wouldn't even realize she'd been drinking when she was high as a kite. Vodka was her go-to beverage if she didn't want anyone to know she'd been drinking. She thought people couldn't smell it on her breath. Thank God she was on the wagon when she was pregnant with Kira. Only problem was, she fell off it not long after Kira was born. I mean, maybe she wasn't an alcoholic. But she sure abused alcohol.

"You have to understand: The effects of alcohol on a fetus are devastating. It's like receiving a traumatic brain injury in the womb. Gracie had a very low birth weight. She didn't sleep well, or eat well. As she grew, there were other issues. Hyperactivity. Poor impulse control. She had trouble telling time. She'd fly into rages when she became frustrated. And the weirdest thing for me was, she never seemed to be able to learn from her mistakes.

"The morning Hannah came to the farmhouse to talk to our mom about it—to run the diagnosis past her and discuss how she should tell me—I was there. I was working in the barn, rehabbing it for my mom after my dad's death. I walked into the kitchen and heard part of their conversation. I asked what they were talking about. Hannah pretty much had to tell me. I listened, tried to take it in, and then I left, roared off in my car. I made it home in five minutes flat. Delia was in the kitchen, unpacking groceries. I came in and started screaming at her. I mean, I lost it. Our daughter was suffering because of her drinking. Grace would struggle with these problems for the rest of her life because of Delia's selfishness. I followed her around the house. She said that Hannah was a quack, that she didn't know what she was talking about. That Gracie was difficult, sure, but it had nothing

301

to do with her having a glass of wine every now and then. She just refused to hear what I was telling her.

"She tried to change the subject, she said she'd been to counseling with Father Mike, that he had such an obvious crush on her—wasn't that hilarious. She did admit that he'd helped her understand what she really wanted out of life. Her conclusion was that she did love me. She wanted to make it work between us. She went back into the kitchen, saying that she planned to spend the rest of the day making Christmas cookies. As she was emptying out the last bag, I noticed a couple of white boxes with pink lettering on them. I picked one up. It was a pregnancy test. I shoved it at her, demanded to know why she had it. She got all lovey-dovey, said that she had a really special Christmas gift in mind for me. I loved children so much, she thought we should have another.

"I started shaking. I asked her if she was already pregnant. She said she wasn't, but she'd been off the pill for several weeks, so it was only a matter of time.

"I don't even remember what I said after that. I think I hit her. We were running through the house at one point, and then we were out on the deck. I had my hands around her neck and I was squeezing and squeezing. I remember her going limp. How disgusted I was by the sight of her, how I just wanted to erase her. I must have dumped her over the railing because the next thing I knew, I was standing there, looking down at her body in the ravine. Reality eventually sank in. That's when I rushed back to the kitchen and called my mom. I told her what I'd done. She made me promise to stay where I was, said she'd be right over."

Jane watched in silence as tears streamed down his face.

He scraped them away. "So now you know. Does it change anything?"

She shook her head.

"You can freely hate me."

"I don't hate you."

"You should." He picked up the bar towel and wiped his face.

The copy she'd made of Walt Olsen's letter felt like a burning coal inside her pocket. Part of the reason he'd come clean with her so easily was that he was sure Jane had no proof that he'd murdered his wife. She reached into her pocket, touched the paper.

A loud knock interrupted them.

Turning around, Jane saw a police officer standing at the front door, the strobe lights on his squad car lighting up the dark street behind him.

"What did you do?" demanded Kevin, desperation filling his voice.

"Nothing," said Jane. "Honestly. I have no idea why he's here."

Wiping his face one last time, Kevin went to open up.

Jane strained to hear the conversation, but they were talking too quietly. After nearly a minute, Kevin closed the door and came back inside. "I have to go."

"What is it?" asked Jane, moving off the stool.

"My brother. They've got him in the cruiser. Seems he was running around the trailer park where he lives, buck naked except for his hiking boots, knocking on doors and cursing people out."

"Is he drunk?"

"Blitzed out of his mind." He grabbed his coat off a hook by the cash register. Stopping before he reached the front door, he waited for Jane. "You know, this may be hard for you to believe, but except for that one horrible act—for which I know I should rot in hell forever—I'm the most normal person in my family." His smile was sad. "The truth never sets anyone free. I'm glad you're okay, but I hope to God this is the last time I ever see you."

All Jane could do was nod.

41

By six the next morning, Jane had loaded up her backpack and taken it down to her car, paid the motel bill, and was standing in front of Guthrie's room, knocking on his door. It took him nearly a full minute to answer. When he did, he looked tousled and sleepy, his robe loosely tied around his waist. He put a finger to his lips. "Kira's inside. She's still asleep."

Jane was happy to hear that'd they'd been able to spend the night together. "Everything okay with you two?"

"More than okay."

She smiled. "I'm leaving, driving back to Minneapolis."

"So early? I though we could have breakfast together—the three of us."

"I dug my Honda out of the snow last night. Had to leave your car in the lot behind Kevin's bar."

"Kira can drive me over."

She reached inside her coat and drew out Walt Olsen's letter. "I have something for you."

"What is it?"

"Proof that Kevin murdered his wife. Turns out, Walt Olsen left a letter. He told his daughter about it just before he died. She said she read it, thought about burning it—or turning it over to the police—but couldn't make a decision, so she gave it to me yesterday. It details everything that happened the day of Delia's death. The cover-up. What Walt did. What Brian Carmody did."

Guthrie stared at it as if he'd just been handed the holy grail. "We should take this to the police."

"Should we? Have you thought about the ramifications? Everyone in the Adler family, and that now includes Kira, is part of a cover-up. They could all do jail time."

He wiped a hand across his mouth. "I've thought about all that. I don't think anything serious would happen to Kira. She hasn't known that long."

"For your sake and for hers, I hope that's true."

"I mean . . . a murder was committed."

"That's right."

"Kevin should pay for what he did."

Everyone, thought Jane, had been doing nothing but paying since the day Delia died. "If that's what you believe, then turn it over to the police. But before you do, let me go home and write up my notes. You need the full story. In fact, I could come in right now and tell you both everything."

"No," he said quickly. "I need this time with Kira."

"Fine. You should have my report in a couple of days."

His eyes narrowed. "What are you really saying to me?"

"I'm saying that . . . that you hired me to do a job. I did it, and this information is what I was able to dig up. It's up to you to decide what to do with it."

306

"You're passing the buck, just like Walter's daughter."

"Apparently I am."

"That's not fair."

She put her hand on his shoulder. "Oh, Guthrie, if you want fair, you're going to have to find yourself another planet." She stuck out her hand. "Good luck."

He shook it, and then said, "Thanks, Jane."

The last thing she wanted for presenting him with that letter was thanks. As she walked back down the hallway, she couldn't help but think about Kevin, about the entire Adler family, and what kind of horror one tragic decision could create. All she wanted for herself right now was to get the hell out of the peace and safety of small-town America with some part of her heart and soul intact.

On her way out of town, Jane stopped at a QuikTrip. She needed to fill the gas tank, and also clean the CR-V's windows. As she worked, she hummed a particularly bad rendition of Three Dog Night's *Joy to the World*.

Walking around inside the store, she found a section of sweets that looked like they might be homemade. A chocolate-frosted Rice Krispies bar caught her attention. After grabbing a cup of coffee, she moved up to the cash register and handed the man behind the counter her credit card.

"Beautiful day," he said. "Blue skies and no snow in the forecast."

"It's warmer, too," said Jane. "At least, warmer than it has been the last few weeks."

"Not really." His hand hovered above the card reader, waiting for it to print a receipt. "It's been pretty much in the high twenties and low thirties. We won't even make it out of the teens today."

"Huh," said Jane, signing the receipt.

"Drive safe," said the man, handing Jane her card.

Back in her car, she set the coffee in the cup holder and the Rice Krispies bar on the dashboard. She adjusted her sunglasses as she gazed up at the intense cobalt sky. She had no intention of sleeping at Cordelia's house tonight. After rounding up her dogs, she would spend her first night in weeks back in her own bed.

She started the engine. The heat flooding from the vents felt almost too warm. Easing out of the front seat, she took off her sheepskin jacket and tossed it across to the passenger's side. And then she climbed back in, put on her seat belt and smiled.

She was going home.